USA *Today* Bestselling Author

Dale Mayer

EGAN 03

SHADOW RECON

EGAN: SHADOW RECON, BOOK 3
Beverly Dale Mayer
Valley Publishing Ltd.

ISBN-13: 978-1-773367-28-6
Print Edition

Books in This Series

About This Book

Deep in the permafrost of the Arctic, a joint task force, comprised of over one dozen countries, comes together to level up their winter skills. A mix of personalities, nationalities, and egos bring out the best—and the worst—as these globally elite men and women work and play together. They rub elbows with hardy locals and a group of scientists gathered close by …

One fatality is almost expected with this training. A second is tough but not a surprise. However, when a third goes missing? It's hard to not be suspicious. When the missing man is connected to one of the elite Maverick team members and is a special friend of Lieutenant Commander Mason Callister? All hell breaks loose …

Shit happens but at the arctic camp, it's happening too much and too often for Egan. The mess from the scientist camp has left a pall over the training camp. And still there is no sign of Teegan, Mountain's brother. The surrounding tundra has been gridded and searched but so far, nothing… except another body…

Berry's sister convinced her to try a new experience and apply for this training camp with her. Except none of her training prepared her for what lay ahead. Being in close quarters and cooped up due to the ugly weather, several people struggle to stay calm and in control. When her sister shows a side of her personality she'd never seen before, she's wondering what she can do to fix this, but was it even fixable?

And if she'd been taken in, how many other team members had been as well? And did it have anything to do with the nightmare happening right under their noses. Egan and Berry need to find out, before they become the next victims…

PROLOGUE

MASON STARED DOWN at the phone. "Damn."

Mountain responded, "I know. I know." His voice booming through the phone. "The trouble is, we're still not getting to the core issues," he said, with a brewing anger deep inside. "Plus we're still missing the other scientist team. At this point, although we don't have any answers, I have a suspicion that Anna may have done something to that team, taking them out as well."

"Christ," Mason muttered, running his hands through his hair. "This is not what we expected."

"No way we could have known there would be these problems," Mountain noted. "I understand that the university is planning on sending somebody to clean up the scientists' camp. They'll stay with us, unless we can get their camp up and running soon. However, they really don't want to engage with any of us, as they have suspicions of their own about the entire base. Regardless they want a few days, four, five, maybe six days up there. I think they're also looking at sending out their own search-and-rescue team. They have different coordinates and are potentially looking at finding Dr. Amelia. She's an important member of that community but has ties up here and is a bit of a wild card. I did try to get them to share those coordinates with me—maybe they will but later—and to promise that they would alert me if Amelia and her coworker were found."

"So, either she's got powerful friends or somebody else is financing this?"

"Her brother is some dot com wizard, and he doesn't believe she's dead. And I have to admit that, if there's a chance she's alive, I'm encouraged to believe there's a chance that Teegan's alive too. I know there isn't another soul up here who believes that, but, in some way, this missing Dr. Amelia is giving me hope."

"Good," Mason said. "It's not that late for her yet. Teegan has been longer though," he added gently.

"No, it isn't too late for Amelia. Again that's not our main problem. And I'm not shifting on Teegan," Mountain growled stubbornly.

"Fine. And, no, Dr. Amelia sure as hell isn't our main problem, yet it's not that easy." Mason groaned. "Anyway, thanks for the update. Have you had any luck with the new arrival?"

"Hardly a new arrival." Mountain laughed. "But Egan has been pretty busy being friends with everybody. He enjoys socializing with everyone."

"Sometimes that's a good thing too."

"Sometimes, and, as long as he can get information from people, … I am good with it."

"That's Egan's specialty," Mason noted, "and exactly why he was assigned to be there. Give him a chance."

"Yeah, believe me. He's got all the chances he needs up here. People are more than interested in something to take their minds off the hell that's been going on all around them," he shared, "and everybody is more than happy they're not the ones involved."

"Of course," Mason agreed, "but we've still got several

dead people and too many who have gone missing. So, short of something else going wrong, how about the next time you call me, it's with a positive update?"

"Yeah, I'll try that next time." Mountain gave a hearty laugh. "So, besides Magnus, Rogan, and now Egan, do you have anybody else up here?"

"I do …" Mason hesitated. "Yet I won't tell you who that is right now."

"*Great*," Mountain muttered. "You really think I don't need to know?"

"I think that this person is not the person you would expect, but they're very good at what they do." And, with that, Mason hung up.

MASON EYED HIS wife, a small smile playing at his lips.

"What is that look for?" Tesla asked.

"Rogan's one thing, and Egan is the newest addition to our SR team," he began. "However, Mountain also has a covert female operative up there, which Mountain won't like. It will supercharge his instincts to protect, maybe even to overprotect and to distract him. So better to keep that secret from Mountain for now."

DAY 1

Arrived. Weather is a bitch. Shit, it's cold. Taking a snowcat to the base. Will check in soon.

Egan Crosok hopped up into the snowcat, tossed his duffel bag behind the seat, sat down, and slammed the door shut. He looked over at the driver and recognized Magnus. He gave him a hard grin. "Lovely weather you've got up here."

Magnus snorted. "We haven't had lovely weather since I arrived," he muttered. "Mother Nature hates us."

"I don't think she gives a damn, to be honest," Egan noted cheerfully.

"Yeah, that's obvious," Magnus grumbled.

"Any more problems?" Egan asked, looking over at him in concern.

Magnus shook his head. "No, not since the last bout, but that's been bad enough. We've had our own troubles, without the scientists' camp running amok."

"Did you ever find their missing team?"

"No, and now we've been asked by the scientific community, specifically the research department at Dr. Amelia's university, to look for her. They sent us a new set of map coordinates too, which we hope are more accurate than what we had, which wasn't much. She is well-known for living off the land, having spent a lot of time in the Inuit communities. From what I hear, she's got a solid reputation, but still, being totally out of communication isn't normal for her."

"*Great*," Egan uttered under his breath. He couldn't imagine being out here isolated for weeks.

"Right, but your job is completely different."

"Hey, my job is whatever it needs to be," Egan admitted in a quiet tone. "Plus, I understand search and rescue in these temperatures." When Magnus glanced at him, Egan nodded. "Another reason I was chosen to come up."

"Who gave you the okay to be here?"

Egan knew what Magnus was asking but gave a clipped nod. "Let's just say not the normal division."

"Mason?" Magnus laughed.

"Yes, Mason," Egan confirmed, "but I'm very short on information."

"We all are," Magnus stated. "You probably know as much as I do."

Surely they had better intel than just this. Particularly after Magnus had been the first one up here—other than Mountain, searching for his missing brother, Teegan, for the last two and half weeks or so. "In which case, we're in trouble." Egan eyed Magnus.

"Yeah, we are in trouble all right. We've got somebody dangerous on the military base, and nobody knows exactly what the problem is. Trouble is, there is no indication of who it could be or what it's about at all. So far we've had a killer nurse named Joy stealing drugs, and then a psycho scientist called Anna trying to kill all of them at their camp. And we're still no closer to finding Teegan or other missing persons, nor what happened to the various others who met with accidents, some fatal, all in this training program."

"And are these guys who have gone missing, are they

missing on their own, or is this a case of having gone missing without a vote in the matter?"

"If we could find any of them before they die, we could ask them," Magnus replied in exasperation and then pointed up ahead. "Regardless of the whiteout happening all around us, the base is up there."

They came to a rise, and Egan saw the lights down below. "Interesting little valley."

"It works well for us here," Magnus stated. "It keeps us out of the worst of the wind, and it helps us to somewhat control this little valley here."

"Valleys are good," Egan admitted. "Except for when you have planes that need to come in. Or avalanches that could bury us."

"That was taken into account when they set up the base. The airstrip is on the flats up here. Most supply runs are done by airdrop, unless we have fuel or people brought in. We're on short supplies now, unless it all came with you."

"Please tell me that they have coffee," Egan replied in mock horror. As he'd helped load the snowcat, he knew a lot of the supply orders had come with him.

"They do"—Magnus laughed—"but it is one of the things we tend to run out of when supplies get low."

"I brought a couple pounds in my personal gear," he shared comfortably.

Magnus shot him a look. "Glad to know that."

"Oh no, you didn't hear me say a word about my private coffee stash," he added, with a big cheerful smile. "Besides, hopefully I won't be up here all that long."

"Oh, so before your personal coffee runs out, you'll come in, solve our problem, and get out, *huh?*" Magnus asked in a dry tone.

Egan winced. "Sounds arrogant when you put it that way."

"Yeah, you'll be here for a month probably," he murmured. "Yet, depending on what you end up sussing out in this place, it could be longer."

"Oh, I hope not," Egan stated. "A month would be okay though. Besides, it goes by quickly."

"And not fast enough sometimes," Magnus noted in an odd tone.

"I hear you and the doc paired up."

"We did." Magnus grinned.

"And that's working out for you?"

"It is at the moment, yeah. Can't wait until this is over, and we get some time to enjoy it. Someplace warm sounds awfully good about now."

"Yeah, to you and me both." Egan laughed. "However, I'm heading back to Norway for a few weeks after this."

"Any particular reason?"

"Family, there's always family."

"As long as it's a happy family issue, then it's all good."

"It is, at least it's supposed to be." Egan hesitated. "Any news on the latest missing man?"

"No," Magnus replied, his tone hard. "Not a word on Ron. Nobody has seen him anywhere in the most probable locations and that—"

"Why am I thinking we'll find an ice cave somewhere, with all these bodies stacked up?" Egan muttered.

"We sure as hell better not." Magnus shook his head vigorously. "We've checked with all the locals, and nobody's seen him either."

"I understand that the others didn't take any equipment or safety gear, so those missing guys probably didn't head back home the hard way then, *huh?*"

"No, they sure as hell didn't," Magnus confirmed. "And if anyone had stolen some equipment or supplies, we would have noticed."

"So, we presume that Ron and the others are lost out there in the Arctic tundra?"

"Theoretically, but I'm not so sure. Yet we've seen stranger things happen. However, I'm afraid Ron's already dead. We just need to find his body to confirm that suspicion. I'm beginning to wonder if we ever will find him. Sure would help to have more answers. And that is taking too long to please me."

As they made their way closer to the military base, Egan added, pointing to the back of the snowcat, "Those boxes are supplies for the kitchen."

"Yeah, I saw that," Magnus said. "I'll get them in to the chef."

"And an envelope is there for the colonel."

"You can hand deliver that," Magnus stated, with an evil grin, "on your own."

He rolled his eyes. "Thanks. I heard this CO's not the easiest."

"No, he's not, but then he's been given this shit job here, and, so far, it's been nothing but hell for him."

"Yeah, that sucks, doesn't it?"

"Yeah, it does. Everybody expected a clean house, and instead? … Colonel's got people dying and disappearing on his watch, left, right, and center."

"I'm surprised he hasn't been replaced."

"I'm thinking this job might be his intended punishment already."

"We hear about those things, but I wonder if it's something the brass does."

"I think it is," Magnus suggested, looking at his newest Shadow Recon member. "Wait till you meet him."

It didn't take long, as the colonel was waiting for them to show up. Egan walked into the colonel's office and handed over the envelope. The colonel accepted it, then asked him how his trip was. "It was fine, sir."

"Good. Get to your room, take some time to recuperate and settle in," he noted in a businesslike tone. "Tomorrow we'll start off with a bang."

And, with that, Egan was dismissed.

Not sure where his room was, he looked for someone by the name of Dave who was in charge of accommodations. It didn't take long to roust him, and the room assignment included comments on the previous occupant, Myles. Egan already knew for a fact what had happened to that scientist. The name Myles had come up in Egan's briefing, and the fact that Egan was given a dead man's room just made the situation on base all a little creepier.

As he walked into it, the chill was unmistakable, but it was his room and his alone, and that was good enough for him. As he dropped his bag, he turned around to see another guy staring at him, a grin on his face.

"You get the haunted room, *huh?*"

"I wasn't given a choice."

"Somebody's got to stay here. Everybody else has been avoiding it."

"Right, that's nice to know." Egan shrugged. "Can't say ghosts have ever bothered me."

"Maybe not, but not all ghosts are harmless."

Surprised that he would say that, Egan stared at the guy with a raised eyebrow and got a shrug in return.

"I was raised with a lot of voodoo in my family," the stranger explained, with a half smile. "My beliefs and thoughts are a whole lot different from most people here."

"I'll keep that in mind," Egan replied, with a laugh. "Anyway, you want to show me where the kitchen is?"

"That I can do." He held out a hand. "Garry," he introduced himself. "Garry Boon."

"Nice to meet you, Garry Boon. I'm Egan Crosok," he responded, with a smile, stretching his name out a bit as he pronounced it.

Garry looked at him with interest. "Part of the Russian team?"

"No, I'm as American as they come," Egan stated. "I was born in Norway though."

"Interesting." Garry eyed Egan intently. "Why the hell would you be on the American side if you were born in Norway?"

"Dual citizenship." He shook his head. "Sometimes I often wonder what our families were thinking. Then again, sometimes I don't think they were thinking at all, at least not at the time of conception."

At that, Garry laughed. "God, isn't that the truth. Anyway, come on down. The kitchen is this way." He pointed it out up ahead.

They walked through the hallway, multiple closed doors on each side.

"We all gather in this room over here." Garry nodded toward a dining area, where people huddled together. "The kitchen has a serve-yourself buffet area. It's small but has just enough room if we all squeeze in close." He shrugged. "For that reason a lot of us tend to eat in staggered groups, so it's not so crowded at the chow line. Then there's a common area nearby where they don't really want us eating, but, hey, with everything else going on, nobody gives a shit anymore."

"That's a good point too," Egan noted. "Did you know the missing guys?"

Garry nodded. "I knew them, and I also had a little bit to do with the dead scientist Myles." Garry shook his head. "None of us understood that Anna, one of the scientists, was something of a loose cannon. Imagine coming up here just to kill off all your teammates. Freaking mind-boggling."

"It doesn't really bear thinking about, does it? And yet, if we don't, we don't learn anything from it," Egan noted.

Garry walked over to the sideboard. "There's always hot water here, or, if there isn't, you can ask for it. We keep big kettles on the stoves, and you can usually get tea or instant coffee anytime you want. However," he added, with a slight grin, "the good coffee comes out in the morning and at dinnertime—or sometimes in the afternoon, if we're lucky."

"Good to know." Egan walked over and made himself a hot instant coffee. Seeing the hot chocolate there, he added a good spoonful to make it a hot mocha.

Garry laughed. "I guess you're accustomed to your treats."

"I've done some pretty hard roughing it myself," Egan admitted, "but I do recognize the benefits of having something good and enjoying it when you have it because, next time you turn around, the supplies will be gone."

"Yeah, I don't know how many times Chef has told us he's running out of groceries."

"I think that's a common refrain," Egan agreed, looking over at his new friend and smiling.

"Anyway, I'm heading over to the commons to play some cards, if you want to come join us," Garry offered.

"Otherwise you're on your own." And, with that, he walked back out again.

Egan normally would have gone along with Garry, except Chef glared at Egan from behind the counter. He walked over to introduce himself.

Chef shook his hand. "Why the hell do we have new people coming in, when others are dying?"

"Maybe that's why," Egan clarified his point. "We have to replenish the numbers. I am Egan."

Chef winced at his casual comment. "Chef Williamson. You can call me Chef." He took a deep breath and added in a hard tone, "God, it just seems so wrong to bring in more people, when the ones already here keep dying or go missing. It's so frustrating."

"It does, and I'm sorry if my presence upsets you."

Chef shrugged. "It doesn't upset me in a personal sense. I just don't want you to be fresh meat for the grinder."

"Do we have any idea who's operating the grinder?" he asked casually.

"No, and, if I did, believe me. I'd have mentioned something."

Egan nodded. "It's hard watching the people around you go down, isn't it?"

"It sucks," Chef added, "and no way to know who is behind it. I never, ever would have pegged Anna …"

"To be a serial killer?"

The words struck Chef oddly, and he took a deep breath. "She was this timid thing, always after a hot cup of tea," he shared, with a headshake. "What BS is that?" And, with that, he stormed off into the back of his kitchen.

"If you need any help sometime, let me know," Egan offered in a friendly tone. "If I can, I'll come and give you a hand."

Chef poked his head around and glared at him.

Egan smiled and nodded. "Yeah, I can cook. I'm not a chef by any means, but I can certainly put two and two together and make a decent meal."

"Well, good, because my last guy managed to get himself injured and got shipped out after a damn fire in the kitchen. A bloody idiot is what he was."

"Are you here alone?"

Chef glared at him. "Yeah, I'm here alone, and, yeah, I can cook, and, yeah, it doesn't matter. I can manage these numbers easily enough." He gave a dismissive wave of his hand. "Just don't expect anything too fancy because I don't have the supplies."

"Doesn't matter." Egan shrugged. "Hot grub and lots of it is worth more at this place than fancy foods."

"Best not to get your heart set on either of those," Chef replied, with an evil grin, and, with that, he disappeared.

Smiling, Egan stirred the hot mocha in his hand, then turned around and saw two women walking into the dining room, their tones low, as they conversed among themselves. When they looked up and frowned at him, he smiled and nodded. "Good evening, ladies. I just arrived. I'm Egan."

At that, one of the women's eyebrows shot up. "They let somebody new in here? I understood nobody was to come and go."

He nodded. "You also have a lot of mechanical and electrical issues," Egan explained. "So I'm here to help out with that." He was trained as an engineer, though that's not exactly the reason he was here. However, nobody else needed to know about it.

"Oh, so you'll probably help with the scientists," the

same woman added, with an eye roll, "as if we haven't got enough headaches."

The other woman eyed him intently. "My name is Berry, and this is my sister, Cherry."

He nodded. "The resemblance is hard to miss."

"I wouldn't think so," Cherry stated, a hint of attitude in her tone.

"However," Berry added, with a smile, "we're obviously not identical twins, and sometimes, when we're apart, people do still get us mixed up."

"I can see that," Egan noted, studying them both. They both had a honey-colored skin tone, and both were five-eight, slim, and obviously fit. "Interesting that you're up here."

"We're doing some survival training, like everybody else here, and I requested this," Cherry shared, with a groan. "Then I convinced my sister to get onto the same team, so we could come up together."

"Any particular reason that the frozen north interests you?"

"All of it interests me," Cherry replied. "The whole world, everything and every place I can travel to. I spend a lot of time in tropical temperatures, so I thought this would be a nice change. But, since I hadn't had any experience at it, and you never know where you'll get shipped these days, I thought it would be a good idea."

"How do you feel about it now?" he asked, with a twinkle in his eye.

"We were doing fine, until people started to go missing, and others started to die," Cherry admitted. "That's completely changed the atmosphere, and it's not a good change."

"No, of course not," he agreed immediately. "I'm not

trying to minimize the danger. I get it."

"You were told?" Cherry asked sharply.

He nodded. "I understand some of the issues and decided I would be willing to come anyway."

"Why? Do you have a history of investigation too?" she asked in a snarky voice.

He did; he'd been a cop a long time ago, although it was so long ago that it didn't seem to make much difference. But there was another reason he'd fit the bill, as far as Mason was concerned. "I do have some investigative experience." Egan chuckled. "Maybe that's why they sent me up here."

At that, Berry looked at him, the questions evident on her face.

He shrugged. "I was a cop. I joined the local police force at eighteen," he explained, "and at twenty-five, I joined the Navy."

Cherry frowned. "Not the usual pathway for this."

"I don't think anything demands *usual*," Egan noted. "No right or wrong, but that was my pathway."

"Whatever," Cherry replied, as she poured herself a cup of tea. She turned to her sister and asked her lightly, "Do you want one?"

"No, I'm good," Berry said, with a quick wave to Egan, as the two of them headed back toward the door.

He asked before they left, "Where does everybody go at night, in the evenings?"

"Their rooms," Berry told him, with a laugh, "especially now."

"You're on a curfew here?" he asked because he hadn't heard anything about it.

"It's not curfew, just common sense."

"Right." He nodded. "Let's hope that there's no need."

"There's always a need," Cherry snapped, glaring at him. "But then you're male, so the world looks different from your point of view."

And, with that, the two of them were gone.

"YOU AND YOUR usual short-tempered personality," Berry whispered to Cherry.

"I just want out. I can't believe I got you into this."

"It's fine," Berry stated. "It's an experience and one that we'll look back on someday and laugh about."

"I hope so," she muttered. "The last thing I want is to end up in this frozen world forever."

"Hey, don't even start talking like that," Berry admonished her sister, reaching over and rubbing her back. "You were getting close to the one guy before he disappeared, but that doesn't mean it'll be you next."

"Maybe," Cherry mumbled, "but still, it makes it very personal for me."

Berry couldn't argue with that because it *was* very personal. Cherry had been devastated when Yegorahn hadn't shown up again. Especially after they'd finally spent their first night together, after dancing around for the first couple weeks. He'd gone missing the day after. "I'm sorry," Berry said, for the umpteenth time.

Cherry shrugged irritably. "For the umpteenth time, it's not your fault. So you don't have to keep apologizing."

"Maybe not. I just wish I could have done something to ease the heartache."

"That would take finding him and finding answers," Cherry snapped in a hard tone, "I just …" She shook her head, as she stared out at nothing. "I can't imagine what would have even triggered this. And the scientists have had what? … two deaths besides ours?"

"Two deaths that we know of. We can blame Anna for the one guy who came with her, Myles or whatever. And, for the other one, we still don't know."

"I really like Sydney too," Cherry added out of the blue. "It doesn't hurt that she's one of the few women here, and she's hooked up with Magnus, which … he's yummy. Yegorahn didn't care for him at all though. I never did know what that was about."

Berry laughed at that. "Magnus is yummy, and he's also taken."

"Yeah, well, I made my choice, and look at how that worked out for me."

Berry winced. They reached their room, and, as they stepped in, her sister stopped and looked up and down the hallway.

"I always get a creepy feeling that we're being watched. There's no reason for it, but it still doesn't stop that sensation."

"If you ever understand where it's coming from, you can always tell somebody."

"Yeah? But who, who would I tell?"

"You can mention it to the doc, or maybe the colonel, if you have a chance to talk to him, or maybe … I don't know, maybe mention it to Magnus. He seems to have his hands in all the cookie jars around here."

"That's hardly something I'll do, is it? That would just make us sound like flighty women."

"Maybe, and yet you don't know what the doc's been through, so you don't know what Magnus might say is the issue."

"Possibly. I don't know. I'll see."

And with that, they went in and settled in for the night. They had books, which they read under emergency lights, and cell phones to play games on. They had some card games that they played a lot, but her sister was distracted tonight.

Finally Berry looked over at Cherry and shared, "I didn't get tea earlier. Maybe I'll go grab one."

At that, her sister hopped up. "Sure, let's go get one."

Berry hesitated. "You don't have to come with me, you know?"

Her sister snorted. "We have enough problems without us splitting up."

"That's ridiculous. Absolutely no way we need to worry about going and getting tea," Berry protested.

Cherry glared at her sister. "This is a really good chance to sort it out."

"Sort what out?"

Cherry muttered, "I just don't feel comfortable letting you go on your own."

Berry held up a hand. "Stop. I'll be back in ten minutes, and, if I'm not back on time, then you can come looking for me."

"Ten minutes? You can't even go there and get a cup and get back again in that amount of time."

"Fine, make it twenty then," Berry said in exasperation.

At that, her sister pulled out her watch and hit the timer. "Now go."

DAY 1, EVENING

ROLLING HER EYES, Berry slipped out of the room and headed down the hallway. She heard the wind whistling outside. It seemed to be a never-ending sound, just one of those background noises that didn't stop. It was frustrating, yet Mother Nature forgot to ease up. They had some good days originally, and then came a period of ugly rough weather, which may have had an awful lot to do with the mental state of some of the people here, when these other things went off the rail. But it was just as likely that, whatever the headache, it was an issue with the people themselves, and Berry couldn't blame the weather for that.

She really enjoyed the break in the weather a few days ago, but now it seemed it would take another dark turn again. She had a vast amount of respect for the people, the civilizations, who had gone before them, handling Mother Nature when she got to be too much. It still sometimes amazed Berry that civilizations had grown enough to survive on this very inhospitable rock.

Much of the time this place was a thing of beauty, and the rest of the time, as she had learned, it definitely was not. It was quite a challenge to even be here. She'd only come because her sister had really pushed for it, and, while neither of them had enjoyed it, Berry was getting acclimated to the gorgeous whiteness and the amazing life that survived through what appeared to be completely uninhabitable conditions.

She found the local village nearby to be fascinating. The twins had been there a couple times to visit, and it had really been quite interesting. As a race, present-day humanity was used to the easy comforts of so much, and yet these people out here survived with so little—and, to top it off, they were happy. Berry often thought everybody could learn an awful lot from these locals.

Berry entered the dining area and then into the kitchen and quickly found the teakettle. Thankfully it was already hot enough for her needs. She poured herself a cup of green tea and quickly put the kettle back on the hot stove, checking for wood to go into it. As she stoked it and closed it again, someone spoke behind her.

"That appears to be a natural habit."

She turned to see Egan standing here, and she smiled at him. "It's amazing how quickly things do become a habit," she replied, with a laugh. "I've spent a lot of times in some fairly faraway corners of the world. ... Although it's different here, and it's not something that I thought I would enjoy. Yet I've come to love what it has to offer," she murmured. "It's not a place I would choose to stay right now, but I am very grateful for the experience."

He nodded slowly. "It does give you a completely new perspective on nature, doesn't it?"

"And on people," she added impulsively. "The perseverance, strength, and adaptability of our race as a whole." She shook her head. "Don't get me started. My sister would tell you that I never shut up about the topic, once I get going." She smiled at him. "Hopefully you're getting settled in okay."

"I found my room, then decided to come back and get another hot drink." He waved his hand at the kettle. "Having just arrived, liquids are important."

"Liquids are really important," she agreed, "and, of course, there's a limit to what we have, but there's never a limit to the snow."

"And snow is great. as long as it's not overwhelming," he added, with a nod.

She smiled. "In the evenings, we all tend to go to sleep early because it's so cold, and we have to ration our light usage."

"And yet a number of people are always around, either playing on cell phones or God only knows what else, I bet."

"True, but cell phones can't always get charged up here," she shared, with a note of warning. When he frowned at her, she nodded. "We're having generator troubles, so sometimes we can't all get charged up. So, if it's important for you to have it, … you need to preserve it."

"Got it. Thanks for the tip."

She smiled. "You're welcome. It won't take you too long to get used to this."

"No, and I don't know how long I'll be here," he noted casually. When she tilted her head at him, he shrugged. "I'm here to help out. I'm not sure that I'm here to stay."

"That's nice for you," she said, "but I wouldn't pass that around because an awful lot of people here have been trying to leave. However, because of all the problems, the brass isn't letting them go."

"No, because, if somebody here is responsible for murder," Egan acknowledged, "they don't want to let them out. We may not track them down again."

"That just blows me away," she replied. "How could

anybody here do that? We're all part of the same team."

"Did you know any of them?"

"I've been here since the beginning of this training session," she explained carefully, "so I knew them to that degree. I've been on teams with them. I've worked and done some overnight survival training with them, but obviously I didn't know them. I didn't know them before I got here, so I've only gotten to know some people during these first few weeks here. My sister, on the other hand, did know one guy quite well, and they'd become an item, but he disappeared one night. It's left her with more than a few questions and a lot of uneasiness."

"Of course," Egan stated. "She was with one of the Russians?"

Berry nodded. "Although it sounds bad when you say that. His name was Yegorahn. I forget his last name."

"So, she has no idea what happened to him?"

"No, and honestly they spent their first night together. Then, on the very next day, … he was reported as missing, so she's been beside herself ever since."

"I'm sorry. That's tough."

"It is tough, and she's not handling it well."

"No, of course not." He hesitated and then asked in an undertone, "Was there any chance that somebody was jealous of him?"

She looked at him. "What do you mean by jealous?"

"That somebody else may have wanted your sister's affection and decided to kill off a rival?"

Her jaw opened in shock, and then she slowly closed it. "Wow."

"Wow?" he repeated, looking at her. "What do you mean by *wow*?"

"That was not even a question brought up so far."

"Did people know that they were an item?"

She winced. "No, you're right. They probably didn't. I shouldn't be telling you all this." She looked around, with a worried expression. "Why the hell am I even telling you that?" she asked, turning and glaring at him.

He didn't say anything, just smiled at her gently. "I'm not trying to get you in trouble, but it's a valid question."

"Of course it is," she agreed, stumped. "And it never occurred to me that her relationship should be questioned. We were asked if we knew of any reason why someone would want Yegorahn dead, but I didn't have any response because I didn't think anybody would want him dead."

"How about now that you're considering it from this point of view?"

She blinked at him several times, trying to process the information. "I don't know what to say."

"Was anybody else around your sister, spending time with her?"

"A couple guys are pretty interested in her, and she's beautiful." At that, his eyebrows shot up, and she stared at him, confused. "What's the matter?"

"You both look very much the same," he pointed out, smiling. "You stated she's beautiful. Yet it seemed as if she was beautiful, and yet you are somehow not."

She flushed. "I didn't mean that at all," she replied defensively.

"Yet that's what you told me."

"Fine, it was just a phrase though," she muttered, as she waved a hand. "Regardless, some people were pursuing her, but never anybody who seemed to be over-the-top about it."

"Did you have any arguments with Yegorahn over it?"

"Over his relationship with her? No, not at all," she responded in an apprehensive tone, "and they seemed to be truly happy, although they were keeping it very quiet." He just nodded. Immediately feeling as if she'd betrayed her sister, Berry added, "I've got to go back to our room, before she comes looking for me. She set a timer when I went to get tea."

"Is there a reason for that?"

"Yeah, our safety, and she's probably panicking now." She winced. "Christ, I've got to get away from you. I don't know what it is, but I don't normally talk this much."

"It's not as if you're breaking any secret code," he noted, "and I'm not trying to put you in a position where you feel you're betraying her. I'm just trying to get up to speed on what's going on here."

"My sister would say, *Watch your back because nobody saw it coming.* Nobody, not a single person. Nobody has a clue what's going on, and the fact that somebody as big and as physically fit as Yegorahn was taken down means that nobody here is safe."

"Is that what you would say?"

She sighed. "I don't have quite such a negative view of the world or of being here, so it's a little hard for me to be as negative as my sister. Yet I do understand where she's coming from. I get that pain is doing the talking right now for her. But it's still good sound advice, so watch your back."

And, with that, she smiled up at the man, who, for whatever reason, was way too easy to talk to. "And now I'll definitely be in trouble." And, sure enough, as she turned to face the door, her sister stood there, glaring at her. She threw up her free hand. "I just told him that I had to get back, before you decided to come look for me."

At that, her sister grabbed her by the arm and marched her back down to their room.

"Seriously?" Berry protested. "I'm not a child."

"What are you doing talking to him?" Cherry muttered, then stopping at the doorway, she looked back to see him staring at them, frowning.

"Do you see how you treated me just there?" Berry asked her sister, with a clipped tone. "Why would you do that? That just brings attention to us."

"That's fine. I don't care," Cherry stated. "I'll do whatever it takes to keep you safe."

"This has nothing to do with keeping me safe," she cried out. "I'm fine."

"No, you're not fine, and you were talking to him. We don't know anything about him."

"Yeah, he just arrived, so that also means he didn't kidnap Yegorahn," Berry snapped. And, with that, she entered their room, carefully placed her tea on the floor, and crashed on her bed, waiting for her sister to say something. When all she heard was quiet sobs, Berry groaned, then rolled over to face her twin on the nearby bed. "Look. I'm sorry, but you have to stop panicking."

"I can't," Cherry wailed. "I just can't. I see him everywhere. I feel guilty because I didn't do something to stop it."

"You didn't know, so what could you do to stop it? And why are you even saying that? You must have a guilty conscience to feel guilt, but you didn't do anything wrong."

"No, but I slept with him." Cherry sighed, then walked over and sagged down on the other bed, beside Berry.

"It doesn't matter, and it was an adult relationship. The two of you were happy. You were excited that you found each other, and life was good. That's not against the rules.

It's not as if you broke any mandate here. Nobody cares about fraternizing up here."

"And yet we kept it a secret."

"Yes, and how much of keeping it secret was because it was special?" Berry pointed out.

Her sister smiled through her tears and nodded. "It was special. I had really high hopes. And now? … Everything is lost."

"It's not lost," Berry corrected. "Even though he may be lost temporarily, don't you even think that."

She shook her head. "How can you be so positive all the time?"

"Well, for one thing, I don't focus on all that negativity you keep spouting," Berry replied. "We're twins, but, jeez, in some ways, we are so opposite."

Her sister groaned. "You keep saying that."

"People tell us that all the time, that—outside of our looks—we really have nothing in common. I'm not sure that *nothing in common* fits either, but our life experiences have changed things."

"They have, whether that's a good thing or not."

"It doesn't matter because it's in our past. Our life experiences up to this point in time are what made us who we are. It doesn't matter that we have what we have," Berry stated. "You must start somewhere, and you start by getting over that fear."

"I'll get over that fear when I'm out of here," Cherry snapped through her teeth, rubbing the streak of tears off her cheeks. "Somebody here *killed* Yegorahn," she muttered under her breath, "and, damn it, I'll find out who."

"But, Cherry, we don't know that he is dead," Berry replied. "He's treated as missing, and people are out there every day searching for him."

"He's dead," she wailed. And, with a huff, Cherry scrunched against her pillows, pulled the blankets up over her head, and wouldn't say anything else.

Day 2 Morning

THE NEXT MORNING Egan woke, the chill of the Arctic in his bones. He quickly dressed and headed to the cafeteria for some coffee, and, if not coffee, hoping at least for hot water. He wouldn't complain regardless; coffee would be awesome, and, if not, he would adapt. He wasn't here for the coffee after all. And, if he didn't have to stay the full term for this survival training, at least the original twelve-week term, then he didn't have to stay, no matter what other people said, thought, or speculated.

As he walked into the dining area, several other people were eating breakfast. As expected, a lot of them stopped and stared.

He smiled at everybody and lifted a hand in greeting. "Yep, I'm new. Name's Egan." Then he grabbed a coffee and a plate of food. When he sat down at the table with a dozen other guys, they slowly introduced themselves. Even as they kept eating, their gazes were on him.

He nodded. "I heard. Nobody else is supposed to be coming in, but I'm an exception."

"Why the hell would you want to be an exception?" one of them snapped, his English heavy with a Russian accent. "People are dying up here. You know that, right? Our countries have forsaken us and have left us here to rot."

Egan winced at the vehemence in his tone. "I'm sorry to

hear about the deaths and the missing people. I'm an engineer, here to help with the mechanics of the generator."

"Right, of course, you'll help them keep us here. You're here to keep this miserable jail functioning," he bellowed, followed by a snort, as he got up and slammed out of the room.

With the agitated man gone, the atmosphere eased up a little bit.

Egan looked over at the others as he ate. "I gather he's not too happy about being here."

Several of the men shook their heads in unison. One of them shared in a sympathetic tone, "That's Raffi. His teammate Yegorahn is missing and feared dead."

"Ah, sorry to hear that, although I'd assume maybe Raffi would want to stick around until we can find his brother-in-arms."

"With absolutely no progress and the weather so ugly, I think he's given up, thinking his brother will just be buried out there in the middle of nowhere."

"Which would be pretty rough," Egan admitted.

"So, you won't be staying here? Is that the deal?"

"I don't know. Maybe it was a trick to get me up here and help boost the numbers, and they won't let me go home again," he suggested, halfway joking, though he'd seen that happen before.

One of the men nodded. "Salmo's my name. I wouldn't be at all surprised—a typical brass tactic."

"Right." Egan groaned. "Once I was sent to a camp in north China that they were working on, supposedly for forty-eight hours, and it ended up being forty-eight days." He shrugged. "But what do you do? You go where they tell you to go."

At that, the others laughed. "I'd take China over this too."

"It was also damn cold there," Egan muttered. "Some parts of China can rival this region pretty well."

At that, their conversation turned to geography, temperatures, and weather.

When a shadow fell across Egan and Magnus sat down beside him, Egan asked, "Are we heading out to work on generators today?"

Magnus nodded. "Yeah, and we also have to check up on the scientists' camp to confirm that Amelia hasn't shown up again."

"I don't understand that," said one of the men in an irritated tone. "If she has shown up and was capable of showing up, then why the hell isn't she down here already, where we have heat? Why are we wasting supplies by going back to the scientists' camp again and again, plus sending out search parties looking for her?"

"It's not just her," Magnus corrected. "Two of them were together, as best we know. It's hard to say exactly what's going on there and why she's not contacting anybody, especially if she's okay. If she could, she would. So, if she can't, that's why we presume we haven't heard from her and why we continue to search for her. Just as we do for missing base members."

That shut them up for a while, and, when their table emptied, just Magnus and Egan remained sitting here. He looked at Magnus and murmured, "Definitely some hard feelings around here."

"Yeah, did they hate on you about you coming in?"

"A little bit." Egan shrugged. "Mostly because a lot of them just want to get out and don't want to see new people coming in—especially one who can maintain the facility and then bulldoze their hopes of getting out of here fast."

"Yeah, I get that," Magnus agreed comfortably. "I'm not leaving because Sydney won't leave."

He smiled. "I heard about you two."

"All good things I presume?" he asked, with a smirk.

Egan nodded.

"And she's worth a dozen of a lot of people I've met in my lifetime," Magnus shared. "She's good people, so, if you need anything, you can count on her."

"Good enough, and if I can't get a hold of you?"

"Yeah, she'll probably know where I am," he said, with a fat grin. "Unless we're out on a mission, and that's a whole different story. Anyway, finish eating, and let's get going."

"I'm done already. Where are we starting this?"

Magnus stood. "First, we'll ensure we've got gear for you. We'll be out there for the better part of the day."

"Not inside the base?"

"We'll be inside for a while," Magnus confirmed. "That will give our bodies a bit of a break from the cold, and then we'll be back outside. Have you ever done time with the dogs?"

"I have. Will we take a dogsled team?"

"Yeah, we're a little low on gas," Magnus noted, a bit too cheerfully, "so we'll take the dogs. We'll also walk the two dogs—Toby and Benji—that were injured and need to go stretch out a bit. Then we'll be hauling them the rest of the way on the sled. Toby's my favorite. Kinda hoping to convince Joe to let me keep him, when this is all over."

"Sounds good."

They headed over to get the dogs, stashing their supplies to fix the generator in a sled.

Joe nodded at Egan. "Hey, I know you. You're Egan."

Egan smiled, reached out, and shook his hand. "Hey, Joe. How are you doing?"

"I feel better now, if it's the two of you taking my dogs. I can get behind that." But then he glared at them. "But, if you hurt them, you better—"

"The dogs'll be fine," Egan declared. "You know as well as I do that, if need be, I'll walk back and carry the damn dogs."

He laughed at that. "Just like old times, *huh*?"

He nodded. "Just like old times. Especially if we're supposed to be exercising the hurt ones."

"Yeah, one got a bullet in the rump and the other a bullet to his leg," Joe uttered in a dark voice. "That didn't go over very well."

"I'm sorry to hear that."

"The dogs are healing up, but both must be walked to build their strength," Joe explained in a somber tone. "So, you go ahead and use Toby and Benji for a little bit. However, as soon as you see one of those two flagging, you take him off his feet, give him a rubdown, and keep him warm," Joe instructed in a strictly businesslike tone. "We can't have any dog getting chilled out there after a workout, especially these two injured ones."

"Got it," Egan stated, and Magnus gave Joe a thumbs-up.

Within minutes, the two of them were heading out with the dogs toward the scientists' camp. With Magnus riding in the sled and with Egan skiing along at the back of the sled, it was hard to talk, so Egan kept quiet and kept notes in his head about locations, landmarks, and directions, the navigation first and foremost in his mind. When he saw the camp building up ahead, Magnus raised a hand.

Egan slowed the dog team, noting Magnus was now pointing to a broken-down sled off to the side. Egan immediately changed directions but also realized that one of the injured dogs was slowing. He stopped, and the two men quickly shifted Benji onto the sled and covered him up. With that done, Magnus took control of the team, while Egan skied beside the dogsled, as they headed toward the broken rig.

As they neared the wreckage, Egan's heart slammed against his chest because, on top of it, bundled up and strapped down, was a body.

DAY 2, MIDMORNING

IN THE COMMUNICATION center hub, Berry looked up from the data she had been inputting, watching a hard and fast discussion going on in front of her.

Her sister sat beside her and nudged her, then murmured, "Something's up. Look."

Something might be up, but the twins sure weren't privy to whatever was going on. As they waited, other people raced over, then quickly disappeared again. She looked over at Dave, who oversaw the data collection and reports. She asked him, "What's going on?"

He walked closer to her and replied, "They found a broken-down sled at the scientists' camp, complete with a body wrapped and strapped on top."

"Wrapped and strapped up? As if someone …"

"Yes, as if somebody was traveling with the body."

"Maybe trying to bring it back to scientists' camp then," Berry guessed.

"Maybe," he murmured. "We don't have any answers yet."

She nodded because answers were elusive up here and had been since they'd first arrived. It was frustrating to know that everything the investigators were working toward had come down to this problem. Yet she also knew that they were doing what they could.

Berry turned to her sister, who sat completely still, as if frozen. Berry smiled at Cherry reassuringly. "Hey, it's all right. … Don't panic. No need to."

"I'm not panicking," Cherry snapped, "but I know that look all too well, and it means that somebody else is dead."

"Or," Berry suggested, "somebody was trying to help, and they were bringing him in. At least this way they could be found."

"Maybe, and yet it makes no sense that they didn't find anyone with the body."

"We don't know that yet," she stated, looking at her sister. "This is just the first communication. They're going through the scientists' camp right now."

Cherry nodded but seemed completely unconvinced.

Berry wasn't exactly sure what was going on. However, with an awful lot of the essentials stripped from the scientists' camp, once all were evacuated due to no heat, Berry couldn't imagine that anybody bringing back a body, with the intent of picking up supplies, would be terribly happy.

Berry pondered that, and, when no more news was forthcoming, she walked over to Dave. "We cleaned out a bunch of the scientists' supplies, since their camp isn't livable now. What if somebody went back there, looking for supplies for other injured people?"

"Let's hope, if that's the case, they're pretty good at handling whatever life tosses them," he replied grimly. "Our search team didn't meet anybody heading this way, and that's a concern."

She winced at that. "It's a concern but not the end of the world." When he frowned, she shrugged. "If this was Amelia's team, and she's out there, trying to help somebody else, we don't know for sure that this is really a problem."

"And yet, if it isn't, she should be coming to our military base with them."

"Maybe she's trying. Maybe that's what this is about. Maybe she did several trips and didn't know about what happened at the camp. Don't forget that she's been out in the middle of nowhere all this time."

He nodded. "The good news is—at least, if we have a body—hopefully we can get some answers."

Berry wasn't so sure about that but returned to her work, though the atmosphere was uneasy the rest of the morning. When another increase in noise and excitement came, she realized that Magnus and Egan had likely returned.

Leaving her sister to continue the paperwork, or to at least stare at the computer screen, Berry bundled up and headed outside toward the search group, where the conversation was happening. When Egan saw her, he smiled. She walked up closer and asked, "And?"

He shrugged. "We found one of the missing men," he told her in a low voice. "Bundled up on a sled, as if the sled had been deliberately packaged with him on it, but nobody was with the sled, and the sled itself was broken."

She nodded. "So, nothing conclusive, except that we have retrieved one of the missing men. Do we know who? And there was no sign of Amelia?"

"No, none," Egan replied. "Sydney is taking a look at the body right now, hoping to make an identification. For an informal one, I can tell you it looks to be Yegorahn. However, beyond that first glance, we just don't have enough to go on."

"Oh, I get it," she murmured, shocked but relieved to have some closure, yet knowing this would be a terrible blow for her sister. Still, it's what they suspected, so surely having answers would be better than none. And now his family would have some closure as well. "As much as I don't like it, I get it."

He nodded. "How will your sister handle it?"

"She already thought he was dead, since he had been missing for so long. However, getting confirmation today will still be hard for her to handle. His death will bring up all her fears again, so it's certainly not a great situation."

"I'm sorry," he murmured, "but I'm not sorry we found a body."

"No, of course not. It's much better for all of us if we find everyone who's gone missing. It would certainly give us an opportunity to get some answers, which is the hardest thing."

"I agree with you there," Egan noted. "Having no answers is brutal."

"What about at the scientists' camp? Did you find anything?"

He shook his head. "No, but now we'll keep a closer eye on it."

"Why?" she asked. "If the sled made it that far, and somebody now knows that the scientists' camp is unlivable right now, they would have come here, if they could have."

He nodded. "And what if somebody is injured and can't be moved, or what if it's Amelia who is injured, and she went there looking for supplies?"

"Wouldn't she have come here then?"

"Sure," he agreed, "but it also depends on how far she can travel back and forth in a day. Plus you must consider what else might be going on in her world. The bottom line is"—Egan paused—"you have to consider why Amelia wouldn't be coming here."

Berry stared at him in shock and then slowly nodded. "I guess if you take it from that perspective, it changes things, doesn't it?"

"It sure does," Egan said, "though we must give her the benefit of the doubt at the moment."

"I don't think too many people will be prepared to do that."

"Maybe not," he acknowledged, "but it doesn't take a whole lot of guesswork to suggest that she must have a good reason for not coming in."

"Yeah, but most of the people here will just say that she's guilty, and they won't give her much of a chance."

He stared at her, then asked in a quiet tone, "Is that how you feel?"

"No, not at all," Berry stated. "I don't even know the woman, but she's got a lot of experience in these conditions, and she's pretty strong-willed, I hear. Therefore, if something were going on that she doesn't like, as long as she's capable of staying out there, that's probably where she'll stay. I'd probably be right there with her."

He smiled. "That was my take on it too. So let's give her the benefit of the doubt and maybe remind the others here to not be so quick to condemn her, while we catch up with her. Since we now have some tracks, finding her seems more likely—at least as long as I get back out there before the tracks are gone."

"How did the dogs react?" she asked.

He considered her question with a big grin. When she looked at him expectantly, he relented. "Nobody else thought to ask that."

She smirked. "As I've mentioned before, I've spent a fair bit of time out in very unfriendly conditions, and, in those cases, I've learned to trust the dogs."

"I'm right there with you on that," Egan declared. "The dogs were curious and friendly, tails wagging and all that. They weren't terribly happy about the body, but, inside the scientists' camp, the dogs were fine and raised no alarms."

She nodded and kept that info to herself.

Egan added, "You do seem to understand humanity."

"I don't know about humanity," she corrected, with a shrug, "but, if there were a K9 psychology class, I'd sign up and be right there to study it." Berry laughed. "I really enjoy dealing with the dogs."

"We took the two injured dogs with us, the pair that had been shot a while back," he reminded her, his tone dark.

She looked at him curiously. "Why would you do that?"

"Just for the workout." He smiled. "All on Joe's orders of course. Once the dogs got winded, we switched them out and gave them a ride."

"Oh, I would have loved to have seen that. I'm all for animals getting treated better in this world."

"You have to remember. These dogs love to run, and they love to be out here," he said. "So it's not as if they were suffering or anything."

"No, I understand, and Joe's dogs are always well looked after. I spend as much time over there as I can, particularly recently." She grinned, with a glance back at the base.

"Yeah, I don't imagine your sister is that easy to be around right now."

"No, but she's a good person, and I won't desert her in her time of need. Yet it helps to get a little bit of time to myself," she murmured.

"Of course. That's important for anyone."

She smiled up at him. "So, all in all, an interesting day?"

"Interesting, yes. Successful? … Not so much, but definitely interesting. Although no sign of anybody at the scientists' camp. We did repair their generator and got some work done on that. So they can get it back up and running again—at least for a little while, depending on their gas supply. I had brought some parts with me, based on what information I'd been given about their generator's prior problems. So, with what Magnus already knew, and having some parts and a good understanding of what was going on, we managed to make good progress on that and got it back up and running. So—"

"But you didn't leave it running."

"No, not while the camp is empty. Plus it seems the university is getting more involved with backing the search and updating the camp, so maybe it won't be shut down indefinitely, as they had assumed. There's even talk about some of the group who left coming back in—at least for a few days, to close up and to shut it down properly."

"That would be a good idea," Berry noted. "Some of them ended up in a pretty bad state, didn't they?"

"Yeah, especially the ones who were airlifted out," he noted. "I think most of them want some closure. Some don't really want to come back, but understanding what went wrong is how you learn from this. Anyway, that's a discussion for another time, and, if you'll excuse me, I have to get ready to head out again." And, with that, he gave her a gentle smile and was gone.

His smile was way gentler than she had expected, given the size of the man. He was also extremely cooperative and straightforward, and she appreciated that too.

As she headed back into the comm center, her sister glared at her.

"So," Cherry said, "what did he say about Yegorahn's death? Did you get anything out of him?"

"Get anything out of him?" Berry asked in a confused tone. "What does that even mean? I did ask for information, but I wasn't trying to pry it out of him because that can get us into trouble. Me anyway."

"You know perfectly well he won't be allowed to talk," Cherry stated crossly. "So it wasn't helpful to talk to him."

"You can say that if you want," Berry replied, "but I'm certainly not against talking to any of them."

"As long as you don't get involved," Cherry ordered, with a tone of warning. "Chances are he'll end up dying on you too."

Berry sucked in her breath at that. "That's hardly fair, Cherry. And I don't think Yegorahn wanted whatever happened to him anyway, so let's just shelve those suppositions, please." Her sister sniffled several times, and Berry groaned. "Look. I'm not trying to be mean, but we don't really know what happened to Yegorahn, and it would be very nice if we could stick to the facts and not just theories at this point."

Her sister sniffled several more times and then finally nodded. "*Fine*, but I won't be happy until we get out of here."

"I get that. I do, and I'm sorry that it's turned into such a nightmare for you, but we will get out of here safe and sound. Don't you worry."

"I'm glad you're so positive because you know how I feel about this."

Unfortunately Berry did, and it seemed she could do absolutely nothing to get her sister to change her attitude, and that would just make it all that much harder going forward.

Still, even though it was absolutely horrific that they had found the body of one of the missing men out there, it would be a huge boon to Yegorahn's family to know for certain that he was gone and to have a body to bury. Although his death was not the answer they had hoped for, it was definitely a good answer for someone faced with the uncertainty of a family member just disappearing forever in this place and under these harsh weather conditions.

Day 2 Late Morning

GIVEN THE CIRCUMSTANCES, it was at least a possible answer now on Yegorahn. As far as the still-missing Amelia went, that was just one big mystery that Berry didn't understand at all, but she had to trust that this woman— who had such a reputation with her vast Arctic survival experience—was doing what she felt she needed to do. Yet maybe she was doing it under pressure for the wrong reasons, which certainly made Berry more alert than ever.

Then she steeled herself to handle her sister. Since nobody on base was supposed to know about Cherry's relationship with Yegorahn, people here wouldn't offer Cherry condolences. However, many would ask if she had heard the latest or if she had heard even more information. The gossip grapevine would not be appreciated by Cherry.

"Hey, I'll go grab some tea and come back," she told Cherry, who sat frozen, staring at her computer screen, not inputting anything. "You want some?"

"Grab me a cup too," her sister said.

Berry headed to the cafeteria, not surprised to see Magnus and Egan there, warming up before their second Arctic outing of this morning. She walked over and sat down directly across from them. "I know this may sound like complete bullshit, but I'm not trying to stir up anything or cause any trouble for you," she began in a whisper.

"Speak freely," Magnus stated.

"All I can tell you is that I'm wondering if, … what if Amelia is doing whatever she's doing under pressure?" At that, both men slowly lowered their coffee cups and stared at her. She nodded. "Okay, so I'm crazy, right?"

"I'm not sure you're crazy," Magnus replied, "but why would you consider it?"

"I don't know anything about the situation really, but why else would somebody do this, dropping off the body at the camp and not here at the base? Either that or because she doesn't trust anybody here. She has to have a reason for not contacting us, and is that because she chooses not to, or because she can't?"

"One hell of a good question."

EGAN TOOK A sip of his tea, while he studied Berry over the rim of his mug.

She twisted to look at him and shrugged. "Go ahead. Tell me that I'm crazy."

"Coming here is a logical and available option, but you're right. Either she's choosing not to come in or she can't, and, in this case, either choice could be the same thing."

"Right, choosing because there's another reason for her not to do so," Berry noted. "However, what if somebody else is pulling her strings, with consequences we haven't considered? What if one of these guys who've gone missing is too injured or being held hostage by somebody else?"

Egan let out his breath very slowly, as he turned toward Magnus, wondering what his thoughts were. And Magnus, as always, kept his face a blank slate and didn't let anything through.

"The bottom line is," Magnus replied, "we'll have to wait and see. It's good to consider the broad range of what it could be, but no point in beleaguering the details until we find her."

"So, you're going back out to track her then?"

"We are."

Egan asked her, "You guys will be okay here, right?"

She nodded. "Yeah, my sister's not doing all that great, but, hey, what else is new?"

"I'm surprised she wasn't allowed to leave," Magnus noted.

"She didn't want to mention her relationship with Yegorahn, as it was her secret, so she couldn't very well ask to leave because she lost her boyfriend," Berry explained. "And, even though I might have mentioned it to a person or two, it wasn't something Cherry was prepared to broadcast in an effort to get out of here because it wouldn't get me out anyway." Berry shrugged, with half a smile. "And she wanted to stay with me more than she wanted to leave."

Magnus nodded, then looked over at Egan, who still stared at her, wondering at her words.

She smiled at him. "And I hope I'm wrong about Amelia being coerced into helping somebody who is a danger to us all."

"I hope you are too," Egan agreed, "because that

wouldn't be good."

"No, it wouldn't be. And I came here to get tea, but I was hoping to see you guys before you left." She paused, then added, "I was thinking about something that you mentioned earlier to me, and I think a few names might be of interest to you."

Egan nodded. "In that case, want to make a list while we're out?"

She winced. "That's fine, but I really don't want that list to be known as coming from me."

He chuckled. "That's fine. When I get back, share that list with me, okay?"

She nodded, got up, poured two cups of tea, and quickly escaped.

As soon as she was out of earshot, Magnus looked at Egan. "What was that all about?"

"The Russian called Yegorahn? He was having an affair with her sister." At that, Magnus's eyebrows rose. Egan nodded. "So, the question really is, was somebody else not happy about that relationship?"

Magnus let out a low whistle. "I hadn't really considered jealousy as a motive, and yet we should. It should always be considered. I wasn't looking into that death as much as some people might be," he added. "I had a bit of a run-in with him myself. I need to introduce you to Ted soon. He is the face of the investigation up here and the leader of that investigation team."

"Ted Nugan?" Egan asked.

Magnus nodded. "You know him?"

He frowned. "Yeah, I do."

"Doesn't sound as if you know him in a good way."

He shrugged. "I know him, and I'm not sure that it's a

good or a bad thing. I've seen him on other missions, and he doesn't always get along with that many people."

"Maybe the job doesn't allow him to get along," Magnus corrected, "as you and I both know all too well."

"Yeah, isn't that the truth. Anyway, it's something to consider, if we get a list from Berry at the end of the day. I can always give it to Ted," Egan offered, "and that will get both of us out of it."

Magnus laughed. "If you think that will stop our responsibility for it, you're kidding yourself. The problem with a place like this is that too many people are up in everyone's business, and, with no place else to go, we get hot tempers, too much stress, and no release."

Egan added, "That's a recipe for disaster, and relationships are one of the biggest banes."

"It could also be one of the biggest boons," Magnus pointed out, with a grin.

"Absolutely, but I've seen a lot more bane than boon in places like this. We probably need to get some grub and get going, *huh?*"

"Yeah, let's go." And, with that, they headed over to the first hot dishes of lunch coming out.

Chef looked at them, then shook his head. "Will you guys be the first off into the tundra every day?"

"Today for sure we were," Magnus stated. "And now we're heading right back to the scientists' camp to see if we can come up with any usable tracks from the broken-down sled."

At that, Chef's expression turned somber.

As they began their second trip today to the scientists' camp, Egan realized that, with the noon sunshine, it was warming up to temperatures that were really pleasant out here. They were both on skis, carrying packs, having left the dogs behind for this revisit.

As they reached the camp, they stopped and studied all the tracks. There had been quite a wind earlier this morning, so blowing snow had covered some of the tracks, but still enough were visible. They headed off to follow them.

After they'd been tracking for a good hour, Egan asked Magnus, "So, why would it be this far away?"

"I don't know," he admitted.

"I've been thinking about what Berry told us. Not only her words but what she was implying."

"I don't want to worry about what she's implying," Magnus declared. "We've got enough on our plates right now. Yet we definitely need to keep an open mind."

As they moved forward, Egan pointed out where the tracks swerved off to the side and stopped, almost for a break. He pondered that for a moment. "So, she's not traveling quickly, and she's dragging a sled behind her, but she's on skis, though that could be because that sled broke down. I wonder if she brought it deliberately or if she broke it down afterward."

Magnus stopped, considered that, frowning. "Now why would somebody do that? Although it could be fixable. I didn't take that close of a look at it. Did you?"

Egan shook his head. "No, and, if it was fixable, she would be looking for it for later. Yet I'm thinking maybe she brought the body here so it could be found, knowing that, even if there were issues at the scientists' camp, somebody still should have been around there."

"And yet we moved everybody out, and the sign was still on the door. Although the facility was locked, Amelia had her own keys anyway."

"Exactly, so we don't know if any of this is part and parcel of the problem with the base."

"It's all part and parcel of our problem," Magnus stated, as they picked up the pace again.

"But one of the concerns is more about what's going on here at the scientists' camp and how it's impacting everybody else at the base, especially considering all the other problems we have on base."

"No doubt that it's having a huge impact on everybody else," Magnus stated, as he kept pace with Egan. "What I don't understand is what's going on in Amelia's world that she would need to do this?"

"Which brings us back to Berry's comment from this morning."

"Exactly," Magnus confirmed. "It was nagging me in the back of my mind, but I was ignoring it."

"Did you tell Ted what Berry mentioned?"

"No, I haven't had a chance yet. I was thinking we'd talk to him when we got back later this afternoon. We just won't mention Berry's name in all this."

"I'm looking forward to seeing that list myself," Egan murmured.

"You really think it could be a jealousy thing?"

"It's an easy answer, and I guess an easy answer is as good as any, don't you think?"

"Maybe, maybe not, but it's at least an answer, and something that we don't have yet," Magnus acknowledged, "and we really need it. We need something to fall into place here."

"I won't argue with that," Egan muttered, looking around. "The tracks are fading fast in this weather."

"That's not good because, if we can't track where she

came from, we can't follow her back."

"And what are the chances that she knew that?"

Magnus turned to Egan and nodded. "That just gives more credence to what we were looking at earlier."

"I know," Egan agreed. "Right about now, Dr. Amelia is raising all kinds of alarms in my mind. This move is really suspicious. … Unless she's a victim herself somehow."

At that, Magnus nodded. "We'll keep going up here for another hour or so, but after that …"

"Yeah. We're starting to circle around," Egan noted.

"I noticed that too." Magnus nodded. "So, was that done deliberately to lead *us* away or to lead *somebody else* away?"

"We can't know until we find her, so let's keep going."

With that, they headed on again. Magnus spoke up a bit later. "We keep assuming this is Amelia, but what if it's not? What if this is someone else altogether?"

His remarks hung in the air, as they moved ahead because neither had an answer to that.

DAY 2, AFTERNOON

B ERRY FOUND HERSELF waiting the rest of the day for the men to show back up again. In the meantime, the dead body was medically confirmed to be Yegorahn's. Word got around the base fast enough for Cherry to hear all about it. Again. In the meantime, Berry struggled with questioning her sister about the many men who had appeared interested in her. Any comment about it was guaranteed to set off Cherry, and that was the last thing Berry wanted to do. Peace and quiet was important for everybody, but, in this instance, her sister had the tendency to get way too upset over the small things. Plus it just emphasized her loss right now, and grieving was hard enough, without people pushing these questions at her.

Finally her sister glared at her and snapped, "What is bugging you?"

Berry frowned. "I was wondering whether Yegorahn's death may have been jealousy related."

Her sister stared at her in shock, then shook her head. "Why would you even think that?"

"How can I not think something?" Berry replied in a bitter tone, more than she intended. "Everybody is wondering what the hell's going on and how this all happened." Berry shook her head. "So to not try to think of potential ideas is foolish."

Cherry stared daggers at her. "I don't want to be asked those questions," she snapped. "I didn't cheat on him, if that's what you're asking."

"That's not what I'm asking," Berry stated. "I know you didn't, and I know how it worked out, but I also know there were a lot of other men coming around."

"So?" Cherry raised her hands in protest. "I didn't want or like any of those other men."

"Good, I get that, but then I still need to know who those other men were."

"No, you don't," Cherry declared, glaring at her. "I just want to put this to rest. So the last thing I need is for you to be poking around at any of those other guys."

"Of course not," Berry acknowledged.

Just then, one of the men they worked with in the data center walked in, carrying a tray with coffees and sweet rolls.

Berry looked up and smiled. "Hey, Henry. Are some of those for us?" she asked in delight.

He shrugged. "Hey, they just came out of the oven, so I figured that, before the rest of the place discovered them and we lost out"—he winked—"I'd grab us some."

"Thanks, that was nice." She quickly gave her sister a coffee and a cinnamon bun, hoping that would appease her. However, from the expression on Cherry's face, caffeine and sugar wouldn't go very far.

Still, Henry sat down beside her sister, staring at her intently. "Hey, Cherry. I know you're still struggling. I just wanted to let you know that I'm sorry."

Her sister frowned, but then her face cleared. "Yeah, I know. Sorry, I haven't been very friendly since it happened," she murmured.

"You were close to Yegorahn, and losing anybody is

tough," Henry noted. "My wife and I lost a best friend one year ago," he shared, staring off into the distance. "Now, when I think of them, it seems to be a fond memory, but, at the time, it was really tough."

"Yeah, it is," Cherry agreed, as she sipped her coffee and smiled at him.

"Besides, lots of other people are around here are interested in having a relationship with you, if you want to step out again."

"God no." Cherry gave a headshake. "That was bad enough once, but to see a repeat? God no."

"It wouldn't be a repeat," Henry said, staring at her.

Cherry just smiled and didn't say anything.

Yet it made Berry wonder how many people really did know about her sister's relationship. As he got up to clear away the dishes, she called out to him. "Hang on, Henry. I'll give you a hand." She helped him with the dishes and headed back to the kitchen with them. "I didn't realize you knew about her relationship with Yegorahn."

"Yeah, I saw the two of them one evening," Henry replied. "They weren't trying to hide it." Then he stopped and frowned at her. "Or were they?"

Berry shrugged. "I just hadn't realized."

"I think most people know. It's just one of those things that's hard to hide in a place like this, but I can understand her not wanting to be the butt of all the conversations."

"No, of course not," Berry agreed, "and I appreciate the discretion on your part."

He nodded. "Your sister is a good person, and I'm sorry for her loss."

And Berry left it at that. What else could she say? Everything he said sounded right, but, because of the circumstances, Berry was taking it the wrong way. And, even then, she had absolutely no reason to take it any way at all. She groaned at herself, as she headed back to her sister.

Cherry immediately stood, left the data room, and headed for their assigned bedroom. "Did you ask him?" her sister snapped. Cherry was beyond furious. "It's obvious you were just dying to ask him a bunch of questions."

"I did ask him some questions. I didn't realize he knew about your relationship."

Cherry shrugged, trying to control herself, and took a deep breath. "Yeah, he saw us one evening."

"That's fine," Berry noted. "As Henry mentioned, you didn't need to keep it secret."

"And yet it felt as if we did."

"So you had to, or did you just want to?"

Her sister gave her a gentle smile. "There is a difference, isn't there?"

"There is, indeed."

"We just felt we had something special," Cherry shared, "and we were really enjoying being together."

"And that's great," her sister said. "No reason to feel bad about that."

"And yet when you talk about it, … you make it sound bad."

Berry groaned because sometimes her sister could just get cranky over nothing. "That's not fair," Berry replied. "I have no intention of making you feel bad about anything. All I was trying to do … Look, Cherry. I'm just trying to figure out if Yegorahn's death could have been caused by somebody who was jealous of your relationship."

"Who would even give a damn?" she asked in exasperation. "It's not as if I spent time with anybody else."

"But you did, when we first got here. ... You spent time with a lot of people."

"Sure, but I didn't spend any *private* time with them," she clarified, glaring at her sister. "That was mostly just people trying to be friendly." Cherry shrugged. "After all, we're in a camp, and things can get very old, very quickly, if we go that solo route."

"I understand that," Berry stated, "but it still doesn't change the fact that it's a question that deserves asking."

"Ask away, just don't involve me with any of it," Cherry muttered, frowning at her sister. "I would just as soon you drop it, but obviously you won't. You've got a bee in your bonnet, and that's all there is to it," Cherry declared, with an odd expression on her face. "You'll make my life miserable while you sort this out, won't you?" And, with that, she turned and slammed the door, leaving Berry standing in the hallway, with Cherry in their bedroom.

Astonished, yet not sure why she was really surprised, Berry slowly turned and headed back to the comms room.

As she walked in, Henry looked up and smiled at her. "Hey, I'm sorry. I didn't mean to upset her."

"Anything upsets her these days," Berry stated, with a wave of her hand. "It's a pretty upsetting scenario."

"I didn't even realize she was in that much of a relationship."

"I think she would prefer that everybody just forgot about it at this point," Berry noted, with a half smile. "Nothing quite like thinking people are talking about you all the time."

He winced at that. "I can get behind that. No matter how it goes, none of us want to think that we're being talked about, especially in a place like this. So, you're right. I'll stay quiet."

"Thank you," Berry replied gratefully. "As far as my sister goes, she'll come to terms with it eventually."

"I hope so. It'll make life a little difficult for you the longer she takes," Henry added, with a word of warning.

Berry shrugged. "That's just a fact of life," she murmured. And, with that, she got back down to work, knowing that, if she could do nothing else, at least she could get some data input accomplished.

And that was worth a lot to her.

EGAN AND MAGNUS made it back to the base, as Egan headed straight for the kitchen and the dining room area, knowing he was really just heading toward wherever he might find Berry. He saw the knowing look that Magnus didn't even try to conceal, and Egan shrugged. "What can I say? I'm looking for that list."

Magnus snorted but let him get away with it, and, for that, Egan was grateful. He didn't understand the impulse to go, but, hey, he would follow it because Berry seemed to have an inside track, and he needed that right now. Somebody up here had to sort out what was going on, and Egan still had to report in to Mason. However, so far, Egan didn't have a whole lot to say—except that they'd found yet another body, but at least it was one of the missing men. He knew that a select few also reported in to Mason, but Egan hadn't realized who, not until he stepped into the kitchen area, standing behind an enormous back, so huge it could only belong to one person.

He studied the profile and then said in a low tone, "Correct me if I am wrong, but isn't that Mountain Bear Rode in front of me?"

Mountain spun, still as light and as soft on his feet as a man a fraction of his size. Mountain studied him and then slowly nodded. "Hey," Mountain greeted him. "Glad you made it okay."

"Yeah, I made it," Egan confirmed. "The *okay* part's a different story."

"At least you found somebody we were looking for already," Mountain noted. "That's more than the rest of us."

"Only because I was the lucky one at the scientists' camp at that time," he murmured. "Otherwise, you know perfectly well that Magnus would have found him on his own."

"Maybe." Mountain lowered his voice and asked, "Have you had any armory training up here?"

Egan shook his head at that. "No, and I was wondering how the system worked."

"You'll go on training for the next couple days," Mountain shared. "I want you to keep an eye on who has access to the armory, how the guns are treated, and how some of these weapons may have been taken from the armory without permission," Mountain stated.

"I wasn't aware we were missing any."

"Somebody gave Anna a gun," Mountain shared. "It's not something she would have had access to on her own. At least not if protocols were followed, but, given the scenario here, it's possible she slipped in and picked one. If that's possible, which I suspect it is, then I'd like confirmation."

Egan whistled at that. "I didn't think of that."

"Nope, but we need to," Mountain stated. "So that's definitely on my list for sorting out. Now I've delegated that to you. Report back in a few days."

Egan nodded. "No word on your brother?"

Mountain shook his head at that. "No, but I'm heading out tomorrow morning to track where you guys left off today."

"Okay, you know we went out for several hours today alone."

"That's fine," Mountain declared. "I plan on staying out for several days."

His tone was hard, as if to discourage anybody who would argue, but Egan knew that nobody would. He didn't know what Mountain's public position here was, but, in a situation like this, very few people ever argued with Mountain and survived. He literally was a force unto himself. "You don't have to do it alone, you know?"

Mountain looked at him and nodded. "It's too dangerous to take anybody with me."

Egan shook his head. "And you also know that going out alone in the Arctic is stupid."

Mountain deepened his glare.

"I'm not telling you anything you didn't already know," Egan admitted. "I guess I'm just dumb enough to stand up and tell you."

Mountain nodded. "That makes you special around here. Most people take one look and just tell me to do whatever I want to do. They don't give a crap."

Egan smiled at that. "Yeah, or maybe it's got something to do with your size."

"Maybe." Mountain gave him a shrug. "I really don't give a shit myself."

"Maybe not, but I, for one, don't want to see any more dead bodies around here," Egan stated.

"I appreciate your bringing one back and for doing the

tracking you did today," Mountain said. "With any luck we can sort this out faster than not."

"I'm not so sure about that, but …" Egan hesitated and then looked around. "We were talking earlier today—and not saying this is what's happening of course—but what are the chances that Amelia *couldn't* come back?"

"Either she chose not to or she couldn't." Mountain nodded. "It's got to be one or the other."

"Somebody with the experience that she's got, … I'm betting she *couldn't* come back."

"And that is definitely concerning and also why I'm heading out," Mountain replied. "I do need somebody to keep track of things here, since Magnus is already overloaded and really busy."

"I can do it," Egan offered. "What is it you want me to track?"

"Anything and everything to do with the armory, plus anybody interested in where I'm going and why."

"If they even notice that you're leaving," he pointed out. "Outside of Chef, getting food for you, or Joe, if you're taking his dogs and a sled."

"Sure, the obvious ones in the search and rescue process, but keep an eye out for someone too nosy," Mountain suggested, "and it's easy to make us think that it's nothing, but obviously something much bigger than I assumed is going on here."

"I don't think it's anything bigger at all," Egan shared, "in terms of the Russian Yegorahn. I'm wondering if that wasn't just a case of jealousy."

At that, Mountain turned with an amazing speed, as he snorted. "Why would you say that?"

Egan quickly told him about Berry and Cherry.

Mountain shook his head. "I spoke to both of them myself," he snapped. "They never mentioned it."

"They never mentioned it because Cherry didn't want her relationship with Yegorahn made public," Egan explained.

"And Berry went along with that?" he asked in astonishment. "From the very beginning it was a potential damn murder investigation," Mountain declared in frustration, his face growing all red and puffy. "Why would anybody not want to get to the bottom of it?"

"I don't know about that, and all I can tell you is what I know at the moment. Berry also suggested that Amelia may not have been acting on her own accord, which just adds to our own suspicions."

"Right," Mountain noted, with a disgusted tone. "So *now* she talks. As much as I want to ask her some more questions before I head out, I don't have time, so I'm delegating that to you."

"What do you want me to do?" Egan asked.

"Track it down, sort it out, and find out how much of that is something that we can move on, versus something that's really not helpful," Mountain detailed. "Just because people say they were in a relationship doesn't mean that they were." At that, he looked down at his watch. "I've got to go." And he stomped off and disappeared rapidly down the hall.

Day 2 Dinnertime

EGAN WANTED TO call out and ask Mountain if he'd gotten some food to go before heading out, but it didn't look like it. Maybe Mountain already had his supplies loaded up.

Now, as Egan watched Cherry and Berry step into the cafeteria, Cherry took one look at him, and her face twisted in anger. She immediately turned and glared at her sister, then picked up a plate, filled it, and walked right back out again. He gathered that he'd been pegged as the bad guy in the whole deal.

Berry walked over, sat down beside him, and murmured, "Sorry about that. She's quite pissed off at me for starting this."

"Apparently you both were questioned along with everybody else when Yegorahn first went missing, and somebody is not happy that you lied."

She looked at him and shrugged. "I didn't lie. Really I didn't. At the time I didn't see any value in discussing Cherry's relationship with Yegorahn. As to what I was being asked, I told the truth. However, nobody specifically asked me if my sister was in a relationship with Yegorahn," she replied in astonishment.

"So, that won't wash. Just so you know."

She rolled her eyes at that. "*Great*, my sister's already pissy enough, and now the last thing I need is for her to get questioned once more about it by the authorities."

"Did she get asked point-blank if she knew him?"

"I don't know what she got asked. I was in a different room at the time," Berry explained. "I was asked if I knew him, and I said that I knew *of* him, but I didn't know him well, and that was very true," she stated. "Believe me. I didn't spend any time with him. He was all about my sister."

"And where exactly did they have time and space to be together?"

"Our room," she replied, with a wince. "My sister kept asking me to go for a walk, so I spent a lot of time in the common room, while they got to know each other." She added air quotes to emphasize her point.

"And their last night together?"

"Yeah, that night I found an empty room," Berry explained. "So I bunked in there and left our room to my sister. Believe me. I wish now that I hadn't."

"It doesn't mean that's why Yegorahn is dead though," Egan reminded her. "It's easy to take on guilt, but it's not your fault. The only person who's at fault here is the one who killed Yegorahn."

Berry wanted to believe that, but she was not quite sure that she could let herself off the hook. Then she slowly nodded. "I keep telling myself that, but my sister's so broken up over it." Berry groaned. "So I keep wondering if I could have done something else."

"Of course you wonder," Egan agreed. "But, in this case, finding Yegorahn's dead body, we've got to question everything, and that's what we'll do now. We've got to start at the beginning and question everything, and unfortunately that means we'll also talk to your sister."

Berry nodded slowly. "She's likely to be quite combative. She doesn't like authority in the best of times."

"Which doesn't make any sense," Egan broke in, "since the military is all about authority."

"Yet she fit in quite well, as if she understands the whole system, as if she understands how it works, and she's been good with that. Still, when people step out of that box she's constructed, she doesn't like it. So, if you have an official standing that puts you in this position, then she'll probably be fine. However, if you don't, you can expect her to tell you to shove it where the sun don't shine."

He nodded. "And I'm sorry about that, but this is well

past the time to worry about her feelings. So we will question her regardless. We just have to make it happen and get whatever information she has, whether she likes it or not."

Berry winced. "Probably better if I came along," she suggested. "I can't guarantee that she'd be any kinder or easier to get along with, especially with me there, but it might be a little easier on her afterward."

He nodded. "In that case, we'll start with her."

Berry knocked on their door, only to have Cherry snap, "Stay out."

"I won't," Berry said, fatigue in her voice. "I need a good night's sleep too, and this is my room as well."

"Go get another one," Cherry growled.

Instead Berry just opened the door using the key she'd picked up before heading out for her day, just as a precaution. "No, I won't. This is *our* room. If you want to change it up somehow, ask Dave for a new room assignment."

Her sister just glared at her, then turned and threw herself to the other side of her bed.

Berry sighed. "You won't like the next development because you'll have to talk to Egan."

Cherry snorted. "Why would I do that?"

"He's been tasked with taking a fresh look into Yego-rahn's death," Berry explained. "And apparently your statement didn't mention anything about knowing him."

Cherry stiffened. "It's none of his business what I know and don't know," she stated, with a sneer. "Ted's running the investigations."

"So, did you tell Ted the truth?" At that, Cherry didn't say anything. "Is there a reason you're avoiding talking to them about it?"

"Of course there's a reason." Cherry turned to look at

her sister. "You know that perfectly well."

"How is it that you feel more concerned about looking after your reputation than finding out what happened to Yegorahn?"

Her sister burst into tears at that, but they were angry tears. But rather than screaming and shouting, aware that the walls were damn thin here, her sister pulled the covers over her head and muttered, "Go away."

Going away tonight was one thing—but still not happening. However, "going away" wouldn't work in the morning, not when Berry knew that Egan would be here, ready to talk to Cherry. If she didn't want to talk, that was fine, but it was only fine to a certain point. Then it would just become a bigger problem for Cherry.

DAY 3, MORNING

WHEN THE NEXT morning came though, Cherry got up and left their room very quickly, and Berry warned Egan at breakfast. "She's not cooperative, and I have no idea why, but I'd say she's more combative."

He nodded. "That's fine. She may not like it, but it doesn't change the fact that it'll happen."

"She says that you have no right to do any investigation and that this is Ted's thing."

"Oh, Ted's a part of it. Believe me, but I've been assigned to reopen the investigation from scratch again." She just looked at him, even more confused, so he had to clarify. "Starting fresh, just in case there has been some bias," he pointed out, with a shrug.

Berry winced. "Cherry *is* good friends with Ted."

"*Great*," Egan muttered. "Nice to know that I've already got to start with that problem."

"Sorry." She nodded. "Cherry won't cooperate. She tried to keep me out of my own room last night, and I didn't get a whole lot of sleep. Thankfully I grabbed the key before I left that last time, otherwise …"

"It's supposed to be your room too. If there are any issues, go see if there's a spare that you can use. I can't say I would be against having a room all to myself under your circumstances."

"Of course not," she agreed, with a smile. "It really does help to have your own space sometimes, doesn't it?"

"It does, though it's not typically how it is on these military bases, so I'll appreciate it while I can." He looked down at his watch and frowned. "I'll keep you out of it as much as I can, and I'll make it as official as possible for Cherry's sake, so she doesn't think she's been railroaded into something. However, the fact of the matter is, … she's not getting out of it, regardless of how much she objects."

That's what Berry was afraid of.

EGAN WALKED OUT of the colonel's office with a notebook in hand and headed straight for Ted Nugan. More to the point, his quarters, that he was using as an office as well. But that was part of the problem with doing the work that Ted did. It always had to be in private, so he couldn't work in communal areas.

As Egan knocked on the door, it opened under his hand. He pushed it farther open and stuck his head around the corner to find Ted glaring at him.

"Yeah, I already heard," he snapped.

Egan shrugged. "Hey, not trying to step on any toes."

"Whatever." Ted raised both hands. "Jerry is around here somewhere too—and of course Magnus," he said, with an eye roll.

"And Mountain too."

At that, Ted snorted. "Yeah, it's getting a little ridiculous, if you ask me."

"And yet it sounds as if you need help."

"I don't need help," he stated briskly. The older man

bristled under the implied suggestion that maybe he wasn't doing his job. "The problem is very much a case of the shit just doesn't stop, and nobody's talking."

Ted had a point. "I'm here now regardless," he declared, dismissing Ted's concerns because, no matter his rank or efforts, so far they hadn't had any breaks. Sydney, Magnus, Mountain, and Rogan had cracked some of it and had found some other problems, but Ted hadn't had any luck on the main case so far. Trying to control his thoughts, Egan continued. "Obviously I must talk to everyone on base again, now that we know Yegorahn has been killed. I'll ask that everyone keep the details to themselves."

"Ha. In gossip central? That won't work. You'll still have to make it somewhat official for anybody to talk to you about it."

Egan pondered that and then nodded slowly. "I'll just say that I've been directed to collect information."

Ted snorted at that. "You need to talk to Jerry about it, and I can assure you that he's pissed."

"I understand he was hoping to go home."

"We're all hoping to go home." Ted rubbed his face. "It's never comfortable to be in a situation where we're the ones investigating everybody else, … but, when we're not getting answers and when people are dying and when more things are running off the rails, you can bet that we're getting more than sideways looks."

"Right, I really hadn't considered that pushback," Egan muttered.

"Don't consider it now either. Go do whatever it is you think you need to do," Ted stated, then frowned. "What is it you think you need to do?"

"First off, I need to talk to the sister about her relationship with Yegorahn."

"Berry?" he asked.

"No, the other one, Cherry."

At that, Ted shook his head. "Oh hell no. I talked to her. She didn't say a word about any relationship."

"I now know that she had a relationship with him of some sort, and she's pretty heartbroken over his death. That's what I've gathered so far."

"See? That's the problem with a situation like this," Ted complained, half standing up. "Everybody lies. Damn it. I am sick and tired of this hellhole."

"I think it was more a case of, if the question leaves any opportunity, they don't feel as if they need to volunteer anything more. They don't even classify it as a lie. Yet, at the same time, they're clearly withholding evidence or information that might have made a difference earlier."

"Jesus," Ted muttered. "Cherry had a relationship with Yegorahn?"

"Her twin, Berry, states that Yegorahn and Cherry spent his last night alive together."

"I'm pretty damn sure I asked when she'd last seen him." He backtracked through his notes and brought it up on his laptop. "Yeah, here it is." He then read through his notes and swore. "I asked her point-blank if she'd seen him that previous day."

"What do you want to bet she split hairs because she hadn't seen him during the day but during the night?"

"I wouldn't be at all surprised." He swore profusely. "And having found out that much, now I do want to make sure that we aren't missing anything else." He sat here, tapping his finger on his desk for a long moment. "And you think you'll get better answers alone?"

Egan tilted his head. "Yes, let me just tell Cherry and other interviewees how I've been asked to go over all the interviews done to date and to follow up with some questions that have come up since then. I'll point-blank ask Cherry about her night, and, if she continues to lie, then I'll suggest that I bring her down to talk to you, and I'll sit in on that."

He snorted at that. "Be still my beating heart," he muttered. "Of course she'll lie."

"That brings me to my next point. The only reason to lie is if she is hiding something."

"Seems as if by now everybody is hiding something. Haven't you figured that out yet? Anyway, it doesn't matter. Go do your best, and, if she does lie again, you can bet that I want to talk to her myself," Ted stated, "and we'll make this beyond official. You go get your answers now. I'll be waiting to hear them when you return." And, with that, he waved at Egan to get out.

Egan smiled, stepped out of the small room, and headed where he knew Berry's and Cherry's room was. He didn't know whether Cherry was in or not. When he knocked on the door, he heard a muffled response, but, unsure what response it was, he knocked again. When the door opened, he saw a tear-stained, sniffling, and red-faced Cherry.

As soon as she saw him, the tentative half smile dropped off her face, and she glared at him. Snapping, she asked, "What do you want?"

His eyebrows shot up. "I've been assigned the task of going over everybody's statements regarding one of the deaths at the camp, and I have a few more questions about yours."

She shook her head. "I ain't answering nothing."

"Either you talk to me or you talk to Ted and me. So basically it's me, or, if you don't cooperate, a full panel of investigators. Regardless," Egan stated, staring into her eyes to emphasize his point, "you *will* talk to us." With an authority that came naturally to him, he added, "Just in case you think this is not still a military operation, get that out of your mind because you're on base, still under military law." Before she retorted, red in the face, he snapped again, "Think again."

Biting off the sharp retort, she stared at him in shock. "Why are you being so mean?"

He shook his head. "I'm not being mean at all, but I fully expect you to come to attention and to follow through on orders as they're given." She glared at him, and he nodded. "So, what is it then? Me or Ted and the full panel? Choose wisely."

She snorted. "You say that as if Ted is some a threat. He's not a threat. He's nothing."

At that, Egan shook his head. "No matter what you think of Ted, he is a ranking officer, and he deserves respect, particularly from you."

"Why from me?" she snapped, glaring at him. "This isn't my fault."

"No, but you definitely withheld information, and Ted has every right to report you to the colonel, and that can also go on your permanent record."

"Permanent record? What do you mean I withheld information?"

"Your statement," Egan replied, pulling it up on his phone, as he repeated it back to her. "You were asked if you'd seen him the previous day." He paraphrased the question, and she glared at him, as he remained standing at the door.

"That wasn't the question."

"Then what was the question?"

"It was whether I'd seen him that day. Nobody asked me about that night."

"So, you're splitting hairs when a man's been murdered. Instead of willingly coming up with information to help solve it. Why would you do that?"

"Because I hadn't seen him the previous day, and he was out all day."

"And when does a day end, Cherry?" he asked her immediately, and she again glared at him.

"I don't know. When is a day over? Four o'clock, five o'clock, six o'clock, nine o'clock?"

He shook his head and stared at her. "That response doesn't go a long way to bolster your own credibility. So let me rephrase the question for you and see if we can clean it up. When did you last see Yegorahn before he died?"

Sighing, Cherry allowed her shoulders to slump.

He nodded. "That's what I thought. Now shall we get to the truth here? The *real* truth that you've been trying so damn hard to cover up?"

She shook her head. "No, we can't talk about anything." She crossed her arms. "Besides, you're not here in an official capacity anyway."

He turned, saw one of the MPs lurking at the far end of the hall and stepped back a bit so she could see. Turning back, he looked at her with a gaze that could split stones. "Listen to me, and listen well. You'll either answer my questions or I'll order him to escort you to Ted right now," he stated, his tone clipped. "What'll it be?"

She gasped and stared at him.

"Yeah, that would be quite public, and everybody would know something's up. So, if that's the way you want to do it, that's your choice."

"I hate you," she spat.

"I don't give a fuck," Egan replied, stressing every syllable as he glowered at her. "Believe me. All of this will be on record now too."

When a voice broke in behind him, tentative, almost like soothing oil on troubled waters, he knew it was Berry.

"What's going on?" Berry asked.

At that, Cherry turned to her sister and snapped, "He wants me to go down and answer more questions about Yegorahn's death."

"I didn't say questions about his death," Egan snapped back. "I simply asked you for the truth as to when you last saw him, and you immediately gave me nothing but flack, which is why I've brought in the MP to take you down to talk to Ted and the panel—just in case you still feel I don't have the credentials to have this conversation."

She glared at him, then looked at her sister and whispered, "I don't want to go."

"Jesus, Cherry, then why aren't you talking to him here? Because he will take you down there, past everybody, with an MP, and you'll just be in trouble for obstruction too. You know what gossip around the base will start then."

"All of this is starting talk," Cherry stated, glaring at him. "You didn't have to come here at all."

He stared at her nonplussed. "Seriously? Do you really think that nobody will find out that some of these interviews were missing information?"

"Maybe Ted should have asked the right questions then," Cherry retorted, with a sneer.

That was the last straw. Egan had had enough of her BS. He reached up a thumb and signaled to the MP, who came immediately down, and, on Egan's orders, Cherry was grabbed by the shoulders and escorted down the hallway.

She protested the whole way, and Egan turned to look back at Berry, knowing she would find it hard to forgive him for that. Instead, she chewed on her bottom lip, as her sister was hauled away.

"I'm sorry," Berry said. "She's her own worst enemy."

"Ya think? We could have done this nice and quiet."

"Did you have to do it at all?" she asked.

"Yes, I did, because, in her recorded statement, Ted asked her point-blank about Yegorahn's last day, and she stated that she never saw him the previous day at all."

Berry gasped. "Seriously?"

He nodded. "Apparently, according to her, nighttime is not the same as the previous day."

She closed her eyes at that and nodded. "She's always been a little spoiled."

"Always been a little spoiled, even in the military?"

"She handles the military because it's an enforcement system she understands, but she doesn't acknowledge any other authority outside of it. And," Berry admitted, "Cherry's good at getting around all authority anyway."

"And how does she feel about …" He looked down at her, then left it unsaid. "Look. I have to get down there. Ted's expecting me."

She nodded and asked, "What about me? Can I come?"

"Nope," Egan replied. "Nothing you can do to save your sister. She's gotten into this on her own."

Berry nodded, but crossed her arms and stared up at him. "I know it's too much to ask, but go easy on her."

He raised his eyebrows at that. "You do know that we're not the bad guys here, right? We're just trying to find out what happened to somebody that Cherry was apparently close to, yet she's not making any attempt to help us get answers or to even cooperate," Egan detailed. "That makes everybody suspicious of Cherry—even her friend Ted."

At that, her eyes rounded. "Oh my God. No, no, no. You don't honestly think… You don't think she had anything to do with Yegorahn's death, do you?"

He shrugged. "Doesn't matter what I think. The fact of the matter is, her actions make it appear as if she's guilty as hell." And, with that, he gave her a nod. "I'm sorry it's your sister, but now I have to go deal with her and Ted, who won't be very happy either."

DAY 3, LATE AFTERNOON

U PSET AND NEEDING something to distract herself from
what Berry knew would be a difficult conversation for
her sister, Berry headed outside over to the dogs. She didn't
bundle up quite the same, just putting on her heavy parka,
some warming packets, and gloves. By the time she burst
into the area where the dogs were kept and where Joe had
made his home, she already felt the chill. Still, it was
beautiful and sunny outside, so the snow-blindness reflection
came off the snow all around her.

As she hopped inside, Joe looked up and grinned. "Who
are you trying to avoid now?"

She winced. "Do people only come here to get away?"

He nodded. "Usually, yeah, unless we're out on training,
and that's a whole different story."

"*Great*," she muttered. "So, yeah, I guess I'm trying to
find something to take my mind off what's going on. And
hoping some dog cuddles will do it." Just then Queenie
appeared, an almost white dog with a few black markings
around her cheeks. Berry dropped to her knees and cuddled
her.

Joe's eyebrows shot up. "What's going on?"

Berry winced and then shrugged. "I guess you'll find out
anyway. My sister was having an affair with the Russian who
died, Yegorahn."

Joe nodded. "Can't say I'm surprised. She's a good-looking woman."

"Yes, she is, but she didn't tell the investigators that she was with him the previous night, so she's being interviewed right now."

He winced, then shook his head. "Ain't no point in hiding shit like that," Joe stated, with a careful look. "You can bet somebody else around here knew about it, and it would have gotten out eventually."

"That's the thing," Berry murmured. "I think my sister fudged a bit by making the question a little too literal in order to not effectively lie." Queenie head-butted her, a reminder to keep scratching her head.

"Same thing as a lie," Joe declared, "and shame on her for not cooperating to the fullest to try and find out what happened to him. If he was good enough to sleep with, surely he was good enough to tell the truth about and to help find out what happened to him, right?"

"I think she was afraid that people would judge her for it."

He snorted. "So, she's more afraid about saving face than worrying about what happened to this guy that she supposedly liked enough to sleep with?"

"And that's why she'll have a hard time today," Berry admitted, with a groan, as she stood up, still rubbing Queenie's ear. "I guess people will judge her for that then too, won't they?"

"Sure, they will," Joe snapped, "and I will too. That man didn't deserve to die out here, a long way from his home. Plus, if somebody really cared about him, they sure as hell should have been first in line to cooperate to ensure that— while there was still an opportunity to catch somebody who might have done this to him—they had all the information they needed to do so."

Berry walked toward where one of the injured dogs was curled up on the hay. "How's this guy doing?" She was trying desperately to change the conversation, knowing it would likely be foremost on everybody's minds after this got out. "This is Benji, right?"

"Yeah. He's doing pretty well," Joe replied, his voice softening. "At this point we all will be happy to go home though."

"And yet for you this is what it's all about anyway, isn't it?"

"Sure, but it's not the same as being at home with my wife," he noted, with a half smile. "I'm here for the duration though. I signed up, and I'll stick it out," he muttered, as he shifted on his chair. "But the weather is not being very cooperative, so we're not getting out as much as normal. Thus, everybody here is getting pretty antsy." Joe looked out the little slit they called a window. "It doesn't help that we've had people go missing, people showing up dead, murdered even, and people with information deliberately not sharing it."

An awful lot was packed into that statement, but Berry understood what he meant. A beautiful husky with two different colored eyes came in through the dog door, a blanket of snow on her back. She launched herself at Berry.

"Stay down, Bella," Joe barked, but the dog was too happy to see Berry. Within seconds she was wearing the snow brought in by Bella and was laughing at the dog's antics. "She's beautiful." Berry sighed. "I'm sorry for my sister though. I think, when it happened, when Yegorahn first went missing, she was just so shocked and grieving that she didn't quite know what to say." She cuddled Bella.

"The truth would have been a good choice," he pointed out.

She winced. "Yeah, and I think she'll feel the impact of that decision for a while."

"Yeah, you're not kidding." Joe shook his head. "I won't say anything to her, but you can bet a bunch of people around here will be looking at her suspiciously now—especially the Russian team."

"And yet she didn't have the physical strength to do anything to hurt Yegorahn."

He frowned at that. "Women more likely use poison. No strength needed. Plus Sydney would know something more about Yegorahn's cause of death. However, I don't think she had anything definitive at this point. They didn't release much in the way of details, and yet speculations and rumors are everywhere you go. So your guess is as good as mine."

She nodded. "So, it may not have taken any strength at all."

"That's another reason why they'll have to question everybody again because now Yegorahn's movements will get filled in a little more, and they'll refine their questions a bit to try and get at the truth and to fill in more holes."

"Right." She groaned. "I don't even know when he was killed."

"And that's why they need to know where he was because, up here in these conditions, his body would have frozen over much faster, making the timeline of his death much harder to pinpoint. Cherry's lies have lost them valuable hours. And remember, Yegorahn isn't the only missing person out there. So Cherry's gonna have a lot of haters on her now—and deservedly so. People who lost loved ones and just people with morals and empathy and humanity. You two may be twins, but you ain't nothing like that Cherry. And you should thank God for that. And you need to stop coddling her. Your sister is a liar, putting her own boyfriend at risk of death, and I hope she is punished accordingly."

Taking another round of hits for her sister was not something Berry was up for, so she just nodded, straightened, and repeated, "I just came out here to get away, knowing that the interview was happening right now."

"Cherry's made this mess, and Cherry's gotta take her lumps. Nothing you can do for her. Just let her take her lumps," Joe stated briskly, "so you might as well help me with these harnesses."

She walked over to him and asked, "What are we doing?"

"We're oiling them up. Everything out here cracks in these temperatures, so I do this daily."

She grabbed several of the leather harnesses.

"We're inspecting them for any wear and tear, cracking, or any fraying on the edges," he explained. "All of that matters when we're out there. It's all about safety."

And, with his lecture tone firmly emphasizing various points about caring for the dogs and their equipment, she realized that, while they'd been talking, several others had joined them. He nodded. "This is a safety session, one of the sledding lectures I'll be giving," he told her. Then raising his voice, he called out, "So, everybody grab a harness, and let's go over it, piece by piece."

For the next several hours she helped him through the class, making sure that all the harnesses were in good shape and that everything was oiled up and ready to go, just in case they needed a dogsled in an emergency, in case the weather broke, and they could get back out sledding again.

When the class ended, Berry smiled at Joe. "Thank you."

He nodded. "Keep that damn sister under control—if you can."

And with that reminder that people would expect just that, Berry replied, "You do know that's not possible, right?"

He sighed and then nodded reluctantly. "And it wasn't fair of me to say it. It's not your responsibility. Your sister will face the consequences of her actions and inactions on her own," he muttered. "And, up here in these close confines, that could be a little harder than she's expecting."

"Maybe they'll ship her out," Berry suggested, a question in her tone.

"I doubt it. Why would they? She might as well suffer here, with everybody else." Joe chuckled. "Not that we're suffering, mind you. It's just the weather being what it is has everybody cooped up and makes for very short tempers and frustrated people. I don't see them shipping her out."

"I'm not even sure we can blame the weather for the attitudes as much as the circumstances around right now."

"Exactly, which is why your sister's actions are beyond questionable."

With that, Berry took her leave, feeling as if she'd had more than enough exposure to how people might react to Cherry. Waving at Joe, she said goodbye to the dogs and quickly stepped outside. The wind had picked up, and the snow blew heavily. There was always a safety line from this building to the main base. They were connected, but it was pretty damn easy—even with the safety line out here—to get turned around, especially when you couldn't see anything but white. Grabbing the safety line, she quickly made her way back to the main building. As she stepped inside, the change in temperature was shocking.

She quickly took off her parka, stomped her feet out of the mukluks, switched into her inside boots that she wore, which were packed with heavy felt, then headed toward the kitchen to get a hot cup of tea.

As she walked in, Chef looked up at her, then quickly glanced away. She looked around at several other people, noticing that their glances immediately shifted away from her as soon as they caught her looking at them, and she groaned. "Nice day out there, isn't it?" she asked in a sarcastic tone.

One of the men snorted. "Hey, at least you're alive."

She wasn't sure if that was a beef about her sister, the dead Russian she had dated, the temperature outside, or just because too many people had died. Deciding to refrain from answering, she carried her tea to one of the tables.

Almost as soon as she sat down, the people at the table got up and left. She sighed, not waiting long until the room completely emptied, then looked over Chef. "So am I a pariah now?"

He glanced at her, turned away, and shrugged.

"I'm not my sister," she stated in exasperation.

"And yet you knew," he declared, turning to look back at her. Such force filled his words that she stopped dead for a moment.

"I didn't know that she didn't say anything. … We were interviewed separately, and nobody asked me. I told them when I had last seen him, and I didn't realize Cherry didn't tell them about her last night with him."

He stopped, considered that, and then nodded. "That

might help *your* case," he admitted in a clipped tone. "At this moment, however, people are looking at you as having enabled her."

"I didn't," she argued. "I just didn't know she hadn't told them they were together. They didn't ask me, and I knew that they were talking to her, so I figured she would tell them everything, but apparently she told them nothing."

"How did they find out?" Chef asked.

She winced and, in a lowered voice, replied begrudgingly, "That would have been me."

"That would have helped if people had known early on."

"Yeah, it should have been earlier," Berry admitted. "Believe me. I feel terrible now because of all the time that's gone by. Maybe they could have learned something else."

"Maybe, but I have to admit I'm pretty damn glad they are taking another look at it."

"Any idea why they're taking another look at it?"

"Because that missing man is now a dead man. All because the searchers and the investigations had inconsistent information."

She winced at that. "Yeah, that would be my sister." She shook her head. "She was just trying to keep private something that was personal to her."

"For the wrong reasons," Chef snapped, putting down the pan too hard. "A man died, and you'd think that somebody would give a damn, particularly somebody who slept with him."

"Yeah." Berry held up a hand. "Look. I get it, and I get that people will hold that against me. That isn't fair because I didn't have anything to do with it, and I did my part as soon as I realized there was a problem," she explained. "Which is precisely why my sister is getting raked over the coals right now."

"And she deserves it and more," Chef declared, pointing a spatula at her. "So, if you want to stay in good stead in any way with those around you, don't try to make your sister look like anything else but a selfish liar."

"I'm not trying to. … Honestly it saddens me to think that it went this far."

"Damn right," Chef declared. "I don't know what they might have missed because of it, but you can bet that they'll be pissed at her about it." And, with that, he went back to his cooking. Without another glance at her, he muttered, "Food will be about an hour."

"Good enough," she replied and took that as a dismissal. She got up and refilled her teacup with more hot water, then headed back to her room. She didn't pass anyone on the way, which suited her just fine. She already felt completely ostracized.

When she opened the door to her room, her sister sat on the edge of her bed, crying her eyes out.

Cherry looked up and groaned. "What the hell are you doing here?" Cherry asked in a shriek. "Haven't you caused enough trouble?"

"Really? This is how you want to play it? Do you realize that I'm now being ostracized because of *you*?" she asked in anger. "I went to the dining room, and everybody got up and walked out, just from looking at me," she snapped. "So, thanks for that too, as if it wasn't hard enough to live here with you already."

Her sister stared at her in shock. "Don't you even care what they said to me?"

"I rather imagine that they're talking about court-martialing you," she snapped, her voice hard. "You withheld important information, and that'll never go down well."

"I didn't kill him," she muttered, "so I didn't think it mattered."

"How about now?"

At that, her sister subsided and shrugged. "They seem to think it mattered quite a bit."

"At least maybe now they have a better idea of when he died, since you should have been able to give them that much."

"I told them what I knew, but he left while I was asleep."

"Sure, and yet when was that, when you last saw him?"

She glared. "I don't have to answer your questions too," she retorted in a snippy voice.

"Maybe not, but you probably should because I don't have anything to tell people, and right now they're not being very friendly to me either. So I'm taking the heat *for you*, and I can't say I appreciate it." And, with that, she stormed out of the room. She stood here against the hallway wall, as she had no place to go. She wondered if there was a spare room left in the place and headed to check with Dave, the man in charge of the accommodations.

When Dave found her lingering around, as if looking for him, he immediately frowned.

She frowned right back. "Look. I get it. Everybody thinks I'm to blame, but it would be nice for people to realize that I didn't know my sister hadn't come forth with vital information," she snapped. "And believe me. I'm well aware that everybody's holding that against me too, and yet I didn't have anything to do with it."

He shrugged. "It's not as if anybody will believe that."

"I get it. Thank you very much for that piece of precious information, but I also have to deal with my sister, and right now I'm seriously hoping you have an empty room that I could have to myself."

Dave stared at her. "Why?"

"Because my sister is pissed at me, and everybody else is too."

"Why is *she* pissed at *you*?" he asked, staring at her.

She sighed. "Because I don't have any sympathy for her. She lied, and I guess I'm probably the one who broke the news because of the fact that I didn't know that she hadn't told the truth."

Dave nodded at that. "If you didn't know she lied, then you shouldn't feel guilty."

"I don't feel guilty, except by association. She's my sister, and she did a shitty thing. So, yeah, of course I feel guilty." She raised both hands in frustration. "The fact that I walked into the cafeteria and sat down, and basically everybody got up and left to get away from me says a hell of a lot."

He nodded. "Yeah, it sure does. Nobody likes liars when people are being murdered around here."

"Liars?" she repeated, aghast.

"Liars. Plural. Both of you," Dave declared. "For now at least, until you redeem yourself. You have to understand how we still have several people missing, and one of them died, and your evil twin sister—who was sleeping with Yegorahn and didn't feel anything—wasn't ready to help find out who did it."

"I didn't know she lied about it," Berry cried out.

Dave sighed. "People may believe that over time. I don't know. And I'm going to tell you one more thing. You may be the good twin, but you are guilty of projecting your goodness on your evil twin. Just saying. Stop giving her the benefit of the doubt. This lie here? This whopper? At this military base? About a dead man she slept with? Can you look me in the eye and say that is the only lie you've ever caught Cherry telling?"

At Berry's stunned silence, he nodded. "Don't keep enabling her by failing to call her out on those repeated lies. … I do have an empty room, at least as long as nobody else comes in. If we get any more people or if we have a real need for it, you will be the first to get bumped out, do you hear me?"

She nodded, almost numb at the attack she hadn't expected. Was he right? Had she been enabling her sister all this time? Anything she'd done had been more for peace than anything. But maybe in this case … it was the same thing? "Yes, thank you. I would really appreciate just being able to have some space from everybody right now."

"Yeah, well a lot of other people would too," Dave replied, "and this will just make it look as if your sister is even guiltier and being held in her room."

"I don't know what the end result from the questioning even was," Berry admitted. "I really don't. My sister is in my room, our room, and she's crying, but I can't be in there with her. Yet apparently *wherever* I go, everybody else has to leave. So, if you have another room, where I can be a prisoner, hey, that would be just fine."

He checked his books and then looked up at her somewhat apprehensively, yet still sympathetically in his own way. "You can have the single bedroom at the back by the storeroom." She nodded, and he warned her, "It'll be colder than normal."

She winced and nodded.

"There is additional bedding on the bed for that reason. Remember. It's an *extra* room, so just be aware," he stated, his voice rising with that note of warning. "If I have to reclaim it, you get dumped back with your sister."

"Got it." She nodded in agreement. As she walked out of the room, she turned and said, "Thank you."

He nodded, but his gaze was piercing as he added, "I sure hope you're right about your sister not being a killer."

"I'm right. She's a fool, but she's not a murderer."

Dave snorted. "Now all you have to do is convince the rest of the base of that."

Her shoulders slumped, as she headed to what would now be her new room. She wanted to go back to their room and get all her gear, but she didn't want to deal with her sister right now, and that would be the next problem.

WHEN DINNER WAS called, Berry wasn't sure her sister would even go to the dining room. Berry waited, hanging back, only to realize that Cherry was hanging back too. As Berry walked down the hallway toward the dining room, and Cherry walked past her and headed right for the food, Berry figured her sister would probably grab something and come back to eat it in her room. Therefore, Berry took this opportunity to slip into their shared room, grabbing her personal gear and her bags, taking it to her new room.

By the time she was done and headed back to get her own plate of food, she saw no sign of her sister in the cafeteria. She looked over at Chef. "Was she here?"

He nodded. "Yep, and she got the silent treatment."

"Of course," Berry noted. She loaded up her plate, then looked around and decided she didn't really need to be dealing with angry, upset people any more than she already had. Therefore, she took her plate and sat down at an empty table this time. When a shadow crossed over, she looked up to see Egan there. She gave him a lopsided smile. "What? You'll bear the stigma and sit with me?"

He frowned at her, as he plunked down with his plate. "What does that mean?"

"I've been ostracized. So has my sister."

"Ah." Egan nodded. "In a base like this, that's always a

possibility."

"Maybe so, but why me too?"

"Presumably they either think that you lied for her, covered up her actions, turned a blind eye, or in some way were implicated yourself."

"And yet I wasn't, and I didn't," she stated bitterly.

He didn't say anything and then nodded. "It'll blow over soon."

"You think so?" she asked. "I'm not so sure. Everyone is so on edge right now."

"I went to your room to see if you were there," he shared, "but nobody answered."

"That would be my sister who ignored you, particularly if she heard your voice …" Berry let the silence finish her thought.

"Yeah, I wondered. Then I came down to get food anyway and saw you here."

"I didn't plan to even eat here tonight, but there was an empty table. So I thought, *Screw them. I'm staying.* I can't hide forever."

He smiled. "Maybe if they see us sitting together, it might help."

"Maybe, and maybe they'll think that I'm also part of the enemy, especially if you're not well regarded either."

He laughed. "We can change that." As Magnus and Sydney walked in, he waved at them to join them. They collected their food and came over and sat down.

She sighed. "Thank you," she muttered to Egan. "I can't say I was really looking forward to being completely ignored in this place."

As Magnus sat down, Egan quickly explained the issue.

Magnus nodded. "Yeah, we've seen that a time or two."

Sydney smiled over at her. "Listen. You aren't your sister, and you aren't responsible for her actions."

"Now, if only other people would believe that," Berry groaned. "It's amazing how quickly people want to judge, even without any reason to."

"From their point of view, there are plenty of reasons to judge," Magnus declared, "and even that will probably blow over—for you at least—especially if we can get this solved." He looked back over at Egan. "Unless you think Cherry is the murderer."

He shook his head. "No, I don't, but now we have a much better timeline than we had before."

"Does it change anything though?" Sydney asked.

"It does in this case because there was a very short window when he was alive," Egan noted. "Knowing the actual timeline is so valuable. Now all we have to do is map out everybody's movements during that one-hour window."

"Is that all it was?" Berry asked. "One hour?"

"Yes."

Dinner after that was an enjoyable affair, with several other people stopping by to talk to them, and Berry could see that, with their concerted efforts, she might find at least some level of acceptance, maybe, in part of the base again. It wasn't that she wanted acceptance because part of her really didn't give a crap. However, she would be here for several more weeks, and it would be a whole lot easier on everybody if they got along.

Otherwise trust became an issue, especially when they were out on training sessions, and that was not something Berry was prepared to compromise on either. What she needed was to have everything back to the way it was. Hopefully these people's presence at her table gave the others all some reassurance that Berry was not involved in Cherry's shenanigans.

DAY 5, TWO DAYS LATER, EARLY MORNING

BERRY HADN'T SEEN her sister all of the next day, and finally, early the next morning, when she got coffee, she looked over at Chef and asked, "Did you see my sister yesterday?"

He frowned at her. "Didn't you?"

She shook her head. "No, I asked for another room because things got a little tense between us."

He nodded. "I think she came in for dinner last night, but … I'm not sure she did."

Berry stared at him for a moment and knew that shock and fear were surely taking over her expression.

He took stock of that and added, "Don't panic. Just go see if your evil twin is there. Maybe open the door and check to see if she's inside her room, before you go off half-cocked."

She nodded and quickly turned on her heels and headed to her sister's room. When she opened the door just a hair to peek in, she realized that both beds were empty.

She turned slowly inside the small room and realized it didn't look as if Cherry's bed had been slept in at all. Swallowing a rising panic, she snatched her phone from her pocket and quickly texted Egan. **Have you seen my sister? Yesterday or today?** When she got back his **No** answer, it sent her nerves into overdrive, and then her phone started to ring.

Egan quickly asked, "Where are you?"

"I'm in my sister's room," she whispered. "It doesn't seem she slept here last night."

"I'll be there in a minute."

Berry stared at the empty room and wondered if things had really gone so far south that now her sister was missing too.

Missing or murdered?

Day 5 Morning

EGAN RACED OUT of bed and ditched his morning rituals to arrive at the room as fast as he could. Berry stood outside the room, leaning against a wall, shaking. He wrapped her up in his arms. "Don't panic. It doesn't have to be all bad."

"No, it doesn't have to be," she cried out, looking up, "But where is she?"

He hesitated before speaking. "This will sound terrible, but has she spent the night with somebody else?"

Berry winced. "I don't know. She's not talking to me, not anymore. I haven't had a conversation with her since you interrogated her. She won't talk to me at all, so I don't know."

He nodded. "For some women," he replied, carefully choosing his words to not upset her, "some women need that male attention, whether it's for protection or a sense of belonging or just to know she's not alone."

"And that would be my sister," Berry confirmed. "Still, I just don't know who she would have spent the night with."

Almost immediately they both heard the sound of a door

down the hallway. Berry turned to look, and her sister exited a room at the far end, then raced in their direction.

She stopped when she saw them standing there, and then a sneer slipped onto her face. "Of course here you are. Spying much?"

Berry shook her head. "Good God, Cherry," she muttered. "Mom would have a heyday with your behavior."

He watched as Cherry stiffened at that snide remark, then turned to look at her himself. "Whose room did you spend the night in?" Egan asked bluntly.

"None of your fucking business," she snapped.

His eyebrows shot up, then he crossed his arms. "Actually it is."

"No, it isn't," Cherry argued. "This has nothing to do with Yegorahn's death. My relationship is my relationship."

He watched as Berry tried hard to keep her own temper under control. She added, "You know it'll just cause more trouble if you don't answer him."

"I don't give a fuck, and he's got no right to ask me questions anyway. And according to—" Then Cherry stopped, as if to prevent a slip of the tongue. "To somebody, he didn't have any right to question me the day before yesterday either."

"You want to take that up with the colonel then?" he asked, his voice hard. He'd already had enough of her BS. "Because that's where you're headed right now."

"What? So you'll call in an MP again? Have me hauled down there in front of everybody? You liked that, didn't you? Big he-man, abusing the little woman?"

"You're hardly a *little woman*, Cherry. A liar and a cheat? Yes," he stated, with his own sneer. "But a helpless little woman, innocent and honest, no way," he declared, matching her venom. "So, you will tell me where you spent the night. You were down at Richard's room, weren't you?"

She flushed. "What makes you say that?"

"Because that's his room, but he was also bunking with Steve."

She glared at him. "And?"

"And were they both there?" he asked.

"Oh, so you want to check into my sex life too?"

"Stop it," Berry cried out. "Jesus, do you have to be so crude?"

"What? He's the one who's asking where I spent the night."

"You just came out of Richard's room," Berry wailed. "Do you think everybody doesn't know who stays where?"

"It's also Steve's room."

"That's right, so that's why he's asking because it gives more than one alibi to whether you were there or not."

"Oh, so now I need an alibi, do I?" Cherry asked, turning on Berry with a speed that stunned Egan.

"Wow," Egan noted, "you really hate your sister, don't you?"

Cherry glared at him. "I don't hate her, but she used to be on my team. So, the fact that she turned traitor and went to the enemy makes it a different story."

"Enemy?" Berry repeated, aghast. "Is that how you view me now? As your enemy? You lied over somebody's death, and I told the truth, not knowing that you had lied about your evening with Yegorahn. So don't blame me that I outed you. I said something completely innocently that outed you. That doesn't make me the enemy. That just makes you the liar."

"Yeah, well, if you hadn't spoken up, they wouldn't have

turned on me." Cherry sneered.

"So how was I supposed to know what your story even was? You didn't tell me to keep quiet about it. Maybe if you had, I would have known not to open my mouth," she snapped. "But I didn't even know, and so, when somebody mentioned something to me that didn't make any sense, I told him that's where you spent the night. Which you should have done already." She took a deep breath which appeared to help her calm down. "Apparently you forgot to tell me that you needed *me* to cover for *your* lies," Berry stated furiously. And, with that, she turned and stormed off toward the kitchen.

He watched her go, so sorry for what she was going through, but, as for her evil sister, Cherry was something else. "So, you're alienating your sister because she didn't realize that you had avoided the truth, and now you're implicating somebody else? Good job," he quipped. "I'll be sure to tell Ted, and the word will reach the colonel." And, with that, he turned to walk away.

He almost didn't feel the blow, but the second one was hard to mistake. He turned around and caught her fist, as it came back at him a third time. He just held it tight, glaring down at her. She was almost spitting fire and snapped in between the bouts of profanity.

"You've got nothing to do with this. If you hadn't gotten in my sister's face, or is it her pants," she cried out crudely, "none of this would have happened."

"What? Your boyfriend wouldn't be dead?" he asked, giving her a hard shake, "I wasn't even here. Remember? That man died, and you didn't give a shit. As long as you could screw somebody else, you were fine. But the minute anybody asks you for the truth, so they could narrow down a time of death and figure out what happened to the poor sap, you choose not to volunteer any information. And, in fact, blatantly lied about it."

As he was just winding up, ready to blast her again, as a hard voice spoke from behind him. "Egan."

Egan immediately stopped speaking and glared down at her again, before turning to face Magnus. "She threw two punches," he stated. "This is me stopping the third." And he took a step back, throwing her arm away. "She's on the rampage now, including one misdirected at her sister for Cherry's own shitty behavior. I'm not dealing with her anymore." And, with that, he turned and he walked away, leaving Magnus to stare in disgust at Cherry. Egan couldn't hear what was said because Egan was no longer interested. As far as he was concerned, this whole scenario had just gone from bad to worse.

When he walked into the kitchen, Berry walked over and said, "I'm sorry. I just couldn't handle it."

"That's fine. Don't worry. It got much worse after you left." Then he quickly explained.

She stared at him in shock. "She hit you?"

He nodded and frowned. "Twice in the back, and, when I turned around, she was winding up for a third. I stopped it, but yeah. Is she always this physically abusive when her verbal abuse isn't enough?"

She shook her head. "No, she must be really worried about something."

"Either Cherry's afraid that she's guilty of something or she's afraid that people will think she is. Or she killed him, and now she's afraid of getting caught," he snapped. And then he took a slow deep breath, holding up his hand. "Sorry, it's not you I'm pissed at. She spewed some awfully crude things."

"No, I get it," Berry replied, her voice small. "I'm sorry too because I feel as if I started this."

He shook his head at that, then stepped over and picked up a plate. "It's not your fault. Stop taking on Cherry's guilt," he stated. "If she would have told the truth from the beginning, there wouldn't have been any discrepancy in her statements. Since then she's just gone straight downhill."

"I don't remember her ever being this bad before," Berry muttered.

In silence, they each served up an early morning breakfast on their plates, as other people filtered in. Egan pointed toward a table off to the side. Berry nodded, and they quickly sat down. It was close quarters, and there wasn't a whole lot of privacy to talk, which was fine with him. He was still quite pissed off, so it was best that he cool down before he discussed Cherry with Berry.

When Magnus joined them a few minutes later, he looked over at Berry and stated, "Your sister is confined to the medical quarters for the moment."

She winced and nodded slowly. "I'm really sorry that she lost control."

"The question is why?" he asked, his gaze intent. "Now it's nothing major, but I have a few questions for you that need answering."

She nodded immediately and replied, "I'm happy to help. I don't know what I can do about her though."

"Does your sister have a history of drug use?"

She stared at him in shock, her jaw dropping. Then she slowly shook her head. "No, no, not at all, no way. Why would you suggest that?"

"Because Cherry's behavior points to drug abuse," he

stated.

Berry sat back and swallowed hard. "If she did, if she was, … I think I would know about it. However, I don't recognize the woman she is right now," Berry admitted. "So I guess I don't have any good answers."

"But you've never seen her use?"

"No, not at all." And she hadn't, she really hadn't, so the suggestion obviously had shaken her.

Yet for Egan, it made a lot of sense. "Not only drug use," Egan added, "what about withdrawal?"

"Exactly. I also have Richard, Cherry's latest *friend*, talking to Ted right now," Magnus pointed out carefully. "Ted was not terribly impressed with me for getting him out of bed early."

"Yeah, well, in this case," Egan snapped, "better to strike while the iron is hot than to wait another week for people to get around to giving us the information that we need."

At that, Magnus nodded. "Keep up the good work." And he promptly left.

"Keep up the good work?" Egan repeated, as he looked around the dining room, getting more and more packed and noisier by the second. "What work? Be a punching bag for an angry woman?" He looked at Berry and added, "Looks to me as if all I've done is raise Cain."

"And maybe that's what was needed," Berry admitted in a worried voice. "It scares the crap out of me to think that people are looking at my sister as if she could be a drug abuser."

"Which is why she'll be detained in the medical clinic." He eyed Berry and explained further, "In case you didn't make that connection, they'll be testing Cherry's blood for drugs, and I'm guessing you can imagine the rest."

Berry swallowed hard and then nodded. "Thank you, and, no, I hadn't really put that together."

"How about Yegorahn? Any idea if he did drugs?"

Still shocked, Berry stared at Egan and shrugged. "I'm probably the last person to ask. I don't really know anybody who does drugs," she replied cautiously. "So I don't really understand what I might be seeing, but I would have said no as to Yegorahn using drugs as well. I don't know what the rest of his team would say."

Egan didn't say anything for a long moment, just quickly finished his meal. When he looked over at her, he smiled and added, "At least while Cherry's under medical care, they can figure it out. … Maybe it's just grief. I don't know. It hits all of us in very different ways."

"That's true." Berry grasped onto that idea with relief.

Egan didn't think she'd grasp onto it for very much longer, but, as long as he gave her some peace for the moment, that would be good.

"I guess I can't go see her, can I?"

"I'm thinking you should wait, at least until Cherry's gone through the testing, so the doc can figure out a little more about what's happening. Maybe your sister will be ready to talk to you then. Obviously she's very angry right now at everyone," he stated, "and that's not a good time to talk."

"No, but it is a good time for her to spout out some truths that she may not be willing to say at any other time," Berry pointed out. At his raised eyebrows, she shrugged. "Nothing like family to push your buttons."

"And here I thought I was pushing her buttons pretty damn hard," Egan noted.

She smiled at that. "Maybe, but Cherry saw me too at

the same time. Plus I'm the one who walked away from her and got another room. She is no doubt simmering right now."

"And would she have taken that personally?"

"I don't know," Berry admitted, "but I couldn't be in the same room with her. She has become very unruly and aggravating. She just wouldn't give me any peace, so I knew I couldn't even be in there," she explained. "I was rather desperate when I went to Dave and asked for a new room assignment."

"Did you absolutely need to?"

"Yeah, even given the state of my new room. The one I'm in now is cold as hell frozen over, and I can't necessarily even have it full-time. Dave repeatedly told me that I only get it as long as they don't need it for anything else."

"Exactly."

"What about Steve, Richard's roommate?" she asked. "Shouldn't somebody talk to Steve, as well as Richard?"

"I was going to mention that to Ted, if Magnus hasn't already," Egan stated. "I'll go talk to him now. … Look. I don't know when I'll see you again, but just … take it easy, okay?"

She nodded, with the hint of a smile.

With that, he got up nimbly and took off.

DAY 5, LATER THAT MORNING

BERRY WANDERED THE military base for most of the morning, trying to find things to keep her busy. When she finally headed to the dogs in desperation, Joe looked up at her and frowned.

She frowned right back but walked over to the beautiful Bella, who was always willing to cuddle. Finally she turned to face Joe and spoke. "Look. I don't know what the hell is going on, but—"

Joe nodded. "Yeah, I hear Cherry attacked Egan in the hallway."

Berry winced. "I didn't tell you that."

"No, somebody else saw it. Actually I understand several *somebody elses* saw it." Joe smirked. "And Egan will never hit a woman, but she landed several blows on his back, which the brass won't take very well."

"*Right.*" Berry groaned. "I don't know what's come over her. It could be just … I know people don't want to believe it, but it could be grief."

"Could be," Joe acknowledged. "Grief gets to people in all kinds of ways. The thing is, she started this, and she brought it on herself, so it's hard to have any sympathy for her."

Berry winced again because he was right and because his opinion would be the popular one as well. That would just make it crazy around here. One good thing that did come out of this mess was that people were no longer stepping out of their way to get around Berry, so it might make her life a little easier while she was here.

As she headed back to base several hours later, she saw Mountain coming from the generator room. They met inside the anteroom to the main building on base, where they were taking off their heavy winter gear. She stepped closer and asked, "Any other problems out there?"

He shook his head. "It's all clear at the moment."

"What about finding Amelia?"

"I just returned from a two-day search. As soon as the weather breaks again, I'll head out in the opposite direction."

She winced. "Surely she can't still be alive."

"Yes, she absolutely can be," he stated. "She's spent several winters up here. If anybody could do it, I would put my money on her."

"I'm glad you feel that way," Berry replied, "because at least then you'll be fighting for her."

"Absolutely I'll fight for her," he confirmed, "but then I'm well-known for fighting for the underdogs."

"I'm sorry about my sister."

"Don't you be sorry," Mountain told her gently. "Your sister is responsible for her own actions. She gets to sink or swim on her own behavior. You're not responsible for her choices or actions."

"And yet it feels that way up here," she muttered, looking around. "For a while there I wasn't sure if I would be permanently ostracized too because everybody was avoiding me."

"As people sort out which one of you two is the problem, they'll make their own decisions. Keep your nose clean, and you'll be fine."

And with that, he was gone, leaving Berry to spend the rest of her day in her new room. Better to stay apart from the others on the base, other than Joe and Chef, while people here made up their minds as to Berry and Cherry.

Day 6 Wee Hours of the Morning

EGAN WOKE UP in the middle of the night, hearing a strong heavy wind but also an odd banging going on. Wondering just what he heard—and disturbed enough that no way he could go back to sleep—he got out of bed and quickly dressed.

It was only four in the morning, a godforsaken hour, but if that banging noise was the locker room or the storage room door or one of the exterior doors, they couldn't afford both the loss of heat or the winter weather coming in.

As he made his way to an exterior door, he met Magnus.

Magnus nodded. "Not just my imagination, is it?"

Egan shook his head. "What the hell is that?"

"I don't know," Magnus replied. "I couldn't sleep because I kept hearing it."

"Is it here by the sleeping quarters?"

"No, sounds as if it's coming from that way"—Magnus pointed—"back somewhere near the kitchen."

"In the storeroom? That's where Berry is bunking now."

Magnus stared at hearing that info.

"She asked for another room assignment because of the problems with her sister."

"Yet her sister is still in the medical clinic and isolated," Magnus noted.

"I had heard that and told Berry that before bed last night, as she seemed quite depressed. She's looking for as many answers as the rest of us."

"Yeah, but I can tell you that they won't be good ones."

"Shit, I figured as much," Egan muttered.

The two headed down to where the banging was, and, when they got there, through a series of doors, they found the hinges on the exterior door had snapped. Battling against the storm elements blowing hard outside, they finally managed to get the door shut, and, using some sturdy wood beams and some nearby tools, they managed to get it closed and to keep it that way.

As Egan turned and caught his breath, Magnus studied the hinges. "What's the matter?" Egan asked.

"I'm seeing if the hinges snapped."

"The storm could do that, couldn't it?"

But Magnus took a closer look and shook his head. "Come look for yourself. I'd say they were pried off."

After Egan's inspection too, he groaned. "Damn, they sure were." His tone grim, he turned and looked around. "I imagine that some of our food supplies are gone."

"That won't make Chef very happy," Magnus noted, as he turned to study what appeared to be a full contingency of canned food and baking goods on the shelving unit alone, but, with as many people as they had on base, it was quite possible that some foodstuffs were missing. Chef would need to run an inventory to confirm any shortages.

"We do have fewer people here, now that we don't have Anna or anybody else from the scientists' camp here with us," Egan added.

"Right, and, because of the weather, Chef has been trying to keep the food staples stocked up fairly consistently, rationing his stash when needed, just in case we won't get any supplies in for a while."

"And that isn't what any of us want to hear either," Egan noted, with half a smile.

"No, but people here can make do with less, if need be, when it comes to that," Magnus stated, "but too much cutting back wouldn't be good."

"So, who the hell would be breaking in here, looking for supplies? Locals?"

"Maybe."

"The scientists' camp?" Egan suggested.

"Not supposed to be anybody there," Magnus stated. "I'm kinda curious as to what's missing, if anything."

Egan nodded. "Right, it would help to know if it's something that people here can be eating on their own, such as granola bars and snack stuff, versus food that needs to be cooked. And, for that, we'll have to get Chef to do an inventory.

Magnus nodded. "We do, but do we want to wake him up now?"

"I'm already awake," Chef growled behind them. "What the hell happened in here?" He glared at Magnus and Egan, Chef's hair was sticking up all over, as if he'd just rolled out of bed. Plus he hugged a huge coat around him. "Shouldn't be this cold in here," he muttered, as he wandered around, staring at foodstuffs.

"Can you tell if anything's missing?" Magnus asked him.

At that, he stiffened and turned to look at the two men. "Are you expecting something to be missing?"

"Looks as if the exterior door was pried open."

He shook his head at that. "What? Now who the hell would give a shit about food you've got to cook?"

"Is that what's here?"

"Yeah, aside from the quick stuff, I use this area to store baking supplies, canned goods, and such," Chef explained. "It's not where I keep the meat or any of the fresh materials, not that we have any lately," he added, with an eye roll. "You're sure about the door?"

"No, not positive," Magnus admitted. "I need better light to be sure. So, come daylight, we'll check for tracks. Although, if that's a storm out there, the tracks need to be checked out now."

At that, Egan looked over at Magnus. "Let me go get dressed and in some outdoor gear. Then I'll go out and take a look."

"Not alone," Chef snapped, a bit too quickly. "Particularly if we think this was a break-in," he muttered. "God damn this mess."

"Yep. Let me get my gear."

"I'll get started on the inventory."

With that, the other two men headed to get into their winter gear. When Magnus and Egan stepped outside of the outerwear anteroom, they went around to the back of the building, near the kitchen exit and the generator shed, checking out the area, while Chef was inside counting supplies. When they reentered the kitchen via another rear door, Egan joined Chef and asked in frustration, "Anything missing?"

Chef nodded. "Yeah, a couple cases of food are missing." He shook his head. "Not enough to really hurt us, but, yeah, it will have an impact if it happens again. Especially if we don't get supplies in a timely fashion, it could have a major impact. But who the hell is out there who could even be bothered to do that? In the middle of the night in this weather? Who does that?"

"Somebody who's desperate," Egan stated.

Chef nodded. "In that case, I don't really begrudge anybody the food. However, it would be nice if they wouldn't just steal it. I have duplicates of a lot of stuff, which I would have just given them. I won't let anyone starve. But I sure as hell don't want to sleep here to keep somebody from stealing."

"So, it's got to be someone completely unaware that it's safe to come and ask our base for help with supplies—or they don't trust anybody here," Egan suggested, turning to look at Magnus.

Magnus nodded. "I'm afraid to say it, but I think you're right, and I think it's the latter—all about trust. In which case," Magnus added, "that sounds to me as if we're talking about Amelia."

At that, Chef snorted. "Are you telling me a woman did this?" he asked, doubt in his voice.

"It doesn't mean she did it alone," Egan stated. "Tracks are still out here, but they've been brushed with something, maybe a broom or a shovel, something to disguise them. So, that combined with this wind make it tough to track. If we had waited until dawn this morning, we wouldn't see anything from the snow drifts. Even just now we didn't really see much, and that's what the intruders were counting on."

"Yet why didn't they take more then?" Chef asked.

"They probably just took what they needed, exactly what they had to have. I wouldn't be at all surprised if you don't find the *Hey, so sorry. We need this to stay alive* note at the end of the day."

"That would be better than not getting one," Chef admitted. "I don't begrudge anybody foodstuffs when they need it, but it's a bummer to think that they felt this was the only way to get it."

"And the only way that would happen is if they think they're not allowed in our base or that they think whoever is here will come after them," Egan muttered. "So, as soon as dawn breaks"—he looked over at Magnus—"I suggest we make a trip back to that scientists' camp and see if any tracks come from there to here."

"Why up there?" Chef frowned. "The intruder could have come from anywhere."

Magnus turned, looked at him. "They could have, but the going is so much easier in line with the camp because we've already got a track built to there from so many trips back and forth. Thus, even with a storm, there is still a groove to move through. Sometimes it's easier. Sometimes it's not. However, in this case, I would guess that it would make the trip a lot easier. But only if they were coming from that direction," he added carefully, not wanting to stop the open flow of ideas.

"They could have been coming from anywhere," Chef repeated.

"If that's the case, hopefully we'll find some tracks elsewhere, as soon as it's light." Magnus turned, looked back at Egan. "So, an hour, back here in an hour?"

"Make it two," Egan suggested, as he looked outside. "With this storm we won't get daylight very quickly."

"Good. Let me go grab some sleep," groused Chef, "then I'll get the coffee on."

With that, he was gone.

DAY 6, EARLY MORNING

B ERRY STUMBLED TO the kitchen the next morning, hoping the coffee was already hot and ready. She hadn't expected the chill in the air inside the base. As she reached the coffeemaker, she saw Chef, grumpier than usual, glaring at her. She stopped, looked around, found herself alone, and asked, "Have I done something?"

He shook his head. "No, just a tough night." He snorted. "The food locker area, … the storeroom got broken into."

She was in the act of pouring coffee, and she froze. "What?"

He nodded. "The guys have gone out, looking for tracks to see if they can figure out what's going on."

"We know for sure that it was …" She hesitated and then shrugged. "I know it sounds insane, but do we know for sure it was somebody from *outside* the camp?"

"No, we don't know that," Chef confirmed. "I just don't know why somebody in our camp would feel the need to break into the storeroom. They broke the back door to get in here."

"Was anything taken?"

He nodded. "A few cases of food."

She let out her breath slowly. "Wow." The distaste soured her mouth. "Seems every morning reveals another fun day around here."

He gave a hard laugh. "Stick with us, kid, and you'll have a life that you never thought you could have."

"Yeah, but I was hoping for a peaceful one," she muttered. "This here is a shit show."

"Yeah, says you and me both," he muttered, then went back to cooking.

"Did the thief leave us in short supply?"

He shook his head. "It'll be what it is. When we get more supplies in, we'll stock back up, but we're good for now."

"Are we thinking it might have been the locals?"

"I don't think so, but I'm not the one to say. If they're suffering, they should come to us. However, they should be used to being up here in shitty weather. Yet some people just make life difficult and must have certain things. I don't really get it."

"My must-haves are your cinnamon buns. Those you made yesterday were delicious."

Chef rolled his eyes. "You won't be getting those today, but I do have some cookies in the oven."

She sniffed the air appreciatively, grinning. "I wasn't sure what that smell was, but cookies are always good."

"The thing about cookies," Chef noted, "is that they always put a smile on people's faces, particularly when the cookies are fresh and warm. No matter what shit's going on, everybody can appreciate a warm cookie."

She wondered at his words and the wisdom behind them, yet immediately realized he was right. She'd been in a lot of tough places in her life, and a cookie, particularly a hot fresh delicious cookie, always managed to put a smile on her face. In this environment, they worked off all the calories, so that wasn't an issue here.

However, she knew back home a dependence on cookies to elevate her mood could be problematic. But happily, in this military base, it absolutely made a positive impact, with absolutely no downside. So, with her coffee in hand, she headed back to her room, then realized she didn't know which guys had gone out to track the kitchen's intruder.

Instinctively she decided it would be Egan and Magnus, although she didn't have a clue why she decided this. Maybe Rogan was involved too, although he had been down sick for the last little while. Then she passed Rogan on her way down the hallway. "That answers that question," she said, looking at him. "I thought maybe you had gone out."

He shook his head. "No, I caught that flu, and I've been down for a few days. So getting cold and wet would not be a good thing for me right now. Unless they need me?" he asked.

"Other people are here to handle it," she told him, with a smile.

"How are you handling things?" Rogan asked her, eyeing her carefully. "I hear it's been pretty rough, … these last few days."

She rolled her eyes at that. "If you mean my sister? … Yeah, you're not kidding." Since they were not all that far away from the medical clinic, Berry turned and glanced in that direction. "I want to see her, if I'm allowed to visit."

"Get clearance first," he advised. "That would make it easier on Sydney too."

"I did think of that," Berry admitted. "Otherwise, Sydney has to determine who can come and go, doesn't she?"

"To a certain extent." He rubbed his stomach and asked, "What do I smell cooking?"

She whispered, "Don't tell the gang just yet, but it's cookies."

His eyes lit up. "Are they out of the oven now?"

"I don't think so, and, even if they were, I'm not sure Chef will let you have them."

"Oh, he'll let me have them." Rogan grinned, as he picked up the pace and headed to the kitchen. Curious, she followed behind, and, sure enough, when he turned toward the door, he was holding a big fat cookie.

She shook her head. "How the hell did you manage to get one of those?"

"Because I'm good," Rogan stated, "and, if you're friendly, you might get one too."

"But then again, I might be putting Chef on the spot because things haven't been terribly friendly between us."

Rogan rolled his eyes, quickly disappeared, then came back with a cookie for her. "This way you don't have to address it."

"Thank you," she said, as she accepted the cookie. "So, do we have any more information on the break-in?"

"No. I only heard about it when I woke up this morning."

"*Great*, as if we didn't have enough headaches around this place, without having to deal with that too."

"That's what I was thinking," Rogan agreed. "I would think that we'd be past all that."

"I would think so too, but, hey, it is what it is." As he headed back to his room, she called out, "Thanks for the cookie."

He immediately froze, then turned and glared at her. "You did not just say that out loud."

She flushed, but then grinned at him unrepentantly.

"Hey, you're supposed to share with your team members."

"Hell no," he muttered, but just about then, a door blasted open, and a head popped out. "Did you say *cookie*?"

"No, I sure didn't," Rogan quipped, as he walked past, waving the huge cookie in his hand.

"Damn." The man's tone was urgent and high. "I've got to get there fast. Otherwise there won't be any left." Almost as soon as he slammed his door, others opened up and raced to the kitchen. She laughed at their antics, but it put a lighter tone on the day, and that was all-important, considering yet another anomaly in the night. Kudos to Chef for recognizing it.

Later that morning she walked to the medical clinic, unable to help herself. She knocked on the door, smiling tentatively when Sydney opened it.

"Hey," Sydney greeted her.

"Hey. I know you're probably not allowed to tell me very much, but is my sister okay?" Berry asked in a worried tone. Lowering her voice even more, Berry added, "I'm hearing all kinds of stuff, but nobody is talking to me directly."

Sydney stepped back. "Come on in."

Berry saw her sister, curled up, sound asleep on the bed. "What's going on with her?" she asked, as she walked over.

"I'll tell you, but you won't like it."

She stiffened and turned toward the doc. "What's the matter?"

"Drug withdrawal, which she finally confessed to. I guess Yegorahn had his own supply of drugs, supposedly recreational drugs, to calm her down and to deal with the isolation of being here." Sydney gave an eye roll at that explanation. "With his death, Cherry used up the last of his supply, and then slowly went to pieces since, not sure how to get more or what to do about going cold turkey. Her condition definitely worsened."

Berry sat down hard on the spare chair and stared at the doctor in shock.

Sydney nodded gently. "I gather you didn't know."

Berry shook her head, almost mute, trying to think back to when she'd seen her sister with Yegorahn. "I didn't even know that he was a drug user or that drugs were here to use and abuse," she whispered.

"Now we're wondering whether it was also connected to some of the break-ins here at the clinic as well. For example, did he already have the drugs with him when he arrived on base or what? Because we had several break-ins here, stealing drugs, and maybe that is when they started, with Yegorahn. Then maybe Joy took note and followed suit." Sydney shook her head, with a quiet shrug. "It's too early to know the truth."

Berry walked over to her sleeping sister and picked up her hand and whispered, "How bad is it?"

"She's better today, a little bit, but it will be rough for a few more days." Sydney then pulled back the blankets, so Berry could see that her sister was strapped down.

Berry stared at the straps grimly, then lifted her tortured gaze to Sydney, who reached out a hand to pat her.

"I have to. It's the only way to keep her safe. When she's cognizant, and she's clear, then she doesn't need to be strapped in, but, when she's not, we don't have a choice."

"No, I get it," Berry whispered. "I'm just in shock still."

When a murmur came from the bed, she leaned over and whispered, "Cherry, it's me. How are you feeling?"

Her sister opened her eyes and stared at her, bleary-eyed.

"Like I've been hit over the head," she muttered. "What happened?" She went to shift, only to find her arms restrained. She glared down at the restraints and then her gaze landed on Sydney. Groaning, she realized where she was and what situation she was in. "God damn it," she yelled. "Not you again!"

"Yeah, me again," Sydney stated cheerfully. "And, until I know that you're clear of all the drugs you ingested, this is where you'll stay."

Cherry swore several times and looked at her sister. "If I'd realized that Yegorahn was giving me drugs that I would get addicted to, I never would have taken them."

"I can't believe you took them in the first place," Berry cried out.

"It's this place," Cherry snapped. "I was going nuts. I needed something to get through it. Something about the wind and the cold, just that vastness out there, was freaking me out," she admitted. "Yegorahn had something to help me to calm down. I didn't even question it. I just went along, looking for an answer to make life a little bit more bearable."

Berry sighed. "I need to ask you another question. ... Did you start that relationship—sleeping with him, I mean—the night before he died, or was it some other night?" Her sister's gaze immediately dropped, and Berry's heart sank. "Jesus, Cherry. Please tell me that you at least told the truth to Ted and Egan."

Cherry's gaze flew up to her sister's face, and she slowly shook her head. "What difference does it make?" she asked, her voice harsh and raspy.

At that, Sydney walked over, picked up a glass with a straw, and held it up for Cherry to take a sip. She greedily sucked down the water and then sagged back. "What possible difference does it make if we slept together that night or other nights?"

"Because every detail is important. Where was his roommate?"

She shrugged. "He moved into another guy's room. And you didn't even notice me coming and going from our room. I left once you fell asleep, and I came back before you got up, or I was already up and out in the dining room." Cherry yawned. "Not that I cared whether you found out or not, but I didn't want everybody to know."

"And yet, when you were questioned, you lied?"

"When I was initially questioned"—Cherry glared at her twin—"I didn't want everybody to find out. It makes me sound cheap and trashy."

Berry let out her breath slowly. "So when did you first start sleeping with him?"

"About a week before he died," Cherry said. "We'd been beating around the bush for a few days, and, by then, it was pretty easy to hop into bed with him. Not much else to do in this godforsaken place."

"Maybe not, so when did you start taking the drugs?" she asked.

Cherry shrugged. "Probably the first night."

"Oh my God, so you've been hooked for several weeks now?" Berry cried out.

Her sister nodded. "And that's one of the reasons why I changed. I took the rest of the drugs from his room, but I ran out a few days ago—more than a few days ago now. I don't know, and I guess that's when I got grouchy."

"Ya think?" Berry stared at her, staying at her sister's bedside, worrying about her, then noticed she seemed to fade in and out ever-so-slightly. She looked over at Sydney. "Is this normal?"

Sydney gave her a reassuring nod. "Unfortunately, yes." She checked the time and walked over. "It's about time for her to get another dose."

"A dose of what?" Berry asked. "Hasn't she had enough drugs?"

"This is what helps her to get off those," Sydney replied, her voice steadfast, as she put something into the IV strapped to Cherry's arm. "Earlier, with Joy, when I first realized we had a drug issue going on here," the doc explained, "I ordered what I needed, should somebody turn up in withdrawal, so I had it, just in case." Sydney raised her hands in defense. "Believe me. I don't want to use it, but we're past that point now."

And, with that, Berry watched as the medication took hold, and her sister faded off into sleep.

Sydney told Berry, "You might as well go, since Cherry won't even be cognizant for a long while now. It'll take days to get those drugs out of her system. I hate to say it, but she'll need some counseling after this too."

Berry nodded. "She really cared about him."

"Good, I'd hate to think that he died without anybody giving a crap," Sydney declared, although her tone was soft.

"Cherry certainly didn't help her case, but I understand why better now," Berry muttered, as she looked at the sleeping woman. "I just hope the others do too."

"Go on now," Sydney said. "Go get some of the day for yourself. Your sister will be here when you come back."

Berry hesitated, then asked, "Promise?"

Sydney smiled gently, then gave Berry a hug. "I promise. She's doing better already, so every day that she's here under my care is another day that she gets closer to freedom from the demons associated with the drugs. ... When she's awake again, you can talk to her some more, but go now. She'll be asleep for hours."

And, with that, Berry was led to the door and out into the hallway, where the doctor shut the clinic door firmly behind her.

MAGNUS AND EGAN had spent three hours out searching for tracks, searching for anything that would give them answers. They had to use miner's headlamps initially, as they'd come out in the dark. Now it was light, and they still had no answers. When they finally stopped for a break, they shook their heads at each other.

Egan spoke first. "Any chance it was done to fool us?"

"Maybe," Magnus replied, his voice harsh.

Egan groaned. "In which case, whoever the fuck did this did a hell of a job, which would be the reason for doing it."

"Yep," Magnus admitted, "they thought they could do a good-enough job to fool us, which they have. But still, there's got to be a reason."

"And every time we go around and around," Egan muttered, "not exactly coming up with answers. Then we just have a whole lot more questions."

"Questions are good though," Magnus noted.

Egan sighed. "You and I both know that."

Magnus shook his head. "Yet it's so frustrating. When we think we've got something solved, it's only to find out we've got nothing ... again."

Egan smiled. "Sounds like normal life to me."

At that, Magnus laughed and nodded. "Very true. I'll

give you points for that one."

"I guess we may as well head back, *huh*?"

"Unless you've got anything else to suggest."

"No, but we better keep an eye on our storage areas in case these thefts become a regular thing on base, which won't make Chef very happy at all," Egan noted, thinking out loud. "Or the colonel. He is hardly bearable as it is. I'm sure not looking forward to telling him about this. In fact, I'm surprised he's still here."

"I'm pretty sure he's still here until we solve all this, and, if we don't solve it, … there's no safety for him either," Magnus shared.

"I heard rumors that he was here as punishment."

"I don't know whether that's true or not. It would suck if it were, yet it's also kind of—I hate to say it—the military way."

Egan laughed at that. "Isn't that the truth? Anyway, let's head back, and we'll try to figure out our next step from there."

They slowly turned toward the military base, their tracks already mostly covered in the blowing snow.

As they skied, Egan added, "You do realize that they could have quite easily come into the base, gotten supplies, and left, and we wouldn't be any the wiser?"

"That's what they did do, and we wouldn't have noticed if it weren't for the jimmied hinges," Magnus replied, looking at him in confusion.

"I guess I'm wondering if they'd done it any other time. So, if they didn't pry the door off before, how many other times would they have come and gone? Would Chef even know?"

"I would hope he'd know," Magnus stated, his tone

harsh, "because otherwise what would it take for him not to?"

"I don't have an answer for you there," Egan noted, "but it's something to think about."

"Too much to think about right now," Magnus muttered, as they headed home.

"Not only too much to put together but also none of it's making any sense."

"Yet it will eventually. You know it will. We just don't have enough answers yet to put the pieces into place," Magnus added.

Egan nodded. "That's always one of those things that makes life a little more difficult."

"What I want to know," Magnus stated, "is if you're suggesting that this was an inside job just made to look like it was somebody from outside? If so, what was the purpose?"

"To get extra resources, but why?"

Magnus considered that for a few moments. "So, if the insider can't use them at base, the only other reason to steal from the military would be if he's selling them. And who would buy them?"

"The locals," Egan suggested. "Nobody else is here, unless we're also considering Amelia."

Magnus winced at that. "God, I hope not. I would hope that, if Amelia's team were in trouble, they were being overly cautious by not coming in and talking to us. Yet to steal groceries from the base or to buy stolen goods from someone in the village would also be rough."

"And wouldn't say a whole lot about anybody involved, would it?"

"No, but we already know we've got problems here," Magnus noted, "so I can't say I'd be terribly surprised.

Maybe not terribly surprised, but I guess I'd feel pretty sick if I thought that's what was really going on."

Egan nodded but didn't say anything. Yet it was something to contemplate as they headed home, the journey long and cold. Thankfully they were both in good shape, and it was a gorgeous day for this trip.

When they neared the military base, Egan continued with that same line of thought from earlier. "Amelia could have hidden anywhere. She could be out here and relatively close by, and we wouldn't even see them because of the whiteout conditions. She could be out here perfectly happy, munching away at our stores."

"She'd be welcome to it," Magnus stated. "Still, I'd prefer to know that she's okay."

"You and me both," Egan agreed. "I don't like anything about this, especially if the only reason she wouldn't be coming in is because she's too scared. That makes things take an uglier turn yet again."

"Just think about it. Does she know what happened at the scientists' camp, her own camp? We now know that Anna was trying to kill them all, some psychotic murder-suicide mission. But, with Anna dead, was somebody else in the scientists' camp after Amelia too? Or does Amelia even know what happened to Anna and the others, after the carbon dioxide leak in their camp? Or does Amelia think Anna and Myles both wound up dead on our base—which facts, without all the circumstances, sure does point a guilty finger at our military compound. Not knowing everything, maybe Amelia won't come in, thinking someone would go after her again. Again, too many questions, not enough answers, and nothing making sense," Magnus concluded.

When they rounded a bend and came upon the base,

Egan felt a certain sense of relief in seeing it. It represented safety, but a false one at that. Still, when out in the cold like this, day trips could be something incredibly joyous, knowing you could handle whatever was tossed at you because, really, it was glorious out there. A lot of living things did manage to survive in these harsh surroundings, and that just made Egan respect the tundra ecosystem all the more.

As they unpacked and cleaned up their gear, Magnus told Egan, "Don't say anything to anyone in there, will you? I have yet to talk to the boss."

"Better you than me," Egan noted, with a smile.

"Yeah, right? On the other hand, if we can get some answers, then I don't mind in the least."

As they walked inside the main building, several people stared at them, questions in their gazes, but it didn't take long for people to realize that Egan and Magnus hadn't found anything. Egan searched out Berry and found her in the dining area, talking to a group of seeming friends. He hesitated, not wanting to intrude. But when she saw him, she bounded to her feet and came over with a smile.

"Any luck?" she cried out. Then she saw his face and winced. "I guess I should have waited before I asked that, *huh*?"

"It's all right," he said. "We spent hours following what was left of the tracks, but, no, nothing."

She shook her head. "It just blows me away to think that somebody slipped inside the base during the dark of night and took supplies. I don't understand why they would do that."

"The why is easy," Egan noted, with a one-arm shrug. "They needed food."

"Right, sorry, I'm not trying to be obtuse, but why not come into the base during daylight hours then?" He didn't say anything, just nodded. She walked with him to get a hot cup of coffee. As she stood here waiting, she studied his face. He tried not to let on too much of what was going on, but still she saw something in his gaze. "You're wondering about something, aren't you?"

He gave her a dry look. "I'm wondering all kinds of things," he admitted. "Believe me. We have no answers for any of it."

"No, I understand," she replied, "and that's one of those things that the rest of us have been sitting here hashing out. Such as, no need for somebody to steal the supplies, when I don't think anybody on base would care about sharing food, especially not if they needed the food. The question is whether they needed those supplies or not, and, if they didn't, who is it and what are they doing with them?"

"Yeah, all good questions that we want the answers to." Egan smiled wanly. "However, no answers are coming our way just yet."

She winced. "Sorry about that."

"It's not your fault," he noted, with a chuckle. "Definitely not your fault. We've come in from a very long morning of skiing to find not a whole lot, and now we still have to deal with the brass about it."

"Oh, *great.*" She gave an eye roll. "That's probably the last thing you want to deal with."

"Still, it's got to be done." He raised one hand and gave her a half smile. "I'll talk to you later." And, with that, he quickly disappeared down the hallway. More because he knew, if he stayed, he would start talking to her about everything going on. However, the brass must get the accounting first.

Also something was between him and Berry, and he couldn't resist the pull that bound her to him.

As he walked in to join Magnus with the colonel, Egan was ushered straight through, where he found Magnus talking to the colonel, who looked up and glared at Egan. "So, you guys didn't find anything, I hear?" the colonel barked.

"Nothing conclusive, no," Egan replied.

At that, the colonel's eyebrows raised. "I don't play games, so what are you talking about?"

"We're just not sure, … but Magnus and I, … we wondered if somebody inside the base may have done this."

At that, the colonel sucked in his breath and stared at the two men with a hardened look. "And why would that be something anybody here would want to do?" he asked, in a raspy hard voice.

"We don't know that it is," Egan clarified. "All we're saying is that it's a thought that occurred to us, while we were out there. It would be pretty darn hard for anybody to hide this theft."

"But it would also be very hard for anybody to utilize this stolen food, when they are all here," the colonel added. "So your theory or your idea doesn't make any sense."

The two men didn't say anything and just waited while the CO pondered what to do next. Finally he said, "The only reason anybody here would want those foodstuffs is if they were selling them, and we aren't short on rations."

"What if somebody thought we would be short on rations?" Egan asked him.

The colonel stared at him, as if he was out of his mind. "That's a wild accusation."

"I'm not accusing anybody," Egan stated. "All I'm suggesting is that our problem could be slightly different than we were thinking it was."

At that, the colonel nodded. "Oh, I get what you're saying. I can't say I like any of it though."

"Of course not, sir." Egan tried to keep his voice respectful, but it was hard when he was dealing with as much as he was himself.

The older man looked at him, his gaze sharp, and declared, "I want you to keep after this. I don't know who may have done this, but if you think it's worth it, I suggest we do a room-by-room search."

"That would aggravate everybody," Magnus replied immediately, "and elevate the lack of trust to a whole new level."

"You think I don't know that?" the colonel snapped. "There is a complete lack of trust already. In me, in this outfit. I don't want it to get any worse."

"Neither do we, sir," Magnus admitted, "and to accuse somebody of hiding stores here and ruining the door just in order to have a supply in case things go bad, not sharing with anybody else, that's just ugly too."

"None of us will starve," the colonel noted in exasperation. "If nothing else, we can always get stores from our neighbors."

Egan didn't say anything to that because, of course, the locals didn't have a whole lot, certainly not enough to feed thirty extra people.

"As a last resort, we would still ski out of here and get food supplies hauled in. If nothing else, it would be survival supplies."

"We can get those airdropped in," Magnus noted, "so it

makes no sense that anybody on the inside would have done that—not to make an artificially low food supply here."

"Maybe not," Egan added, "and I admit it sounds a bit farfetched, but, with the low morale, with the angry people here, with so many wanting off this base, it could be motive. And, since we couldn't really find any tracks outside, not once sunlight finally came, it just made us wonder."

"Well, wonder something else," the CO said in a snippy voice. "And, while you're wondering, get me some goddamn answers too." And, with that, they were both dismissed.

At the door, Egan looked back to see the colonel staring off in the distance. "Sir?"

The colonel shifted and sent him a hard gaze. "What now?"

Egan then shrugged. "Nothing, sir." And, with that, Egan took his doubts and his questions and quickly made his escape. Out in the hallway, when Magnus stared at him, Egan added, "Something's seriously wrong, and I wanted to have clearance to go check things out, if I needed to. Yet I think it's a bad idea, so that's why I backed off again," he explained, with a laugh. "I've never been very good at talking to the bosses. Can you tell?"

"Oh, some bosses care, and some don't," Magnus replied. "I think, at this point in time, this one's just scared."

"Like all of us at times," Egan confirmed, as he nodded at Magnus.

"That's the problem. Everybody here is scared. So, if they did steal the foodstuffs for themselves and their friends, in a way I understand it. So I disagree with the CO's notion to search everybody's rooms."

Egan nodded. "I don't appreciate it, and I sure as hell won't condone it, but I understand some people here not having the belief that everybody would get the same treatment. We're dealing with a lot of countries, a lot of different cultures and beliefs," Egan stated, carefully choosing his words. "And that can go sideways very, very quickly."

At that, Magnus grimaced. "I hadn't considered it from that point of view, but you're right. Not everybody would have the same confidence in knowing that this would all work out in the end. Some people will have the absolute opposite attitude toward it, something we had better keep in mind. And so I vote that we delay any required search of the rooms for the missing food."

Egan agreed.

And, with that, the two men parted ways for the day.

DAY 6, EARLY AFTERNOON

HOURS AFTER HER last visit, as Berry approached the door to the clinic, she found it open. She stepped inside, calling out a hesitant greeting.

Sydney looked up and smiled. "Good morning again," she called out, as she motioned Berry in. "Or is it afternoon already?" She checked her watch. "Yep, just after noon. You can come in and see her."

Berry knew that she probably could, but that didn't mean her sister wanted to be seen. Berry hadn't heard too many people discussing her sister's drug-addicted condition. Berry didn't know if that particular info was out and in the general knowledge. However, as Berry walked closer, her sister opened her eyes and smiled at her. That was a good sign.

"Hey," Cherry murmured, her voice sleepy, quiet.

"Hey," Berry responded, sitting beside her. "How are you feeling?"

"Like shit. I ache everywhere. Who would have thought getting off some simple pills would do this?"

Berry winced at that. "I don't think those pills were *simple* at all."

Cherry gave her twin sister a half smile. "Yeah? You haven't called me stupid yet."

"And I wouldn't," Berry declared. "I think you've got

enough to deal with *without* my adding anything to it."

"You know Mom and Dad will absolutely hit the roof when they find out."

Berry didn't say anything at first. What could she say? It was true; their parents were extremely narrow in their views. Neither had wanted the girls to go into the military, and neither of them were terribly impressed when the twins had taken this assignment up north, but the parental disapproval was something the twins had both learned to ignore a long time ago. "They will get over it," Berry finally said, "if they even need to know."

Cherry looked at her hopefully. "You won't tell them?"

Berry stared at her sister, her eyebrows raising. "I'm not sure where you've been these last few years," Berry began gently, "but it's not been my habit to tattle on you."

Her sister flushed. "No, … but you did say something about me that was my secret to keep and not yours to tell."

"If I had realized you had specifically avoided telling anyone that information—"

"I get it, though even asking you to hide it wouldn't have been right either," Cherry admitted, "because you're correct. If I cared about him, why the hell would I not want to find out who killed him?" she asked in exasperation. "I guess I felt as if I would get judged, and I'm really tired of being judged."

Berry hid a smile at that. Cherry had always had this thing about everybody looking at her in a negative light.

At Berry's silence, Cherry glared at her sister, then groaned. "I know. I know. I need to work on myself."

"Yeah, you do," Berry agreed, "particularly now."

She stared up at the ceiling. "My military career is over. You know that, right?"

"I don't know whether it is or not," Berry said, "but I do know that you need some professional help, and this is a really good time to get it."

"And how much help do you think I need?" she asked, her tone caustic, as she glared at Berry. "A little bit or will they put me away for this?"

"I have no idea," Berry stated, "and I don't know why they would *put you away*. Seems there are mitigating circumstances, in the sense that you were overwhelmed with loss and fear. However, I don't know how much that would be held against you. Now, would you be allowed to go out on a mission like this again? I have no idea but probably not."

"I don't want to either," Cherry declared immediately.

"Exactly, you just want to go home and to get out of this whole scenario. Therefore, if the brass understands that, … then maybe you'll be fine. I do think you need to seek some professional counseling though."

At that, Cherry rolled her head toward Berry and added a bit too harshly, "Don't worry. Sydney told me the same thing."

Berry smiled. "Good, then, as long as we're spouting the same talk, maybe you'll pay attention and listen for a change."

"Not likely," she quipped, and then she grinned. "Sorry, that was more for fun than anything."

"I get it," Berry replied. "I just don't know if there will be any repercussions for not having spoken up timely about Yegorahn's whereabouts."

"I don't know." Cherry sighed. "I could hope somebody would have a little compassion for me, but really the focus should be on Yegorahn's death and what happened to him."

"I guess I need to ask, ... just for my own sake. So, you have no ideas about anybody who might have wanted to kill him?"

"No, of course not," she stated, staring at her sister. "I get that, for you, ... short-term relationships are never your thing. Yet, for me, they're easy, fun, and I quite enjoy them," she shared. "In this case, it was a little more than that, but, no, I really don't know why anyone would kill Yegorahn," she muttered, banging her head on the hospital cot. "I wish I did."

"How much do you remember of the last night that you saw him?"

"He got up, left me in bed, told me what time it was, and he was going to grab a coffee. Next thing I knew, ... he was missing." Cherry shook her head. "And nobody knew anything about our night together."

Of course Berry wanted to ask why hadn't Cherry come forward at that point in time because that would have been a really good time to have shared what she did know, but her sister didn't deal with her own problems, much less someone else's—even if to potentially save somebody, it seemed.

Berry sat back and nodded.

"Look. I know that you're disappointed in me," Cherry admitted, "because once again it seems as if ... I put myself ahead of others. If I had been thinking about Yegorahn, I would have immediately come forward."

"Yeah, that makes sense—what with your intent to mitigate the circumstances here."

"Which is also why I took the drugs and why I wanted to leave this place. I just wanted to get the hell out of here," Cherry wailed. "You know how I felt about that."

"Yeah, but chances are I'll get interviewed over it all myself."

Her sister winced. "I know you probably want to throw me to the wolves, but it would be nice if you didn't."

She snorted. "Since when have I ever wanted to throw my sister to the wolves? We may have issues, but that isn't something I would normally consider part of our relationship."

"No, it's usually *me* throwing you to the wolves," Cherry replied, with a knowing half smile. "And I do have a tendency to knock you to all the boyfriends."

"You what?" Berry asked, staring at her sister. "Why would you do that?"

She looked at her, flushed, and admitted, "Because—I guess, in a way—I'm jealous, and I'm always afraid they'll come to you instead of me."

"Why the ..." And Berry abruptly shut up and studied her sister.

Cherry shrugged. "I get that, to you, that's probably foolish, but I can't really change the way I feel about it. I can't."

"But it also means that, in terms of jealousy, you're still dealing with a lot of issues that I would have hoped you had long since dealt with."

"When you grow up with a sister who looks almost identical to you, ... you have to do something to ... separate yourself."

"Sleeping with men would do that," Berry noted immediately.

Cherry winced. "Yes, probably that's why I do it, ... but I do enjoy it. So it's not as if I'm doing it on purpose just for that reason."

"I'm glad to hear that," Berry muttered, still trying to

hold back her shock at hearing that her sister used to say nasty things about Berry to boyfriends. "And it would be nice if you would stop saying negative things about me," Berry suggested, "unless you truly believe them. In that case, then we need to have a deeper talk than we are right now."

Her sister jutted her chin out. "It's not that," Cherry stated. "I think it's just jealousy, as always. You're always the smarter one and the prettier one, so I had to be the one who was way more fun."

"Good God," Berry whispered, as she stared at her sister. "You didn't have to be more *anything*. You just had to be you."

"Being *you* when you're a copy and paste isn't that easy. We're a copy and paste of each other," Cherry stated, with a mock chuckle, "and that's freaking irritating."

Berry frowned. "I don't know about *irritating*, and I certainly wouldn't have considered that kind of negative self-talk. I've always enjoyed having you around, and we've been extremely close at various times."

Her sister laughed. "I wonder how much of that *extremely close* we would have been if you had understood how much I've knocked you to the men."

Berry shrugged but still frowned. "They were your men, not mine, and I'm grateful that you stayed away from mine." Berry grabbed a firm hold on her own emotions, as she realized her sister needed this talk. It wouldn't matter to Cherry that she was causing pain for Berry because, when Cherry needed to share damning news, that apparently was all that mattered.

Berry caught Sydney's glance from behind Cherry, and Berry stiffened. "Or was it to my boyfriends as well?"

Her sister slid her a glance and then turned away.

Berry took that as a yes and stared at her in shock. "While you're confessing, could you please confess everything, so that it's right out in the open just how bad this has been?"

"It's not been bad at all," Cherry said, with a careless laugh. "Except that I did break up you and John in high school."

Berry's heart sank at that. "You mean, when I accused you of sleeping with him?"

"Yeah," she confirmed, "and that was a yes. We didn't tell you, but it seemed as if you knew anyway."

"I sure as hell had an ugly feeling about it, but, in my head, I allowed myself to believe that my sister—who loved me—would never hurt me like that," she shared, "and now you're telling me that you absolutely did?"

At that, Cherry winced and nodded. "And it was me, not him."

"You, not him? Really?" Berry asked in disbelief, "and I'm supposed to just accept that?"

"I get it, and it wasn't easy for him. I'll put it this way," Cherry explained, "that he felt terrible afterward. But you broke up with him soon anyway."

"Yeah, because he had changed, and I didn't know what was going on, but something obviously was," Berry declared. "I always had my suspicions, and you just admitted it." She sat back and stared at her sister. "Anybody else?"

Her sister glared at her. "I haven't spent a lifetime cheating with your boyfriends."

"I would be grateful, if that were the truth. However, you didn't even tell me about Yegorahn for the longest time, and, even then, you didn't tell me the truth. I don't know what you were afraid of, but I have never slept with one of your boyfriends," she stated.

"No, because, by the time I was done, they didn't like you," Cherry admitted. "I … whitewashed you out of the picture."

"Jesus, Cherry." She stared at her sister in shock. "All of that … but why? I've never done anything to you, so I don't understand this."

Cherry seemed happy to talk, so not long afterward Berry made her escape and headed to the kitchen area, her energy plummeting at this point. The conversation with her sister had gone from bad to worse, but Berry had remained stoic and had listened to her.

As Berry made herself a cup of tea, Sydney walked up.

"You handled that really well."

Berry glanced at her and whispered, "Maybe outwardly, but I still want to wring her neck."

Sydney nodded and smiled. "But the thing is, you didn't. You didn't attack her. You didn't judge her for it, and I could see that you were really struggling. But, if Cherry has any hope of getting past some of this and healing, then she needs to talk about it, even with you. And you handled it extremely well." Then Sydney hesitated and added in a low tone, "Look. If you need somebody to talk to, please make sure you get help yourself."

"I'm fine," she whispered to Sydney, looking around to make sure they weren't overheard. "But finding out all those lovely little tidbits didn't do anything for my mental health."

"No, and that's why I'm here, … to tell you that I really admire and appreciate the way you handled her. You did very well."

"And yet I don't feel as if I handled anything. I'm in shock and just waiting for it to calm down."

"And it will. It will calm down, but how you want it to calm down will be up to you. Anyway, give her some space right now. You probably need it too."

"Yeah, that'll be easy," she stated. "It may be wrong to say it, but, right about now, the last thing I want is to spend any time with my sister."

And with that, she grabbed her tea and headed back to her room, already looking back over the years with a woman who was identical to her in so many ways, and yet, where it counted, was the complete opposite.

EGAN UNHARNESSED THE dogs and tried to rub Toby down even as Toby rolled in the snow.

Joe stepped out and asked in a guttural tone, "How did he do?"

"Toby did really well." Egan looked over at the older man, with a smile. "You'd never know he'd been shot. Queenie stole the show though. She's quite the dog and a sweetheart to boot."

"She is at that. And, in Toby's case, it's the damn muscle that's causing him so much trouble," Joe shared, as he helped unleash the rest of the dogs from their harnesses and ushered them in. "Is this now a regular thing for you?" Joe asked Egan.

"It is at the moment, yes, until we see whether the rest of those folks from the scientists' camp come in or out. It's a nice quick run, check on their camp, and come back."

"Oh, I agree," Joe said, "and anything like that slow, steady run is very good for the dogs. So I appreciate you working with Toby. And Queenie seems taken with you."

"Believe me. I'm just fine with taking Toby out. And I adore Queenie. Any time the other injured one is ready for a walk, you let me know."

"I was thinking about trying him tomorrow maybe, but I think I want to go out with him myself."

"If you want to come with me, I'll be going back up again tomorrow."

"You're really doing this every day, *huh*?"

"Knowing missing people are out there nobody can find? … Yeah, it's honestly got me a little on the antsy side," Egan admitted, with a half smile.

Joe nodded. "I wouldn't want anybody suffering, if they don't have to. So, if a simple check of the scientists' camp for any fresh tracks is what you need, then I'm all for it. And you guys backtracked the other sled that you found?"

"We did, and the fact that it's broken and just barely made it that far is also a concern," Egan shared. "I presume they had skis, from what we could see, and managed to get back out again. However, if it was Amelia and if she has anybody else who's injured or dies," Egan clarified, "then that's a problem."

"Yeah, and she won't have any way to bring them back and forth."

"Nope," Egan agreed. "Not unless she has another sled or has another method to bring them in. I don't know that it's her, of course, but I'm kind of counting on it."

Joe nodded. "Oh, I agree with you, but it's got to be something pretty severe for anybody to want to stay out there."

"That's what we're wondering about too. Maybe she doesn't have a choice," Egan noted calmly. "And, no, I don't even want to think about what it could be in her world that could be so bad that she doesn't have a choice."

"And yet we all know that's possible."

"Unfortunately, yes. … I just want to be out there in case she needs something."

At that, Joe turned and looked at him. "Do you ever suspect that you're being watched?"

Egan nodded, acknowledging for the first time something that he did intuitively sense. "It does feel as if something's going on that I'm not necessarily aware of, but I don't know that I would say that I'm being watched, per se."

"I don't know what else you can call it," Joe stated. "And, if it is that, then God help us all."

"No, I think it just means that she's terrified to come in, and that in itself is a problem," Egan pointed out. "If she really doesn't trust anybody, what has she heard or seen or acknowledged in some way, and from whom? And why is it that we don't have the same knowledge?"

"So, are you thinking one of her team may have found something they weren't supposed to?"

"Look at who she—or somebody—returned to us. Yego-rahn's body, dropped off at the scientists' camp. One of our own trainees who had gone missing. What if he wasn't dead when she found him? What if she tried to nurse him and couldn't save him, but, in the meantime, he mentioned something?"

Joe nodded slowly. "That's not exactly a thought we want to consider, is it?"

"Yet how is it something we can walk away from?" Egan continued. "Just think about it. All kinds of shit are going on at our base, and we don't have a clue who or why. But she's got some lifeline going on here, and maybe she's just staying on her own as long as she can. Maybe she knows something we don't know, or maybe another team is coming that she's had contact with."

Joe frowned at that. "Why the hell would anybody not bring her in?"

"For safety," Egan suggested simply, "for just straight-up safety reasons. Maybe whoever she has with her is either too sick to travel or doesn't want to come in for some reason, or maybe she's being held hostage for something we don't have a clue about."

"God." Joe swore under his breath. "That's why I stick with dogs," he declared in a harsh tone. "I can understand them at least. When they're hungry, they eat. When they're not hungry, they don't. When they want loving attention, they come get it. And, other than that, you can count on a dog to give the rest of this BS a pass," Joe muttered. "Something's wrong about Amelia deliberately staying out there. It's not an easy life here, no matter what choices we make, but to think that she's deliberately avoiding us and believes *that* is keeping her safe? That's a little scary."

"I agree," Egan replied. "That's one of the reasons I keep going up there, just to check to ensure anybody else isn't left behind."

"Right." Joe smiled. "That's a good model. Nobody ever gets left behind, not in my world."

"Now all we have to do is make sure that whatever the hell is going on stops, so we can get everybody out of here safely," Egan noted. "I still don't quite understand why the brass hasn't just airlifted everybody out or run a heavy investigation into all parts of this chaos, then called it quits."

"Maybe they can't yet. Maybe they don't have enough information," Joe suggested. "Maybe they're just leaving everybody up here to sort it out. Who knows? Maybe they're getting such garbled information from headquarters that nobody understands how bad it is."

"That part I might believe," Egan admitted, with a headshake. "But the rest of it? If the brass talked to anybody here, it would be a completely different story."

"But nobody's talking, right? People are holding back."

"That's also part of the problem. Yet, as soon as that does becomes part of the narrative, then nobody knows who and what to believe."

"It's all bullshit," Joe snapped, as he glared around. Then he groaned. "But it doesn't matter, for I will continue to look after my dogs. However, this time—whenever I get out of here—I may never come back." Joe gave a heavy sigh.

"And you don't have to. That's all part and parcel of everybody making a decision after this, isn't it?"

"Sure, but it feels very much as if we've been left in the wild."

"I think there's probably a lot of investigative work going on, whether we see it or not."

"Just what is happening then? There are still no answers?"

"No answers, yeah." Egan sighed. "At some point in time people will start wondering if someone killed the latest Russian guy, since we now have Yegorahn's body, yet we don't even know what happened to him."

"Sure, and absolutely no idea what killed him."

"No. Hypothermia maybe. I saw no obvious signs otherwise for why he died. So hypothermia becomes a really strong possibility."

"Yeah, it does at that." Joe shook his head. "When all else fails, go back to the basics."

"Up here, it doesn't take long for the basics to kill you

either, as you and I both know."

With that, Joe smiled and added, "Now I'll head over and grab a hot cup of tea or coffee, if there happens to be any left." He gave an eye roll.

"I wouldn't count on it." Egan smirked. "Just enough people are in there all the time that I'm sure they're running out."

"Maybe, but, if nothing else, I'll go and see if all is well."

"Are you not expecting it to be?"

"I'm expecting it to be fine, but, so far, just enough things have gone wrong that I won't count on it."

A little later, after Egan had put away all his winter gear, Egan walked into the main part of the kitchen. He immediately found Magnus staring at him. He shook his head. "All is well?"

Magnus's shoulders slumped slightly, and Egan realized that Magnus was really hoping that this time Amelia and whoever was left of her team would show up—but nothing yet. And it put pressure on all of them in a way. Egan poured himself a hot chocolate, as the coffee was mostly gone, then walked over to where Magnus sat. As Egan sat down, two other men got up and walked over.

One of them got up in Egan's face, and he was not friendly, his voice harsh. "What the hell are you doing going out every day?"

"I keep looking for signs of the missing crew from the scientists' camp," Egan stated, his voice neutral, even as he realized Magnus had stiffened, preparing for a confrontation.

The other guy snorted. "They're dead and gone. Absolutely no point in even discussing that anymore," he snapped. "It's been way too long."

"That's not true," Egan stated. "Amelia is a survival expert, and she's only been gone what, ten days?"

"Ten days is a long time out here," the other man stated, looking at his friend uneasily. "Come on, Budge. Let's go do a workout before dinner."

"Why, Salmo? The food sucks now. It's not as if we've even got enough grub. I want to get the hell out of here."

"Have you asked your boss to be released?" Egan asked Budge.

Budge nodded and turned. "Sure have, and I keep getting the same bullshit answer. *Nobody's leaving.*"

"We don't have all that many more weeks to go in this training session," Egan noted. "You've done fine here so far. Let's just see if we can complete the assignment—you know, finish strong."

"Why?" Budge asked. "I don't even give a shit anymore."

"Maybe, but a lot of people went to a lot of effort to make this happen, so I imagine they do."

"Do they care?" He sneered. "They sure don't care for us. We've got what, two, three dead? Two missing and another found dead again. Whatever the count is now, I'm losing track," he said in a controlled fury. "Somebody stealing supplies from the storehouse too." He turned and stared at Magnus, full in the face. "You didn't think we knew about that, did you?"

Magnus was ready to pounce, but that was not the solution. "Nobody's hiding it," Magnus told Budge. "As far as I'm concerned, the better informed everybody is, the better we all are."

Salmo nudged his buddy. "Come on, Budge. Let's go."

"Why?" he asked, turning on his friend. "I don't want to fucking do another workout," he snarled at Salmo.

"No, what you're looking for is a fight," Salmo stated,

"and this isn't the place. Come on, man."

"Why not? You think they're not up to it?" Budge asked.

"Look. This will just get your ass in hot water."

"So what? What will they do? Throw me in the store-room? It's not as if they have any other place to put us."

"Is that what you want?" Magnus asked, looking at him pointedly, "because that can be arranged."

Budge sneered. "I don't even know who you are or what the hell you're doing here, but the whole thing's damn fishy, if you ask me."

"Good thing nobody asked you," Magnus said, his voice hard. "But you keep pushing, and we'll be happy to oblige. I could stand to kick some ass."

"Jesus Christ, come on, Budge," Salmo said. "Let's get out of here. Go take out that temper of yours on something else." With that, he pulled his buddy away.

Only Budge was still not very interested in being calmed down. But, when both Magnus and Egan stood up and faced him, he sneered. "Yeah, there are two of you *now*," he snapped, "but there won't always be two of you."

"Is that a threat?" Magnus asked.

Budge shook his head. "I don't need to threaten any-body. Consider it a promise." Even as he walked out, followed by his frantic buddy, Budge sent a warning glance back at them.

As Egan sat back down again, he let out his breath. "Wow, I see tempers aren't getting any better in here."

"Yeah, definitely some people are past the boiling point," Magnus agreed.

"The good news is, the weather's set to change tomor-row, and everybody can get back outside again. Maybe they'll wear out some of this feistiness," Egan muttered.

Magnus shook his head and looked over at him. "You still want to get out there and check the scientists' camp first thing?"

"I do," Egan confirmed. "I still feel that somebody is in trouble out there but is just unsure about where to go and how to make things right."

"That really sucks," Magnus said, "because, if you're right, it's got to be Amelia. And, if it is her, where the hell is she getting the information that things here are bad enough that she needs to stay away?"

"The only thing I can think of is the dead man, Yego-rahn," Egan suggested, turning to look at Magnus. "I presume that he wasn't dead when she found him, and she tried to save him. However, in the meantime, he told her what the hell was going on here."

"But just not enough to come in and to make accusations."

"It's possible, or else she doesn't think the accusations will be believed."

"*Great*," Magnus muttered. "That's always the worst, isn't it? When you know something, or at least you think you know something, but you don't think anybody'll listen to a word you say."

"Yeah," Egan agreed, "and, if that were me, I'd probably feel the same way she does. I'm not sure I'd come in either."

Just then Sydney walked over and, giving Magnus a hug, sat down beside Egan. She tilted her head and spoke to him in a low voice. "You may want to go spend some time with Berry."

He looked at her, and she just shook her head. "Problems?" he asked.

"Yeah, you could say so. Her sister is coming off the

drugs and is winding down nicely, but with a case of needing to clear her conscience. Unfortunately the conscience that she's clearing at the moment seems to be a list of things she's done wrong to her sister, including affairs with Berry's old boyfriends, breaking up relationships, that sort of thing," the doc explained. "So Berry has disappeared into her own private space right now to process all that, but I'm not sure it's a good thing for her to spend too much time with it."

Egan stared at her in shock. "Jesus, but they're twins."

"Yeah, and apparently the one twin decided somewhere along the line that the other one was better, prettier, smarter, nicer, and who knows what all, even though they look nearly identical," Sydney recapped. "So Cherry decided to set herself apart by being the *fun* one."

"And being *fun* meant *putting out?*" Magnus asked, with a headshake. "Jesus, how is Cherry doing physically?"

"She's coming down and is annoying as hell, but she'll be okay. It's not a condition conducive to being here though, and I very much want to see her get out of here," Sydney admitted. "We do have supplies coming in, and I believe a couple extra investigators are coming up as well," she added. "Ted mentioned that he wouldn't be handling the investigation going forward."

At that, Magnus stared at her in shock.

She nodded. "I don't know anything more than that, so you'll have to pry it out of Ted. He didn't sound very happy about the whole thing."

"Yeah, I wonder why though. That's his department. How can he leave it just like that?"

"Jerry's been sick since he got up here, so I don't think Ted has had a whole lot of help from Jerry. I'm not sure that either one of them has been terribly cooperative for whatever you've needed either."

"No, and we're trying to do everything on the sly," Egan shared.

At that, Magnus stood and noted in a resolute tone, "I'll go have a talk with him."

Sydney got up too, then looked down at Egan and whispered, "I didn't say anything, right?"

He smiled and nodded. "Got it. I'll go see how she's doing." Then he rose and headed to the back, as he refilled his tea to take with him.

He heard conversations at the table nearby.

"We should just take them out," somebody said. "Nobody would know." There was a round of shushing before he shut up.

Feeling eyes glued to his back, Egan carefully ensured nobody thought he was listening in. Although, in a place like this, any conversation remotely like that was suspicious.

As he walked to Berry's bedroom door, he still felt eyes on his back. Frowning, he turned and casually looked around, his gaze sweeping the corner where the malcontents were seated, only to find one of the men staring at him. The man immediately dropped his gaze and turned away. Egan noted who it was though. It was one of the guys from the Swiss team, which generally they hadn't had any problems with. However, everybody was trying to get out now, and, if one more dead body showed up, it would be an all-out war to make sure these guys got out of here before anybody else was killed. And that wouldn't be fun. It never was, but in a place like this, it could be fatal.

Frustrated in the moment with the circumstances surrounding it all, and knowing that he was definitely part of the problem now, even though he'd come to be part of the solution, he headed to Berry's new room. When he knocked on the door, there was a hesitant "Come in." When he pushed open the door, he saw the relief on her face. He smiled, stepped in, and asked casually, "Hey, are you okay?"

She winced. "Did Sydney tell you?"

"Just that your sister woke up, with a need to bare her soul, and some of it was pretty rough on you."

"Yeah, you could say so," she admitted. "It's mostly ancient history in a way, so you'd think it would be fine, but you know? … It's not fine at all." He immediately sat down beside her and gave her a hug. She curled into his arms, as if it were the most natural thing of all.

"Betrayal isn't ever easy to take, and it doesn't matter how old it is," he shared. "She's your sister, and, if there ever was anybody who should have had your back, it should have been her."

"Instead apparently she went out of her way to damage me and my reputation and to take as much from me as she could," Berry shared. "I'm still sitting here, thinking back on all the times when I didn't understand what was going on around me and blamed myself, only to find out now that Cherry was the problem. … I don't even know what to say."

"You don't need to say anything, and I don't need specifics," he told her. "I'm just sorry it happened."

She looked up at him and nodded. "Yeah, me too. … I guess that's the bottom line. In a way, I wish I didn't know. Yet I think I needed to know because I'd always thought that my sister was there for me, and now? … As you said, betrayal is the worst."

"It is," he agreed.

"But that's okay, I'll get through it," she stated. "Now, what about you? How was your trip out today? They seem to be getting longer."

"I keep going out, leaving messages at the scientists' center. Honestly I really think Amelia's still alive."

"But, if that's the case, she's deliberately avoiding us."

"Oh, absolutely, and, if she's avoiding us, she must have a damn-good reason. I just wish I knew what that reason was."

Berry shook her head. "It's kind of scary to consider that anybody would think that way."

"But when we review everything that's gone wrong here," he noted pointedly, "you can understand the sentiment, and her reluctance doesn't seem to be so bad."

"But the only way that could have happened is if …" And then she stopped, winced, and added in frustration, "Yegorahn said something to Amelia before he died?"

Egan nodded. "That would be my take."

"Damn," Berry said. "That's not what I was hoping for."

"Nope, me neither," he agreed, with a wry look. "But it doesn't look as if we'll be getting any easy answers, so what do you want to do between now and dinnertime?"

She laughed. "Dinnertime? Is it that late? Don't tell me that I've been in here all day?"

"You've been in here for hours, if this is where you came after you left Cherry."

She sighed, then nodded. "I came down and wallowed in misery for a while. I slept too, really hard it seemed. Then, when I woke up, I started doing some work I had, though there isn't a whole lot of it to be done right now."

"No, but keeping our minds occupied right now is really important," Egan shared. "So, if there's anything I can do to help out, just let me know."

"No, it's fine," Berry said. "I need to find a way to make

peace with my sister, though I don't know how to do that. In the meantime, that whole mess will just jiggle around in my mind, and, as new things pop up that I remember, I'll see them from this ugly new viewpoint and feel betrayed all over again. If I can find a way to settle things with Cherry, then hopefully I'll deal with it and put it away."

"I'm pretty impressed that you can even think about getting to that point already."

DAY 6, DINNERTIME

B ERRY STARED AT Egan, wondering at the connection building between them. And glad her sister wasn't here to mess it up, then feeling crappy for having that thought. "Our parents are very not accepting. They're quite hard-nosed in fact, which is probably part of the reason why Cherry did what she did. Anything for a little rebellion," she said, with a groan. "But to go after me? That's where I find it hard to be accepting."

"Of course," Egan agreed. "Siblings are always in a unique relationship, but—in your case, being a twin—it's even more so."

She nodded. "Despite all that mess, I really do love her, and I'm sorry that she's done what she has because I think it makes her feel even worse," Berry explained. "If she had ever talked to me about it, back then or even now, I would have eventually helped her to feel better."

"Maybe," Egan replied, "though, with her in that mind-set, maybe there has never been anything you could do. It's all up to Cherry."

"You're right. I likely couldn't do much, at least nothing substantive. Still, I don't feel any better going over years of our history and seeing how many times people in my life— who were supposedly there for me—were not," she stated. "And that's where I'm really struggling."

"Who wouldn't?" Egan noted. "So don't expect more out of yourself than is reasonable. To even consider the fact that you could forgive her for this is huge already. Do what you need to do for yourself first, then find a way to make peace with it if you can. Just remember. If that peace in your soul doesn't happen right away, don't beat yourself up over it. It is perfectly reasonable to say that you need time to sort yourself out, and you sure don't have to buckle down and forgive Cherry right away." Egan snorted. "As a matter of fact, I'm not sure doing that would be beneficial to her."

"Why not?" she asked, looking at him.

"Because it seems as if your sister has had a pretty easy ride and has gotten away with an awful lot of stuff that she probably shouldn't have. Maybe it's time for her to grow up and to realize that there are consequences to her actions. This wasn't a single act. She did things to hurt you again and again, over a period of many years. So to let her off the hook too easily won't be something she'll learn anything from and will essentially be enabling her."

"Will Cherry learn though?" she asked, giving him an odd look. "If she's been doing some version of this over the course of our whole life, I'm not sure she even gives a crap."

He nodded vehemently. "That's partly why I'm hoping you don't let her off the hook too soon. … I can see that you want to, and it's obvious that taking on her baggage is a major part of who you are, which really just highlights the differences between you two."

"That's one of the things that I've been sitting here suffering through," Berry admitted, with half a smile. "I finally understand, in painful and vivid detail, that, although outwardly we appear to be the same, in reality we are so very different in all the ways that matter."

"I would totally agree with that," Egan confirmed, "at least from what I've seen so far. No offense to your sister, but honestly I really like this twin the best."

She smiled up at him. "You're just saying that to be kind."

He frowned at her, then shook his head. "No, I'm not. Everything I know and have seen about you tells me that you are a really good person. Hold on to that."

"Thank you," she whispered.

"And now we should go see about getting dinner first. Maybe that would be a good thing to do," he suggested, as he rubbed his tummy. "Then we can come back, and, I don't know, find something to occupy our evening."

She laughed. "You mean, something healthy and wholesome?"

"Sure, whatever you want to do." And that's what they did.

When they got back after dinner, he held a deck of cards in his hands. "What card games do you know?"

"Not many," she replied ruefully. "We played several all the time but outside of those ones, I don't know any. Honestly I played them for my sister's sake."

"We'll keep it simple."

"Just don't even begin to mention strip poker," she warned.

He looked at her and then grinned. "I wouldn't, but now that you've mentioned it …" Egan waggled his eyebrows.

"Hell no." Berry laughed. "That would not be my thing. Not at all."

"No, but I gather it would be your sister's."

"No doubt"—she frowned, as she stared off in the distance—"it would be."

"Hey, it was stupid of me to make that comment. And to bring her up tonight. I'm sorry."

"It's okay, and you're right. It would totally be her. Cherry was always the fun one, the one who was up for anything and everything," Berry stated, a bit abashed. "I just didn't realize what *up for everything* means until it turns around and bites me in the ass," she muttered.

She gave a determined headshake, as if trying to get rid of her negative thoughts. "Anyway, we won't talk about her. We'll have a decent evening. Hopefully the weather tomorrow will be completely different, and I can get out and do some training."

"You and everybody else in this place," Egan noted, with a smile. "We're all hoping for a break in the weather."

DAY 7, MORNING

A S IT WAS, when Berry woke the next morning, it was quiet. No storm raged outside. The calm was a gift of peace. She bounded out of bed, dressed, and raced to the kitchen, to find everybody else in the same positive mind-set. She smiled. "Looks as if we will all get out today."

"Absolutely," said one of them, returning a big smile to her. "Even you?"

She nodded. "Even me."

"What about your sister?"

"I don't think she's medically released for that yet," she replied, trying to move right past that conversation. "I'll just grab some food and go see what Peter has assigned me to for the day."

And that's what she did. At least today, she had a smile on her face and hope back in her heart.

EGAN LED A group of sleds and their dogs, while Joe had a second group off to the side. They were slowly walking everybody through the lessons. They were teaching them how to move the dogs, how to command the dogs, how to switch out the dogs, how to understand when one of the dogs was getting tired and when it was time to shift the leader dog, if that was needed. All too often, the dogs didn't change positions when pulling sleds. They were typically quite content to be where they were accustomed to being, so change wasn't always a good thing. Queenie deserved her name, as she was one of the best-trained dogs in the group and was so patient with the newbie trainees.

As they walked their way through the day, Egan smiled and laughed to see everybody in a much better mood. It was really nice outside, and everybody seemed to be at the top of their game.

When they broke for lunch, they all milled around in a group. Egan had twelve trainees in total outside today. It made him feel better that Berry was one of the other group of twelve trainees, working with Joe's group. When Egan heard a shout, he turned to see one of the men pointing in the distance, where another dogsled came toward them.

As they approached, Egan realized it was from the local village.

Several of the military men got off their sleds and walked over to greet the villagers, and two of them on skis were shortly at their side. They all sat and visited for a little bit.

Egan asked the villagers if they had seen anybody from the scientists' camp and immediately got lots of headshakes. He noted one person wouldn't look at him. When he got a chance to get closer, he asked that person in a low voice, "What about you? Have you seen anybody?"

The young man, who couldn't have been more than twenty, jumped up and shook his head, then walked over to stand with the elders. Yet something seemed off in his mannerisms. Egan continued to study him, but the young man still wouldn't look him in the eye and wouldn't say anything.

When the group from the village left fairly soon afterward, everybody smiled and waved.

Joe walked over to Egan. "There's something to be said for living out here."

"There is," Egan acknowledged, "but an awful lot more to be said about going home."

Joe burst out laughing. "Yeah, I hear you there, but they didn't seem to know much."

"No, but that young one? … I'm not so sure, and he didn't seem very forthcoming."

"He may not understand our language. They're also not used to people like us," Joe added, with half a grin. "So, keep that in mind."

"Right, and I wouldn't want to terrorize him any more than he already seemed to be. They don't see many foreigners, and I'm not sure they particularly like the ones they do see," he noted. "Not everybody here is in favor of us coming up and doing trainings and running tests or science experiments either." He shook his head in annoyance. "So far they've been very amiable and generous with their time and energy, so we're trying not to piss them off anymore."

"Yeah, asking that young man any more questions would do exactly that," Joe warned.

"I know, and yet—"

"He's hiding something. You're right," Joe confirmed. "My suggestion would be to let Mountain handle it. He's getting closer to them, without pushing it, from what I hear."

DAY 7, DINNERTIME

W HEN THE TRAINING day was over, and Berry and
Egan were sitting in the cafeteria later, having dinner,
Sydney walked in, right over to Berry, and sat down beside
her. Sydney hadn't even stopped to get food. Berry stiffened
and looked at her. "Problems?" Just enough fear filled her
voice that nearly everybody here could understand where she
was coming from.

Sydney shook her head. "No, but she is asking for you."

Berry stared off in the distance and nodded. "Yeah, I've
been trying to figure out what to do about that."

"Only what you're okay to do," the doc stated in a low
voice. "Forgiveness doesn't have to happen today. Remember
that. It can happen over time. However, even a little bit
would go a long way right now."

"Yeah, but for her or for me?"

"Considering the fact that it's her health I'm working on
right now, and you appear to be *physically* fine," Sydney
clarified, "it would be appreciated if you could find a few
moments to talk to her."

"Oh, I will," Berry declared, "but I can't make any guar-
antees on how that talk will go."

Sydney laughed. "None of us ever get what we really
want in life. All we can do is get something that we're happy
with. And I'll take a compromise on your part any day."

"Fine," Berry muttered. "I'll stop by after dinner."

"Good. I'll stay here a little bit longer then. That'll give you two some private time to talk."

"If talking is something we need to do," Berry whispered, "I'm still not sure what to say."

"Berry, I'm not pressuring you to do anything, other than acknowledge that your sister is still an important part of your life. As for the rest of it? ... You'll work it out over time. None of that has to be today."

"I'm glad you mentioned that," Berry admitted, "because I'm really not ready."

"I get that," Sydney murmured, "and I totally understand. I've seen a lot of people destroy themselves for nothing, and your sister is already in a bad place. She feels she's done something completely unforgivable, so, if you can at least give her a little hope, it might help." Sydney looked around and added, "I'll go grab some dinner." Then she quickly disappeared.

Egan looked over at her. "Are you okay?"

"I'm okay, ... just really sad."

"Sad sounds normal. Sad sounds good," he shared. "Do you want somebody to come with you?"

She looked up, then smiled and shook her head. "Cherry might have been unpleasant to deal with throughout my life in some circumstances, but that's not happening right now. So I'm fine. But I think I will go deal with it now, so hopefully I don't have to take it to bed with me, and it stops me from sleeping," she murmured.

"Got it. If you want to connect afterward, let me know."

"Will do," she replied appreciatively.

Then she got up and headed to see her sister. When she opened the medical center door and stepped in, Cherry looked up, her expression guilty as hell, as she sat at the computer.

Berry closed the door with a snap. "What are you doing there, Cherry?"

She got up, walked over to the bed, and sat down with a shrug. "I'm bored. … I was just looking at files."

"Private medical files by any chance?" Berry asked, with a narrowed gaze, her voice deadly soft.

Cherry flushed. "I couldn't get in," she snapped in a waspish tone. "Sydney logged off before she left."

"*Gee*, I wonder why?" Berry muttered. "Something about trust, maybe? And someone not being trustworthy enough to leave confidential files unprotected?"

Her sister glared at her. "If that's all you came to say, you can leave any time."

"Thank you for yet another mess," Berry snapped. "I came to see how you were, but, if that's the way it is, I'll be happy to leave." She glared at her sister. "I was really looking forward to putting this all behind me, but Jesus, Cherry, trying to access Sydney's computer? That's another huge betrayal of trust."

"You don't know what I was doing."

"No, but you just told me that you couldn't get in, which means you tried."

Her sister flushed and then glared at her. "I've been stuck in here, bored all day, and you don't know what that's like."

"I think most of us are feeling pretty caged-in these days."

"But you got out today," she snapped.

"I did, and it was great," she admitted. "It definitely went a long way to help ease some of the tensions people are feeling."

Her sister suddenly started to sob. "But I didn't get to go."

"No, you didn't, and I'm not so sure you'll ever get to go again. I *will* tell Sydney what you did," Berry declared. "The way you keep nuking yourself at every turn, I have no idea what's happening with you."

"Neither do I," Cherry muttered, "and being in limbo really sucks."

"Have you tried to talk to anybody about it? Have you talked to the colonel?"

"No," she said, with a shudder. "I would just as soon skip that visit."

"Then how do you expect to get anything resolved?" Berry asked curiously. "Obviously I can see why you would be reluctant, but he'll need a first-hand accounting of what was going on. The fact that he hasn't even come by yet surprises me."

"Whatever," Cherry quipped. "According to Yegorahn, nobody respected him."

"And yet you better not show that attitude," Berry said, as a word of warning to sister. "Respect is everything here."

"Sure, but you have to earn it, and he's put everybody at risk by not letting any of us leave."

"Are you sure it's even him who's not letting anybody leave? Everybody's got a boss," Berry stated. "Maybe he's under orders too."

"It doesn't matter. Somebody killed Yegorahn," Cherry replied, tears coming to her eyes again. "How is that fair?"

Berry didn't say anything because she wasn't sure bringing up that whole mess again would help anybody, since her sister had done so little to help at a point in time when that information could have made a difference in solving the case. She sat down on the spare chair and looked at her sister. "How are you feeling?"

She shrugged. "Like shit," she muttered, "but I'm okay."

"I'm glad to hear that. As long as you're doing better, then you should get out of here okay."

"Maybe, and maybe not."

"Meaning?" Berry asked.

"It just feels as if I've been completely ostracized, and it's not fair."

Berry stared at her sister in shock. "*Not fair?* Did you really just say, *not fair?*"

"No, it's not fair," Cherry snapped angrily. "It wasn't my fault Yegorahn got me hooked on drugs."

"But you *took* them," Berry snapped back, staring at her sister, wondering if Egan was right about her. Maybe she shouldn't be let off the hook so easily, since she hadn't seemed to learn anything.

"Sure, I took them, but he told me that it was just to help me calm down. You know how I felt about being here."

"Sure, I also remember you being the one who got me to come because you were so excited about this Arctic training. You wanted to be here then."

Cherry immediately flushed at that. "Should have known you'd bring that up," she grumbled, with a decided pout in her tone.

"Look, Cherry. I came to say hi and to keep you company for a few minutes, but, if we're just going to fight, then I'm leaving. I thought you would have learned something by now and would have toned down your attitude. Yet it's just more of the same." With that, Berry got up and headed to the door.

"Wait," her sister cried out. Berry stopped and looked over at her and waited. It took a moment, but finally Cherry spoke in a whisper, "I didn't tell them everything."

"You didn't tell who everything?" Berry asked, turning to walk closer to her sister. "What are you talking about?"

"I didn't tell them everything about what Yegorahn said."

"What Yegorahn said? You're kidding. Why not?" she asked in astonishment.

She shrugged. "I don't know. I felt as if I was being punished." That was almost more than Berry could handle. She stared at her sister, her jaw working, as she tried to figure out what to say before finally letting the words blast out of her.

"Oh, *you* were being punished, and *you* were being accused, and this will just make it worse because you didn't tell them everything that would have been helpful in the first place."

"I didn't know whether it would be helpful or not," she snapped, glaring, "and don't you start. But if I'm trying to clear the air, then Yegorahn did make a couple comments about some people here. I didn't want to cause undue harm to other people's reputation, but nobody seems to give a crap about mine now, so—"

"So now what? You'll throw other people under the bus?" she asked in a wry tone.

She flushed. "That's not exactly what I'm doing."

"I'm glad to hear that. So what exactly *are* you doing?"

"Yegorahn had some concerns about a couple people here, and I didn't mention them," Cherry stated. "I didn't tell Ted the whole story."

"In that case, it sounds like you should. Particularly if Yegorahn had any thoughts or fears about his life."

"I don't think so, but he thought it was suspicious, and he was going to go talk to somebody about it." She winced at that.

"Talk why?"

"I don't know why." But then she caught Berry's glance and groaned. "Okay, fine, so maybe he wanted in on it."

"Oh hell," Berry cried out, staring at her sister. "And you didn't tell anybody about this?"

Cherry shook her head, nervously chewing on her bottom lip.

After a moment, Berry threw up her hands, pulled out her phone, and quickly called first Magnus and then Egan. When Egan heard, he sucked in his breath, and she asked, "Can you come to the clinic, please?"

As they waited, her sister was still chewing nervously on her bottom lip. "Will you ever forgive me for this?"

Berry looked at her and nodded slowly. "Eventually … I hope to." Relief washed over her sister's face, making Berry realize just how important it was to her.

"But this isn't easy for me, Cherry. Finding out all the things you've done to hurt me over the last decade, and knowing you did it maliciously, intentionally impacting my ability to make friends, keep friends, and just …" She was at a loss for words. Reaching up, she scrubbed at her face. "The hurt and the betrayal runs pretty deep," she finally said. "I will forgive at some point, but it won't be today."

Just as her sister started to say something, the door opened, and Magnus walked in, with Sydney. Sydney looked at the two of them and asked, "What's going on?"

"Just wait till Egan gets here, please," Berry said.

At that exact moment, Egan announced his presence. "I'm right here," he murmured, as he stepped inside.

Walking toward Berry, he put an arm around her shoulders in a show of support.

Her sister saw that and sneered. "You two were pretty quick to hook up, weren't you?"

At that snide comment, Berry stared at her sister. "Did you have something more specific you wanted to say, or are you just going to insult me in front of everybody?" she asked, her voice flat.

Her sister had the decency to flush. "Christ, I don't even know who I am anymore."

"Neither do I, but that's not the point of bringing them here. So maybe you could repeat what you told me."

She glared at her. "I can't believe you just brought them in without discussing it."

At that, Egan declared, "Look. I don't have time for this. I've got meetings, and I have to head out soon, so what's going on here?"

Cherry looked over at Berry expectantly, but Berry just glared back. "It's your story. You tell it."

"Fine. I didn't necessarily tell you everything that Yegorahn told me," she admitted. At that, both men stiffened. "I know you'll just say I was withholding evidence again, but in all honesty you didn't ask."

"No, we wouldn't have asked about things we didn't know about," Magnus snapped, "but obviously you haven't been very forthcoming either. So, what is it that you think that we should *now* know that we didn't ask about before?"

She glared at him, aware of the sarcasm in his voice, but he just glared back at her. Finally she groaned and continued. "Oh, fine, since you all obviously think the worst of me anyway," she replied, taking a defensive stance. "Yegorahn told me that there was some illegal activity going on among some of the other crews, and he wanted to talk to them about getting in on it himself."

EGAN STARED AT her in shock. "And you're just *now* telling us this?"

She spun and glared at him, taking a step toward him, which he answered by taking a step toward her. She backed up quickly and glared at her sister. "Might need some protection from this one, sis," Cherry snapped, with a bite to her tone.

"No protection needed," Berry murmured to her sister, "but it might do you some good to come clean about absolutely everything you know. Right now."

"I don't even know what I know," Cherry wailed. "Yego-rahn just told me that he had a way to make some money and that he thought something really shitty was going on. He wanted to go talk to them before he said anything more about it."

"Why would he want to say anything to you about it anyway?" Egan asked, his tone now under control. "Unless it was something you were also looking to be a part of."

She glared at him. "If there was a way to make money or a way to get out of here, then absolutely I wanted to be part of it," she snapped, "but that doesn't mean I did anything to him."

"Maybe not, but I'm also not sure you're off the hook for what you have already done either," Egan snapped, as he looked over at Magnus. "What do you think?"

"I think she's more than a little behind on providing this information … again." Magnus glared at her, almost as if he didn't quite understand what made her tick.

Egan had no clue what made somebody like Cherry tick. He looked over at her. "What other information did he give you?"

"Nothing," she stated. "That's one of the reasons I didn't tell you. It just seemed to be guesswork on his part, but I'm not sure it was a guess as much as it was some insider information. He told me that he'd seen somebody do something, and he wanted to maybe get in on the act. He did say he was a little worried about it because the wrong step could cost him."

At that, complete silence filled in the room. Sydney brushed the hair off her face, then walked over to Cherry and patted her arm. "Thank you for telling us now."

Cherry looked at her, and her bottom lip trembled. "I should have said something before, shouldn't I?"

"Yes," Sydney agreed. "That would have been very helpful then. At least you've done something now." She turned to look at the two men. "Agreed?"

They both stared at her as if she was off her rocker, but Magnus nodded. "Better now than not at all," he growled, still staring at Cherry. "But we need to know if there's anything else. Anything he might have mentioned, giving you any indication or hints as to who it was, what he even did in the camp, why he thought it might be dangerous, anything," Magnus stated, "because obviously it *was* dangerous."

"If he went and talked to these guys, there's a good chance that's how he ended up dead," Egan added, sick and tired of Cherry.

She nodded. "I guess that makes the most sense out of everything, but still it feels as if I was just passing on gossip," she admitted, "gossip that I can't back up. You guys want answers, and I don't have any to give."

"And yet you were quite happy to throw out lies, innuendos, and falsehoods for the rest of your life," Berry pointed out sarcastically. Cherry immediately rounded on her, and Berry held up both hands. "Sorry, obviously true enough, but this isn't the time."

"You'll never forgive me for that, will you?" she cried out, staring at her sister. "Anytime anything happens, you'll just bring up, won't you?"

"I hope not," Berry admitted. "I hope that, sometime in the future, I'll reach a point where I can trust you, and we'll be past the shocks of all the things that keep coming up here. But, no, I'm nowhere near that place yet and not likely to arrive anytime soon." Then without a word of warning, she turned and walked out of the room.

Egan looked over at Magnus, who just nodded. Egan quickly raced after her. "Wait up," he called softly, hurrying after her, until he caught up with her at the end of the corridor. "I'm sorry."

She faced him and shrugged. "My sister is a piece of work. Unfortunately it's a work in progress." He burst out laughing at that, causing Berry to look up at him and grin. She added, "I'm glad you can laugh about it. I've had nothing to laugh about in a very long time."

"And yet that too will pass."

"I want it to," Berry said. "I'm just not sure I'm there yet."

"You aren't, and you shouldn't have to be. Let it go. Just let Cherry do her evil works, take her lumps accordingly, without guilt on your part, and you try to find yourself some peace amid the storm," Egan suggested.

She groaned. "That's such a commonsense approach, yet, at the same time, so irritating," she muttered, then grinned. "It'll take time, and I can't deal with any of it right now. And, of course, the way I feel right now …" She trailed off.

"Won't be the way you'd feel in ten years?" he offered.

"God, I hope not," she muttered. "Otherwise I'll be a bigger mess than I thought."

"I don't think so," Egan disagreed. "So far, you're the most sensible person I've met."

She smiled at him. "If that were true, I wouldn't have walked out of there."

"I would have," he admitted. "If you can't punch her, what else can you do?" At that, Berry burst out laughing again, and he grinned. "See? You still have a sense of humor in there and more laughter. We just have to remember that they're part and parcel of daily life, and sometimes we have good days, and sometimes we don't." He pressed her hands lightly and let go.

"What about when I'm really tired of the not-so-good days?" she asked, with a sigh.

"Those are the days we have to work even harder," he noted, "to find a brighter light."

"But why wouldn't she have said something about Yego-rahn? She had knowledge of potential illegal activity happening on the base, and she never said anything. Worse yet, she wanted to be a part of it? Good God, … she's so far gone that her judgment has completely gone to shit."

"Maybe because she didn't know anything other than that, no real details," Egan guessed. "If you think about it from her position, there was only so much she had to offer, and, when you only have so much, and you can't provide any proof, maybe it's better that she didn't."

"There's that too. However, I think you're being generous with her just to help me feel better, with my overprotective guilt taking over."

Egan gave her a knowing smile. "Right now we're rather desperate, looking for any information, so hers comes at a very good time and gives us another lead to follow, but not an easy lead. We don't have anything to say, and we don't have any notions. We've got the rest of the people he was involved with and his team, but other than that—"

"If it was his team though," Berry interrupted, "you'd think they would have shared whatever with Yegorahn. It would have been a group activity."

Egan nodded. "I was thinking that myself. I'm going to head to the kitchen and sit down with another hot drink and see if I can source out a group of names. I have a bunch of the earlier interviews, plus the questions that I asked. I have a feeling in the back of my brain that is telling me what I need to know, but I haven't been listening."

"I'll come with you, if that's okay," she offered immediately. "I don't want to be closed up in my tiny room with just my thoughts." She shook her head. "Not a healthy place to be right now."

He studied her for a moment and then nodded, topped off with a grin. "Sure, why not? And I hope you don't take your sister's comments about me the wrong way."

She looked up at him. "I was going to say that to you as well." She shrugged. "I don't want you to take my sister's comments about me the wrong way."

He chuckled. "Nope, I won't. She's just jealous. Plus, when I interviewed her, she mentioned having something that was special, and she lost it," he reminded her. "I'm not sure she takes loss very well."

"I'm not sure she's ever really lost," Berry replied immediately. He frowned at her, and she nodded. "It just seems, whenever there was a problem, she'd always gotten everything, and I waited in the background and got nothing, mostly because I didn't care. However, over time, I think it wears on you," she murmured.

"Of course it does," he agreed. "And that's okay. Everything comes to those who wait."

"Is that the phrase? I don't think it works that way. At least, not in my world."

He smiled. "It can work that way, and we don't need everything to be ours all the time," he clarified. "But come on. Let's head to the kitchen. I need to stop by my room and grab all the statements I've got."

As they walked toward his room, the door ahead of them opened, and somebody stepped out right into them. Egan was a bit taken aback, considering it was his room, and the guy's hands were full of papers. Slamming him up against the wall, but in a very silky voice, Egan stated, "I'll take those, thank you."

As he snatched them from the guy's hands and gave them to Berry, the man attempted to shove him, but Egan turned and clocked him right in jaw, then pinned him against the wall. "Your name's Darren, isn't it?"

Almost stuttering, Darren nodded. "Y-y-yes."

"What were you doing in my room?" Egan asked, his voice deadly quiet.

He swallowed. "The colonel, he asked me to get these papers. So I came here, but, when you weren't in, I opened the door and entered."

Egan stared at him in shock. "If the colonel had wanted

them, he could have asked me for them. So why did he ask you?"

"I don't know. I don't," he cried out. "I just know that he did."

"Let's go down and ask him then. Shall we?" Looking over at Berry, he asked, "You want to make a copy of those?"

She nodded and quickly disappeared.

Darren pleaded, "The colonel was very specific. He wanted me to grab a copy of it, all the paperwork you collected."

"That's interesting. So we'll just go confirm that."

And confirm it, they did. The colonel glared at him. "You were told to turn it over."

"I did turn it over," Egan declared. "I turned copies over to you two days ago."

The colonel stared at him incomprehensively. "You what?"

"You heard me," he stated, trying to keep his voice as respectful as he could. "So, I don't know where they went after that." Seeing the colonel's aide standing here, he asked him, "Where the hell are those copies I brought the other day?"

The aide flushed at him, turning multiple shades of purple. "Sir, I put them on your desk."

The colonel stared at him. "When?" he bellowed. "What the hell is going on here?" Then he turned back to Egan. "So where are they now then?"

"I'm getting a second copy run off of them right now," Egan replied. "And did you tell this guy to go into my room without my permission to steal these papers?" he asked, his tone calm and yet watchful.

"It was hardly stealing when it's work that I had requested."

"Work already received and lost." Egan couldn't keep the flint out of his voice. "But, considering the state of affairs in this camp right now, people walking in and out of other people's rooms and taking investigation information is not exactly a good idea."

The colonel's gaze narrowed. "You're walking a fine line here, young man."

He nodded. "Respectfully, sir, that may be true, but I also understand that we're in trouble here. I've been asked to do a job, and, to do that, we need to maintain a certain level of respect and *confidentiality*. Sending people into my quarters to remove documents without my permission is definitely *not* the way to do that."

"I'm entitled to walk into any room in this complex I want," he snapped.

"You are. But sending someone else in to acquire confidential information …" His words were drowned out when the door opened, and Mountain walked in.

MOUNTAIN STUDIED EGAN.

Egan nodded. "Good evening."

At that, the colonel took one look at them and sighed, waving Egan and Darren away. "This isn't the end of it," he muttered, "but you are dismissed."

As Egan passed by, Mountain patted him on the shoulder. "We'll talk later."

With that, Egan nodded and headed out. But Mountain easily heard Egan in the hallway as he told Darren, "I don't give a shit what the colonel says. If you ever come into my room again, you can expect a completely different reception."

Mountain could imagine the look on the kid's face, but then the only sound he heard was of footsteps running down the hallway. He turned his attention back to the colonel.

"Every day you go out. Every day you come back empty-handed," the colonel snapped. "When will you give this up?"

"Not today," Mountain responded, fighting back the urge to roar his frustration at the man who was happy to sit behind the desk and run slipshod over this camp. "We do have a scientists' team missing as well. So it's hardly a waste of my time."

"And the locals? Are you pissing them off too?"

"I think that is going well. They no longer see me as a useless addition to their world nor as a threat. I won't say they see me as a friend quite yet," he added cautiously, "but they are friendlier and more receptive to talks."

"And that's a waste of time." The colonel glared at him. "If I had my way, you'd be stateside instead of acting on your own private mission. But somehow you got permission, and that came from way above my head. I have no choice, but I don't have to like it."

EGAN WAITED FOR Mountain to exit the CO's office.

When Mountain appeared, he asked, "What's up?"

Egan explained what he had found on the armory issue, as ordered by Mountain. No one was overseeing it. No one seemed to be signing in or out any guns. Maybe it had been delegated to one of the many missing or dead men here. Yet no one had followed up on that. The CO should have been on that, but the CO wasn't exactly known for doing his job. The existing cameras in the armory and outside in the hallway were not always working. So no way to see how Anna got her gun to kill Myles. Therefore, in Mountain's absence, Egan took it upon himself to rotate the SR team in that area, plus to set up additional cams inside, battery-operated ones, what with the generator issues here. However, the SR team just did random inspections of the armory, not having the manpower to set up three eight-hour shifts daily.

Mountain nodded. "Good work. I'll talk to Peter, Dave, and Salmo, see if they are willing to do some extra guard duty, including tracking our armory." Shaking his head, he raised a hand as he left to do just that.

B ERRY SAT BY herself in the dining room, hugging a cup of tea, waiting for Egan to come back. She had the paperwork with her, but tucked out of the way by her feet. When he did finally show, he was still vibrating with anger, unable to sit just yet. She winced, as he approached. "That didn't go well, I gather?"

He shrugged, remained standing. "Sometimes there's just no talking to the brass."

"I know," she murmured. "Sometimes accepting the decisions they make is pretty rough too."

He nodded. "Apparently his aide did give the colonel the paperwork, which I handed over two days ago, but the colonel lost it."

"Or somebody helped him to lose it."

At that, he shot her a look and then slowly nodded. "Could be. Or someone was worried about what we had dug up so far." He stared at her thoughtfully. "I'm going to grab a hot chocolate. Do you want one?"

"No, I'm fine." She motioned to the cup that she was hugging. She watched him, obviously needing to do something, as he grabbed himself something to drink. He spoke with somebody at the counter, who she presumed was Chef, but she didn't turn to look.

When Egan returned, she nodded toward to kitchen.

"Do you always talk to him?"

"Yeah, always." Yet Egan didn't elaborate.

She wasn't sure if that was an off-topics subject or not, but she sat and waited. "Is everything okay?" she asked.

"It will be." Egan shrugged. "I don't know exactly who and what made them lose the paperwork, but now that it's been found—or at least it's been understood that it arrived at his desk when originally requested—things should improve a little bit."

"But you're still pissed because he had somebody go into your room."

"Wouldn't you be?" he asked.

"Yes, I would."

He shrugged. "Doesn't matter though, does it? The brass does what they want to do, and it's up to us to just suck it up and smile."

"And respect it and agree with it," she muttered, with a nod.

He laughed. "Okay, so I'm still working on a couple of those."

She grinned at him. "Particularly when you're concerned about what's happening here. It's a hard one to swallow when he didn't trust you or show you even the slightest respect."

"Yeah, I think that's the bottom line," Egan confirmed. "It feels as if somebody is out to discredit me."

"What's his aide like?"

"I have no idea. I don't know the man," he stated thoughtfully. He looked over at her and smiled. "But we do have other conversations to discuss."

"What?" she asked curiously.

"Your sister and the information that she just provided,

do you trust it?"

"I don't *not* trust it," she noted cautiously. "I don't have any reason to believe her one way or the other. I thought before she wasn't big on lying, but obviously I'm not the one to say that, since I don't really know her anymore."

He nodded. "Do you have the paperwork?"

She handed it to him, and he smiled. "Thanks for keeping it safe."

"Hey, I wasn't even sure who I was supposed to keep it safe *from* there for a while."

"Right, I know, and this is just copies of it. The colonel already had his own set as well."

"That's good then, so he can't get upset at you."

"Oh, he can still get upset over nothing. Plus he's upset because everything's gone to hell," Egan said, with a groan, "and I do understand that." Then he took the folder and flipped through the paperwork.

She offered, "I could help."

"Maybe, but probably better if not so many people see this right now."

Berry nodded. "So what is your working theory?"

"I was just wondering who it was that Yegorahn was talking about. Obviously it would have been nice if he'd left a note saying, 'Hey, so-and-so did this,'" Egan said in a mocking tone. "However, that won't help. The dead man is always blamed. Therefore, if something is going on in this camp, the story will be that Yegorahn did whatever."

"Did you tell the colonel that?" she asked.

"No, that's what Mountain's doing right now."

"Mountain?" she asked, startled.

He nodded.

"The big guy who comes and goes like a ghost?" she

asked.

Egan laughed. "That's a good way to describe him. He's pretty ghostlike in his actions. But, if you're ever looking for somebody to be on your side, he's the one."

"Does he ask questions and shoot later or shoot first?"

"He's a good guy, and, if shit's about to happen, he's the one you want in your corner," Egan shared. "And honestly, given his size, he doesn't have to shoot."

She laughed. "That's a good point too."

He grinned at her. "Seriously, if you ever run into trouble, and you can find him—"

"Which is the problem with a ghost," she pointed out, "in that you can't usually find him, if and when you need him."

"That's true," Egan acknowledged the point. "However, he is somebody you can go to, no matter what."

"No matter what?" she repeated.

Egan nodded. "No matter what. If your sister's done something else, or you find yourself in a pickle, whatever it is, he'll get to the bottom of it," Egan declared. "He's partly the reason why I'm here." Her eyebrows shot up, and he nodded. "As I say, *partly*."

"I thought you were a trainee here, like the rest of us."

He gave her a fat smile. "No, definitely only part of my job."

"Ah." Berry sat back. "And that's why you're doubly pissed about Cherry …" And Berry let her voice hang, as he glanced around to see if anybody heard her and nodded.

"Yeah."

"And the colonel knows?"

"Of course he knows," he muttered, with a half smile. "We're supposed to be all part of the same team."

"And yet, according to what Yegorahn said," Berry noted, "somebody was operating a team all on their own. How often would that happen?"

"If we were in Iraq and or any of our unit bases somewhere else, there's always a certain amount of buying and selling on base. Up here? I guess I wasn't expecting it."

"And yet why not?" she asked. "People are still people." He nodded absentmindedly at that, and she realized he had already glommed on to a specific thought in his head. "So, I'm hearing something, but I'm not seeing answers yet," she added.

He nodded, clearly still caught up in thought.

"But you've obviously picked up on something," she whispered.

He drew his gaze back to her and frowned.

She shook her head. "I'm not saying anything to anybody. Yet it's obvious that something clicked just now with you."

"Definitely something in the back of my brain," he confirmed, "so just give me a few minutes while I read through my notes." Then he turned his attention to the stack of papers and moved through them with a speed she didn't think was possible.

When he set down the papers, she asked, "Jesus, are you a speed reader or something?"

He smiled. "Or something. I've always been good at reading and comprehending."

"Yeah, I'm a good reader too"—she chuckled—"but I can't go through pages like that."

"I was looking for something specific," he said, with a grin.

"And did you find it?"

He shook his head. "Not on this pass. So, that's something else that's bothering me."

She glanced at the notes and then asked him point-blank, "Do you think some are missing?"

"Maybe. I did take copies before though."

"So why did you have me make copies?"

He laughed. "What if they had been changed?"

"If so, then you know you have a bigger problem than when you first arrived. Someone is stealing your notes, even altering your notes."

"That's true. So now I need to go compare." He pulled out his phone and looked at her. "I'll work here for a while, so feel free to leave, if you want to head off and visit with your sister or something." She glared at him, and he winced. "Okay, so that may not have been the best suggestion."

"No, it sure wasn't. I get why you would have otherwise suggested that, for somebody else's *normal* sister, but for Cherry? No thanks."

"Good enough." He gave her a defensive hand gesture. "In that case, let's get another cup of tea or cocoa and see what else I can find." He picked up the papers again with a frown and quickly shuffled through them, until he found what he wanted.

She got up to fix another cup of tea. Several other people came and went, but they ignored him, which was good, considering what his mood was like. When she turned to head back to the table, she noted that Mountain had joined Egan. She hesitated as she approached. "Do you want me to leave you guys alone?"

Mountain frowned at her and then shook his head. "It's fine, but … can you give us ten?"

"Absolutely." She looked over at Egan. "Come by later,"

she invited. "I get that you're busy now. I'll talk to you after a bit." And, with that, she quickly escaped.

She headed past the medical clinic, worried about her sister for some reason, but more so because Berry had just walked off earlier instead of saying goodbye. She knocked on the door and stepped inside to see her sister curled up in a ball, sobbing gently. Berry groaned, walked over, put her tea down beside Cherry, and said, "Have a cup of tea."

Cherry shifted and looked at her, with a groan. "You're talking to me?"

"Of course I'm talking to you," she said in exasperation. "I may not like what you've done here, or what you've done in the past," she clarified, with an eye roll, "and it'll definitely take me some time, but you're still my sister."

Cherry nodded slowly, a smile trying to break free, as she whispered, "Thank you for that. Everybody else seems to just be mad at me."

"Look at it from their point of view. They've been trying to solve a mystery, several murders, find missing people, fix generators, stop people from stealing food, and do it before anybody else gets killed," she declared. "And every time they turn around, they find out you've been withholding information. So, of course they're pissy. Who wouldn't be?"

She shifted the cup of tea closer to her and sighed when she took a big sniff of the aroma. "I was afraid you would never speak to me again."

"Of course I will," Berry groaned, as she pulled up a chair beside her sister. "But it's not easy, hearing all the horrid things you've done to me, against me, and I wonder why I even care. Sometimes I just don't like you," she admitted, "but the bottom line is, you're still my sister. And, in spite of every evil thing you have done, I do love you."

Her sister gave her a teary smile. "Thank you. I really needed to hear that."

"Now that you've heard it, you can relax. … Obviously my shock and horror is not over, not in the sense of all the things that I know and need to come to terms with but—"

"What about the cute hunk you're hanging around with?" Cherry asked, almost enviously.

"What? Egan?" Berry asked.

"Is it serious?"

"How can it be serious? Look where we are."

Cherry nodded. "And yet I had hopes with Yegorahn."

"Come on," Berry began. "You know perfectly well that would have been very much a romance for here and not for later. … So I'm not sure how much you're deluding yourself into that or just looking at him as a lifeline to get out of here."

"Probably a lifeline to get out," Cherry muttered. "God, I hate it here."

"Maybe, but you won't change it anytime soon."

"Yeah, I've come to realize that," she acknowledged. "I need to make the best of it, at least until I'm shipped out," she nodded, "and I don't even know what that'll look like."

"I don't know either," Berry admitted.

"But you can talk to the brass for me, couldn't you?" she asked, looking at her suddenly.

Berry stared at her sister and shook her head. "No, I can't. There's absolutely nothing I can do about this one," she murmured. "Oh, I get it. That's not what you want to hear from me, but, if you only want to be friendly so I can save your ass," Berry spoke frankly, "it ain't happening. It's already too far gone for me to do anything."

"You could ask for leniency," she added.

"What good will that do? I don't even know what the problem is ultimately, except for the drug use, the lying, the obstruction, the attack on your superior officer," she said. "I don't know what they will come after you for, but, whatever it is, you maybe had mitigating circumstances, and hopefully some people will understand that."

"Will they though?" Cherry asked, shuddering. "I don't think anybody'll understand anything about me ever again," she muttered.

Berry wasn't sure what to do with her sister's obviously melancholic mood, but she had to say something. "The important thing is to get well and to get out of here."

"Sure, and how do you propose I do that?" she asked in exasperation. "I'd love to get out of here, but I don't see that happening right now."

"Maybe not right now, but you shouldn't be too much longer in detox here in the clinic," Berry replied, "at least that's what I'm hoping."

Cherry laughed. "We'll be lucky if any of us get out of here alive."

"Yeah, depending on what you had to say about Yego-rahn and the meeting he had set up with this person, maybe *that's* the reason for all these deaths," Berry stated. "I don't know."

Cherry stared at her and shrugged. "Yegorahn didn't seem to think he was in any danger, and he was a big guy."

"But that size often comes before a fall," Berry pointed out. "Big guys tend to think that they can handle everything, until they're up against it, and they can't," she murmured. "So, while I'm sorry he's dead, that attitude wouldn't help."

"No, but he was really nice to be around," Cherry shared wistfully.

"Meaning, he looked after you," Berry stated. She glared at her sister.

Cherry glared right back. "You don't seem to care. You don't seem to want anybody to look after you."

"No, I don't," Berry declared. "Somebody to walk beside me? Yes, but I don't need or want to be babysat. I don't need somebody in my corner all the time," she stated flatly. "I didn't think you had such a poor sense of self either."

"It's not a poor sense of self," Cherry cried out. "However, I think, over time, when I realized that what I was doing was knocking you down in order to build myself up, it was having more of a negative effect on me instead of you," she murmured. "As if the more I did it, … the more I realized just how poor my own self-worth was, and every time I did that, it just made it all worse."

"What did you expect?" Berry asked, staring at her. "It's not a case of just being nice for the sake of being nice but being truly nice on the inside, and that niceness comes through on the outside, and then you find real friends."

"You never did," she pointed out. "You never had boyfriends, at least not for long." At that, Berry glowered at her sister, until she flushed. "Fine, I might have had something to do with that."

"Ya think? When I look back on all the relationships that I cared about that broke up, leaving me confused and heartbroken, I remember you commiserated with me over ice cream, telling me how lots of other men were out there. Now I'm left to wonder how many of those were guys you made sure I broke up with."

"I don't even remember who they were," she said dismissively. "So maybe one or two of them, but not all."

"How do I know that now?" she asked, as she stared at

her. "How do I possibly know or trust anything from you now?"

"You don't have to," she snapped. "I can get out of your life, as soon as I get the hell out of here."

"What do you mean, get out of my life?" she asked, trying to understand what she was saying. "We're sisters, so it's hardly something you can just decide to walk away from. There's still Mom and Dad to consider."

"What about them?" Cherry asked, turning to glare at her sister. "It's not as if they give a shit about us anyway."

"They do, as much as they are able to anyway. They don't understand us. They don't really understand why we do what we do," she clarified, "but that doesn't mean that they aren't there for us."

"I don't think they're there for us at all," Cherry declared. "I don't think they've been there for us since the beginning. It's one of the reasons why we're so close."

"And yet"—Berry glared at her sister—"*so close* that you … did what you did."

Her sister glared right back. "Enough already," she cried out. "Jesus, get over it, will you?"

At that, something inside her just shut down in disbelief. Berry slowly got up and nodded. "Not nice of you to say that, and it'll take me longer than *you* want."

And, with that, Berry turned, walked out, and slammed the door behind her, ignoring her sister's apologetic cries. Berry didn't know how much was the drug withdrawals compared to just the truth coming out now, but the last thing Berry needed was her sister slamming her for not being able to adapt and adjust to all the lovely shitty things that Cherry had already admitted to doing.

God only knew how much she hadn't admitted to.

Sydney walked up to her, as Berry stood outside, trying to regain her breath. "Patience," the doc said calmly.

Berry laughed. "Patience is not necessarily easy in this instance."

"It's never easy," the doc agreed. "Just remember that, in this case, some of this attitude would be from the drugs, though not all of it. Definitely not all of it. She can't use that as an excuse, but some of it is, and some of it will be much harder for both of you to deal with." Sydney sighed. "Yet, as long as Cherry starts to heal, gets some professional psychiatric help, then things will improve."

"I hear you," Berry stated, "and I see the cheerleader in you, but I think some things are just too far gone for any healing. Plus, you need to know. At your dinner break today I caught Cherry trying to read confidential medical records on your laptop." Sydney's eyes widened. And, with that, Berry whispered, "Good night." She walked at a rapid pace to her room, where she locked herself in, hoping and yet almost not wanting Egan to come.

She wouldn't exactly be good company, not with all this mess going on in her world right now. And yet, at the same time, she probably could use a friend, so, with a sigh, she pulled out her phone. She typed and sent a message before she had a chance to change her mind. **If you want to come join me, feel free.**

Then she curled up in bed and waited.

STILL UPSET, BUT at a much calmer level than he had been earlier, Egan looked down at the text for the millionth time, wondering if it was smart to go visit at this hour of the night.

There was a slim chance that they would end up in bed together. They were headed there—at least he hoped so—but, given the circumstances, it was probably not smart on his part to even go there. Not when Berry was as emotionally overwrought as she was with all the revelations from her evil sister.

God, the sister. Wasn't she a piece of work?

He still shrugged as he thought about all the mess going on in that direction, plus the fiasco about his own investigative work that supposedly the colonel didn't know Egan had completed and had handed in already.

Of course the colonel would not apologize; there never were any apologies in these situations. The brass just didn't do that. On the other hand, Egan knew he hadn't done anything wrong, and, once the aide had confirmed that the material had been put on the colonel's desk, then it was over.

Maybe the colonel had misplaced it. Maybe he'd just read it and hadn't realized what it was. Egan didn't know. It didn't make any sense, but he wouldn't lose any more sleep over it. As long as the aide confirmed it had been delivered, then it was off Egan's plate, and that was important.

Now the colonel was pissed at the aide, and Egan didn't relish the aide's position at all. Everybody's tempers were short, as people tried to figure out what the hell was going on in this place, and yet still not having any answers was just frustrating.

Without realizing it, Egan found himself walking to Berry's room, which was isolated from all the rest. He stood outside for a moment, then knocked. When a call came from behind him, he turned to see her smiling and waving at him, coming from the nearby ladies' room.

"I was hoping you'd come," she said, with a genuine

smile. "I was just getting ready for bed."

He nodded. "I figured it was probably too late, but somehow I ended up here anyway." He gave her a lopsided grin.

"I'm glad you did. It's a horrible feeling to see how much we're all pitted against each other here, and I really appreciate having somebody I can just talk to and be myself."

"Always," he said. "I'm just sorry for what you're going through with your sister."

"Me too. … I was sitting here, thinking about what to do about it. Yet I'm just not getting any answers."

"You don't need to find any answers. Remember that. Not right now. It's all too fresh, too raw, and it hurts, the betrayals and everything," he explained. "Forgiveness is a fine tool, but to expect it overnight? That's not an easy thing and not at all realistic either.

"You don't even really know all that she's done in any specific sense, so how could you forgive her? Give yourself a break and just chill for now."

She chuckled. "Right, wouldn't that be nice?" She led the way into her small room.

As Egan looked around, he noted, "I didn't even realize how small this place is."

"It's an overflow room," she shared. "At least I think that's how they look at it."

"And, in tight circumstances," Egan guessed, "this would be quarters for two, if need be."

"It would be warmer for it," she stated, with a groan.

"Are you cold in here?"

She shrugged. "It's definitely not a warm room, but I sure as hell won't complain because I do have my own space."

He frowned at that but nodded. "There is a chill to the air though."

"Sure is, but at least I'm not bunked in my sister's room."

"Even while she is in the medical clinic?"

"Yeah. That just doesn't feel like my room anymore," she stated, looking everywhere but at him. "That probably sounds foolish."

He waved a hand. "Forget about how anything sounds just now. It's all about what *you* need. Just focus on what you need to do, no matter how it comes across."

She laughed. "That all sounds well and good but …"

"It *is* good," he declared firmly. He sat down on the side of the bed and rubbed his face, feeling a level of fatigue that he hadn't really expected to feel.

"How was your review?"

He shrugged. "It's a very strange situation because I handed in the work. Thankfully the aide backed me up, saying that he put it on the colonel's desk. Unfortunately, because the colonel didn't see it himself, he now feels that somebody took the information off his desk."

She stared at him. "Is that possible?" she asked, sitting down beside him. "Are people really stealing things from the brass now?"

"It is possible. The colonel's not there in his office all the time. He's sometimes in the cafeteria, like the rest of us. Plus he's been doing some survival training himself. He's also under the gun in terms of his own responsibility in this base matter, so I think he's been trying to step up a whole lot more, trying to figure out what's going on. I've even seen him roaming the halls at all hours, like he's investigating too. Which, as all this mess rests on his head, is very understandable."

He took a moment to add, "And the fact that this investigative information was there and is now not is a concern. Last I knew, they were actively searching for it, and I don't know whether they found my original copy or not. It's definitely a concern."

"Yeah, I would think so, especially when so much is going on. It isn't so much about one thing going missing, but obviously all the things going on here added together are not to be taken lightly."

"Exactly. I just spent the last couple hours talking to Yegorahn's friends, asking if anybody knew anything about making money on the side here. They were not surprised to hear that something illegal was going on, but none of them would open up as to what it was Yegorahn was supposedly talking about."

"Why not?" she asked, frustrated. "If people have information, why are they not offering it up? This is beyond my understanding now."

He looked over at her with a wry expression.

"I know that my sister's a prime example of it, but I just don't understand that mind-set."

"It's easy to be honest," he noted. "You're not guilty of anything. So, for you to open up and to tell what you know means nothing, and you want to be helpful, if you can. But, if you had something to hide, even unrelated, that's a different story."

"Maybe." Berry frowned. "It still feels wrong to withhold that information when people have died."

"Which is why another round of interviews are starting," he shared, with a half smile. "I did get some done tonight because those particular guys of interest are always sitting there in the dining room. I can't say they were particularly thrilled to hear that we're still talking about all this, but now that Yegorahn's words have come back up again, it's a whole different story."

"What could they possibly be doing illegally here?" she asked. "We already had somebody trying to steal drugs, and we know that Yegorahn had drugs."

"So, maybe it was more about the drugs," Egan noted, "but, if he was sourcing the drugs himself to give to Cherry, then Yegorahn would already know what was going on. Must be something more to that."

Berry swallowed, a fearful expression taking over her face. "*Maybe.*" She frowned and turned toward him. "How many women are on base?" she asked. "I think it's five of us now, isn't it?"

He nodded. "At least. Might be six," he replied, studying her intently, sensing she may be clued in on the next logical thing.

She shook her head. "I haven't heard of any of them getting …" She spoke slowly, as if trying to work her way through this. "What are the chances that somebody has been using drugs for …" Then she stopped. "I don't even want to think about that, much less put it into words."

He nodded slowly. "It has occurred to me too, but that will make for some fairly difficult questioning coming up."

She stared at him in horror. "Good God," she uttered, with a somber face. "Surely it couldn't happen here. Wouldn't people know?"

"How would they know?" he asked. "Particularly if it was happening while they're sound asleep—drugged."

She swallowed and looked at him with such horror that he immediately pulled her into his arms and held her close.

"Was I targeted then?" she asked questioningly.

"I don't know. Were you? Though you were always with your sister, correct?"

"Sure, except for the times that I wasn't because she was with Yegorahn."

"Right, and that is a concern. So, the question would be, have you felt anything odd, unique, terrible, sore, different?" he asked, trying to tiptoe around the issue somewhat gently.

She shook her head. "No, I haven't. Even my cycle has been completely normal up here, and I'd expected that maybe the cold and the physical rigors would change it but apparently not," she shared, followed by a nervous laugh.

"That's a good thing. That just means your body is healthy, right?"

"Sure, though it would be nice if it would forget a cycle once in a while."

"Yeah, unless it was a time when you're afraid you might have ended up in a different state."

"Right," she agreed, "and pregnancy would be something else, wouldn't it?"

"If somebody up here was drugging women and raping them," Egan began, "which is a godawful thought, would the women have noticed something the next day, even if just the loss of time or memories?"

Berry paused and frowned. "I don't know. I can't imagine why anyone, especially Yegorahn would even say something about it to Cherry? If he did..."

"Maybe he realized it must involve a date-rape drug, and maybe he wondered if somebody was being targeted. Maybe it appealed to him to go a few rounds with somebody who was knocked out. I don't know." Egan sighed. "Believe me. I will be checking with Sydney in the morning and having some delicate conversations with her about anybody who may have shown up in the medical clinic, not feeling quite right. But really, without us having any idea that these drugs or any drugs could be a possible problem, we can't test anybody, not now. The drugs may not be present in the body anymore."

"Jesus," Berry muttered. "I really don't want to even contemplate such a thing happening here."

"You and me both," Egan agreed. "Rape is already an ugliness that none of us want to look at, and yet it's prevalent in the military, in all the services sadly."

"Really? How did I not know that? Though, I guess, it's not something anybody would be shouting from the rooftops."

"We will get to the bottom of it," Egan promised her. "I know that there is an awful lot of abuse, verbally and physically, of women everywhere."

"All we needed was one person to show up on this base, with that thought in mind, for all of it go bad."

"We also don't know that just because maybe somebody had the drug on them, that they had a chance to use it."

She nodded slowly. "But to think that they came with it makes me sick."

"And we don't know that for sure. Not yet. Remember. This is just a hypothesis."

"Right, but it's also an ugly one," she whispered. "Jesus."

"Right, but, outside of drugs, what other illegal activity could be going on here?"

"Murder," she stated. "What if there was a witness to Yegorahn's death? Or maybe Yegorahn witnessed one of the other Russians' deaths?"

"Maybe," Egan noted. "That would certainly put everybody on edge, if a witness to one of the previous murders was then killed by one of the other guys, or maybe Yegorahn knew about the other missing men going off into the wild on their own, placing crazy bets against Mother Nature on a dare. Maybe it was—"

"Exactly," she interrupted. "It could be anything."

"So, we're going back through everything again. Unfortunately it's frustrating for those getting questioned again, and everybody's getting pissed about it."

"It goes back to the fact that, if my sister had spoken up in the beginning, regarding Yegorahn's death, we might have known something."

"We also believe the other two Russians know more than they're saying."

She nodded. "They sure won't talk to me."

"Will they talk to your sister though?" he asked.

"I don't know. I don't know anything about that." Berry shook her head. "However, the Russian team is losing members. They may not trust anybody here, even their own team members."

"That should make them want to help out, unless they think they're being targeted, and that's never a good thing. Though, with the unrest going on right now, anybody might feel targeted but especially them."

"What if you flip that around?" she asked, looking at him. "We always tend to think of the Russians as the bad guys, but what if that's true? What if they're the ones out there doing this and setting us up against each other?"

"But what about two of their own men being killed?" he asked.

"What if one of them wanted to target my sister? What if …" Then Berry stopped, sucked in her breath, and asked,

"What if they wanted him to share Cherry, and, if he wasn't willing to, would they do it anyway?"

"Everybody wants to think that the Russians are the bad guys because nobody wants it closer to home."

"So, what if somebody is making it look like it's them?" She raised her hands in frustration. "So how the hell do you ever figure it out?"

He shook his head. "We're working on it."

"Sure, but I can't say that anything you've shared tonight makes me feel very good about sleeping. I would make a suggestion, in lieu of what we were thinking." She looked at him in hope. "Do you want to bunk here with me?" she asked hopefully.

"Ha." He laughed. "That's not quite what I was thinking. I was wondering if you wanted to go back to sharing with your sister?"

"I would much rather you stayed here with me," she stated immediately.

"That's probably not a good idea."

She waggled her eyebrows. "Are you sure? I was hoping that we would get there before any of this happened anyway." He stared at her, nonplussed, and she grinned. "Please tell me that I'm not completely out to lunch and that it's something you've been thinking too."

When he still didn't know what to say and just stared at her, she reached up and kissed him.

DAY 7, NIGHTTIME

BERRY HADN'T MEANT for it to come out that way, but, as soon as she pulled back, he tightened his arms around her, flattened her on the bed, and returned the kiss, sending her senses into overdrive. When he finally lifted his head, they were both panting.

"And no," she said, "I wasn't thinking about that because of what you were saying earlier."

He grinned. "Glad to hear that," he muttered. "I just … After talking about the various ideas of what was going on, I was thinking more about keeping you safe."

"Good, I'm glad to hear that," she whispered, "because this whole thing sucks."

"I know." He leaned over and kissed her gently, this time on the lips and then once on the nose. And then, as if unable to help himself, he left a trail down to her ear.

She shivered in his arms. "Still, I was hoping this would come to pass," she muttered. "My sister's innuendoes were not helping earlier though, and I felt … I don't know. Dirty, cheap, all of the above," she muttered, "but mostly because of her actions in the past. And it sucks because I don't want that to tarnish our relationship."

"Your sister has nothing to do with this," Egan declared, with a smile. "This is all about us, you and me. She's definitely doing some damage, but the reputation she is tarnishing is her own, not yours."

"I know," Berry agreed, "and I keep hoping she's done with these shocking revelations, but I can't guarantee it."

"You think she's still withholding information? Could there be more?"

"I don't know," she admitted, "but, at this point, I wouldn't put it past her. Despite what she's told us, I don't have any faith that she's come fully clean now."

He smiled at her. "That position is probably smart on your part. But, for now, why don't we put your sister out of this conversation and out of this room. It's awesome that you have your own private room," he noted, with a smile, "and that we're turning this conversation back to us, right?"

"Oh, is there an actual *us?*" she asked, looping her arms around his neck.

"Initially I was hoping that we would figure out if we were both interested, during the time that we're here. Then, if so, start seeing each other when we got sent back stateside," he shared. "But knowing now that it'll be a trick to get things all settled enough here for anyone to leave, I honestly don't want to wait that long. I already know without a doubt that you are very special, and I am very much interested in seeing where we can take it."

"We may be here for some time, and I am perfectly happy to work on a relationship while we're here, if that's what you're saying." She smiled. He gently rubbed his nose against hers. "So, let's stop worrying about it then," she muttered. "I'm not trying to hide anything, and, if this is something we wanted enough to actually go for, I would very much prefer to have it be a relationship that is public."

"Good," he agreed. "I wouldn't want to hide it in a place like this anyway."

"No, it doesn't even work," she noted. "I don't know how long my sister would have managed to keep hers hidden to the extent that it was, and I don't even know why she cared."

"I think because the Russians were under a mandate to finish whatever training they had here and to get home. So I presume that Yegorahn didn't think it would be something they were allowed to pursue. Or—" He hesitated, and she nodded.

"Yegorahn didn't really care for her. Cherry was available and why not, right?" she suggested, with a groan. "I already came to that potential conclusion myself."

"Again, can we maybe take her out of the conversation and not go there now? Especially when we are in bed together, I surely don't want to add Cherry to the mix."

"Sure, and, besides, I have much better things to do." Berry unbuttoned the top button of his heavy shirt. "It takes quite a while to get ready for bed, with so many layers on."

"Yeah, believe me. I can shuck layers pretty damn fast, if there's a good reason."

"What more reason do you need?" she asked, batting her eyelashes at him, with mock humor.

He grinned. "I think you're doing a great job of giving me that reason." Egan chuckled, as he shifted and looked down at her. "But you're the one wearing long johns."

"Of course I am. It's always freezing in here."

He laughed, as he stood, and within moments was completely nude in front of her.

She whistled. "Damn, you did that like a pro."

"Are you kidding? You learn to get dressed and undressed in lightning speed in these temperatures," he shared, as he curled into the bed beside her, pulling her up close.

"But you are still wearing way too many clothes." But he took care of that almost as fast as he'd handled his only clothes.

"If that's the case, you'll need to heat me up to the point that I'm okay losing a layer or two." He laughed. She was almost immediately surrounded by the furnace of his body. "Oh my gosh, you're just so warm," she murmured.

"Always. I'm definitely on the hot-body register."

"God, sleeping with you must be like sleeping with a huge thermal weighted blanket." She paused, staring at him intently. "I know we just discussed how we would leave my sister out of our bedroom, until such time as we decide differently."

Egan frowned. "But? Did you remember something?"

Berry nodded. "Unfortunately it's always been really tough to keep her out of my life. She came between me and the one major boyfriend I had in my life. I don't even talk about that really, and it was way back when I was in college and was young and stupid," she muttered. "I had a hard time rebuilding my relationship with her after that, but I did, and I've been really grateful for having her in my life all these years since."

"I don't even know that I want to ask, but what did Cherry do?"

Berry shrugged. "It doesn't matter what she did then, but she saved me afterward, and that's what counts. She's the one who was playing around with my boyfriend, and I was really struggling over their betrayal. However, I let her off the hook, when he was caught with a date-rape drug in his possession. He was convicted for it, I think."

Egan leaned back and looked at her in shock.

She nodded. "Of course she had been sleeping with him

the whole time, which I didn't know, and it hurt both of us."

"Hurt both of you?" he asked. "Only one of you was seriously damaged by it. Did this boyfriend ever use the drugs?"

"No, and he protested his innocence the entire time," she stated, with a groan, "but it didn't do any good. I don't even know if my family knew. We had both moved out by this time. I was living at college and working a job too, while Cherry was living in her own apartment. So all four of us in my family split apart at that point in time, and it was years before my sister reached out to me again, mostly after my parents had talked me in and out of reconciling with her. Like I said, we weren't terribly close."

"Yeah, you're not kidding. She had an affair with your college boyfriend. And you find out at the same time that he's got drugs in his pocket that are not great. I hate to ask but …"

Berry nodded. "Yes, we were lovers at the time, so the drugs didn't make any sense, and I told the cops that, but they figured that, since there had been a rash of rapes locally, then either he was trying to emulate them or he was part of the supply chain or … something." She shrugged. "He wasn't connected to any of the rapes at the time by DNA, so I think they eventually gave up looking at him. He was charged for having the drugs, but I don't know what the charges were."

"What was his name?"

She sighed. "Rick Mendas."

He nodded. "Have you seen him since?"

"No, not at all. That was a relationship I walked away from very quickly, once I found out that he was unfaithful."

"Of course," Egan muttered and looked down at her.

"So, just for the record, I don't cheat or play around."

"I'm really glad to hear that because I don't either." She chuckled. "And you're supposed to be taking my mind off all this, not bring it back up again."

"Sorry about that," he murmured, as he lowered his head and gently kissed her again. "It is really nice to just hold you though."

"It is, isn't it?" she murmured. "There is something very special about just being here with you, knowing that we have a few minutes of privacy, with no prying eyes, no crazy things happening, just some time for us," she whispered.

He squeezed her hand gently, holding her close, then shifted a little lower. "Of course something else could be pretty nice too," he whispered, as he dropped his lips to gently kiss a trail from her chin to her neck to her collarbone.

She moaned softly as the heat inside rose gently. "You're right," she whispered. "Something else could be really nice right now."

He chuckled, as he slowly traveled a little farther down, then pulled the blanket back, and she shivered. He laughed and said, "Just give me a minute, and soon you won't feel the cold at all."

As he slid down and shifted the material out of his way, he took one plump breast into his hand, and suckled on the nipple, pulling on it deeply and heavily. She felt an answering tug in her womb, her hips shifting upward, as she cried out softly. When he was done ministering to that one, he moved to the other plump breast, gently licking and teasing the nipple, before taking it in for several deep long sucks.

She shuddered and whispered, "God, that feels good." He shifted her slightly surprised to find herself nude in the cool air—and not caring one bit as heat curled her toes from the inside.

He murmured something that she didn't hear, but she wasn't exactly listening anymore, her mind caught up in everything he was doing to her. His hands were busy, his tongue was teasing, and, when he separated her thighs and moved on down her body, she cried out, as her body came apart at his actions.

When he moved his way back up and slipped inside her, she shuddered, holding her fist against her mouth to hold back the cries. He gently removed her hand and lowered his mouth onto hers, sealing her cries and swallowing them as he drove steadily inside her. When he finally surged at his own release, she came apart a second time, as he filled his own need deep at the heart of her.

He shuddered, as he slowly collapsed beside her, and whispered, "As I said, there are other nice things to do too."

She gently moved and curled up against him, her heart and mind full, as she whispered, "That was beyond nice."

"Good, then you won't have a problem doing it again."

She yawned. "No, but maybe in the morning. I do like mornings."

He chuckled. "I happen to love mornings myself, so go to sleep and get some rest."

"I'm trying to," she whispered. "That's what I really need, to just crash and forget everything."

"You do that, and I'll make sure you're safe tonight."

She closed her eyes and whispered, "I'd say thank you, but, at the same time, I wouldn't want you to take it the wrong way."

He chuckled. "Not taking it the wrong way. Just sleep."

She closed her eyes and slept.

Day 8 Early Morning

EARLY IN THE morning, he woke her, then made love to her all over again. When she collapsed in his arms and then went right back to sleep, he smiled and drifted off himself. Soon he woke with another thought in his mind, and it was pressing enough that he got up, quickly dressed, and headed out to make himself an instant coffee.

As he sat in the kitchen all alone, he texted Mason with questions about this Rick Mendas, Berry's college sweetheart. It took a bit via text to explain what was going on, but, as soon as Mason got it, he replied.

I'll get back to you in a few minutes.

When the phone rang, thankfully the reception was holding. Mason quickly explained some ugly details. Soon after the breakup, a bottle of the date-rape drug had been found in Rick Mendas's possession. What followed had devastated the young man, and he'd taken his own life, after protesting his innocence and maintaining that he absolutely loved Berry and would never have done anything to hurt her or any other woman.

"The Mendas family professed his innocence the whole time as well, but I guess it drove him to end his life because he just couldn't handle what happened."

"Damn. Look, Mason. This is an ugly thought, but I do need you to check on something else for me." As soon as he explained what it was, Mason whistled.

"Jesus, seriously?"

"I don't know," Egan replied. "I really don't know."

"And none of this has anything to do with Mountain's brother either," Mason noted.

Egan replied, "I just know that we have Yegorahn, a dead Russian, who we just found out had mentioned that something illegal was going on, and we don't know what it was. All I'm saying is that this is another potential avenue that we never checked out."

"Who the hell would?" Mason snapped, his anger rising at the very thought. "I'll get back to you." And, with that, he hung up.

Sensing a presence, Egan looked up to see Mountain, staring at him oddly, and Egan smiled. "That was Mason. I just checked in with him on something. A very unpleasant theory."

"Speak up," he said.

With their voices low enough to ensure they weren't overheard, Egan explained the little bit that he'd discovered overnight.

Mountain shook his head. "That can't have anything to do with this whole mess."

"No, it can't, but, if we can at least get some clarity and clear up some of it, maybe it would help."

"Sure, clarity," he muttered, as he stared off in the distance. "But that's hardly clear, is it?"

"Nope, it isn't, and yet it's something that I need to speak with Sydney about, and we need to have a very genteel interview with the other women on board."

"Good," Mountain said. "You can take that one on, all on your own, but talk to Magnus before you hit Sydney with that conversation out of the blue." He shook his head. "I'm heading out to the locals this morning and another ridge beyond the other side that I want to check out. I thought I saw something the other day, just a glint, a reflection," he muttered, "and then it stopped, almost as if the person was immediately aware of my presence."

"Interesting." Egan stared at Mountain. "You're thinking it's our thief?"

"I think it's Amelia," he stated. "I know that I don't have any reason outside of instincts, but there's a reason why she's avoiding the camp."

"Sure. According to everything she's probably heard, some sick puppy is here. For all we know, there's more than one."

"If what you just shared with me is true," Mountain replied, "it's more than one, and we need that like a hole in the head. And so does the colonel."

"Yeah, I gather he's not terribly happy."

"Your notes were found, by the way."

Egan looked at him, relief washing over him. "Thank God for that," he said with a sigh. "I wasn't terribly impressed at the way the colonel handled that."

"No, he was panicking yesterday," Mountain shared, "and I'm not sure he's feeling a whole hell of a lot better. The brass is really on his ass, and he'll take the fall for this whole mess, if we can't get some answers soon."

"And yet, all we have is a mess going on. One after another really. It's not, … I don't want to say it's not his fault, since it doesn't matter whether it's his fault or not. You and I both know the buck stops with our CO."

"Exactly, but, in this case, I think a whole lot more is going on than we're even thinking of. Yet, at the heart of it," Mountain added, "it'll be damn simple. It always is."

"Sure it is," Egan muttered, as he looked around. "Do you need any help getting ready?"

"No, I'll be out of here soon." He checked his watch. "I want to be out before dawn, so I can catch sight of any smoke out there."

"Surely anybody living off the land must be shutting things down very quickly."

"Which is another safety measure, but, if anybody is left alive out there, and there's a reason for them to be hiding, I need to find out if they're okay and if they need anything. Even if they don't want to come back in again. Honestly I can't let go of the thought that my brother might be out there somewhere."

"And you think that maybe Amelia's got him?" Mountain wore a look Egan could only describe as haunted.

"I find myself hoping so," Mountain admitted. "Yet it makes no sense because Amelia went missing well after my brother did, but that doesn't mean that there isn't anybody else with her. For that matter, another Good Samaritan may have looked after Teegan all this time."

"And Amelia should also have one guy from her team with her. At least that was the last I had heard."

"Exactly, so I don't know what's going on, but none of it's good."

"I hear you," Egan whispered.

And, with that, Mountain gave him a hard look. "Look after Berry, and keep an eye on everybody here. Start those sensitive interviews first thing and see if you've got answers for me by the time I get back."

"Wouldn't that be nice?" Egan laughed. "Not asking for much, are you?"

"At this point, I think you may have something that's about to break wide open," Mountain suggested, "so answers might get easier to come by."

"I hope so," he said slowly.

Yet, as Egan watched Mountain slip out, Egan wasn't so

sure. He started by submitting a request to see the colonel ASAP. When the request came back, he was told the colonel wasn't up yet, but that Egan would be booked in first thing. As soon as the colonel was available, they would let him know. He then moved on to sending Magnus a text, asking if Sydney was up. When the affirmative came back, he sent another message. **I need to talk to Sydney privately, and then you and I both need to talk to Cherry again.**

Magnus called him. "Where are you?"

"Hovering over coffee," he replied, his tone brisk. "I think we need to be looking at something else here."

"Good, because I'm about fed up with the lack of solid information we've got so far."

"I don't think any of this is good information, and I'm not sure how far back it goes, but, if it takes off some layers and leads to a way out of this mess, that will be progress, at least."

"I'll be there in five," he said. And, with that, Magnus hung up.

Egan was still here, contemplating the task before him, when Chef walked in with a huge pot of fresh coffee, then looked at him and shrugged.

"You're up early."

"Yeah, I am," Egan noted, with a bite to his voice. "But I'm hoping that, after what's looking to be a rough day, we might get somewhere."

"I hope so," Chef agreed, as he motioned at the coffee. "Looks as if you'll need some of this to get through the day. Good luck." And, with that, he headed back into the kitchen.

True enough, Egan would need coffee and lots of it. No easy way to get a start on a day like this one was shaping up to be, and, as soon as Magnus showed up, Egan quickly provided an explanation of where he was going with this. As Magnus sat here in shock and stared at him, Egan nodded. "It sucks," he acknowledged, "but I think we have to pursue it as a line of questioning."

"Absolutely," Magnus agreed, shaking his head, as he poured himself a big cup of coffee. "Glad you're here for this one because heads will roll. But listen. I need to tell you about something that happened before you joined us, with the strangled Russian named Helsky, before he died. He got himself all worked up over Sydney and propositioned her in front of a bunch of people in the dining room. She turned him down cold. In front of the whole dining room. Next thing she knew, right after that event, he was waiting for her in the clinic and tried to force himself on her."

"What? Was she okay? Did he hurt her?"

"There was a scuffle, and another one when I turned up, and he was dealt with. So, maybe the date-rape drug idea isn't so far-fetched, not where he was concerned, you know?"

DAY 8, LATER THAT MORNING

BERRY WOKE UP and stretched, noting an uncomfortable soreness in her body, then smiled as she realized where it came from. Relaxed, she curled up under the covers, wondering at how quickly her life had shifted in both good and bad ways.

When her door was flung open, and her sister stormed in, Berry stared at Cherry in shock. Right behind her was Egan, who was apologizing.

Berry looked from one to the other and said, "Somebody want to explain what's going on here?"

Her sister spat, "You! You did this!"

Berry blinked at her, not sure what was even happening. Turning her confused gaze to Egan, she asked, "What on earth?"

He replied, "Sorry, I'll explain in a little bit." And, with that, he jerked her sister out of her room, Cherry screaming at the top of her lungs. Quickly grabbing her clothes, Berry dressed as fast as she could and headed outside to where the commotion was ebbing in his wake, as Egan headed down the hallway, her sister still screaming the whole way.

As soon as Berry got to where her sister was locked up in a room, she asked the guard to let her in to see Cherry, but he immediately shook his head. "Not happening."

She stared at him, nonplussed, then nodded and headed

back, hoping to find Egan. While she didn't locate Egan, she did run into Magnus.

"Come here. We need to talk," he stated, pulling her aside.

"Ya think? What the hell is going on?"

He pulled her into the medical clinic, and she looked over at Sydney. "What's going on?" Berry asked, unable to contain her curiosity.

"Nothing good, that's for sure," Magnus stated. "Hopefully it will end up being a false alarm, but your sister's not cooperating."

"Of course not," Berry muttered, with a sigh. "That's the name of the game with her, isn't it?"

"It is, and unfortunately this is not a good time for her to be causing trouble."

Berry winced. "What has she done now?" she asked fearfully, her gaze going from one to the other.

"You mentioned something to Egan last night."

She flushed. "Yes, I probably did." She stared at Sydney. "Is this something problematic?"

Just then Egan stepped into the clinic and looked over at Magnus. "Give me a minute with Berry, would you?"

Magnus nodded. "You've got a minute, but, as you know, we must get to the bottom of this quickly, so do it fast."

"I know," he said, with a tired sigh, as Magnus and Sydney both stepped out. He looked over at Berry. "You'll think that I completely betrayed you, but I didn't. I'm just trying to get to the bottom of this."

"I get that," she replied, hating the nervousness overtaking her. "Please tell me what's going on."

"The thing is, I got permission to search your sister's

room."

Her eyebrows shot up. "Okay, and why would you need to do that? I'm surprised that it wasn't done already."

"I know, right? It should have been done as soon as we realized she was involved in some way."

"Involved? What do you mean by *involved*?"

He winced. "That, of course, is the next thing. We have a lot of questions surrounding date-rape drugs and the fact that I found them in your sister's possessions."

She stared at him and slowly sagged into a chair. "You found what?" she asked in a faint whisper.

"I found a bottle of it," he murmured.

She stared at him, then shook her head and whispered, "Please, no."

"I'm sorry, but, yes, and it was open. Meaning it wasn't a sealed bottle. And, under the circumstances, she won't tell us anything."

"She won't tell you where she got it, will she?" she asked, the emotional pain stabbing her heart.

"No, she won't. We're presuming it came from Yego-rahn, but we're not sure about that. Since she won't tell us, we're now left to wonder about the extent of her involvement in any of this. As you mentioned last night"—he raised his hand in an apology—"and I'm sorry for not speaking to you about it first because it feels as if I took something special between us and twisted it."

She blinked at him. "I don't even know what I told you last night to bring you to this point," she admitted, bewildered.

"How your college boyfriend had been caught with a date-rape drug."

"Yes, but what does that have to do with anything happening here?"

"I don't know if you even know this, but your boyfriend committed suicide over it and protested right to the end that he was innocent."

She stared at him, as a nasty suspicion entered her heart. "Please tell me that you don't think my sister planted it?"

He stared at her for a long moment. "Would she have?" Berry immediately shook her head, and he motioned for her to calm down. "Think, Berry. Just stop and think for a minute. Don't just react, but think about this."

"I …" She stopped again. "I don't… I don't know. I would never have thought any woman would do such a thing, and I can't even imagine what Cherry's doing with that drug. Maybe it was planted on her here. Like maybe the Russians put it in her room."

"Maybe. We did have some security cameras up, but unfortunately—between the weather and generator issues—they've been sketchy. It's being reviewed right now."

"And that would what? Prove that somebody was in her room?"

"Yes, potentially," he replied, then hesitated. "But remember. It's also your room."

"Oh, Jesus," she murmured, her stomach lurching. He immediately stepped forward and held her, encouraging her to breathe. "Deep breaths. Just try long, deep breaths."

She gasped for air, as the potential connotations rushed forward. "I don't know what you're trying to imply with that," she cried out. "What is it you're thinking?"

"I'm not sure," he admitted. "I'm not sure anybody's implying anything about the women either. We're all just gathering information. What I can tell you is that a bottle was found in Cherry's possession, and your sister isn't talking. But given the history with that same drug, and her involvement at that time, I'm not sure what to think."

At that, Berry's own history played through her mind, like some slow-motion horror film, as she realized just how much they thought her sister might have been involved in. She opened her mouth to refute everything, and then slowly closed it. "I don't know what to say. I really don't."

"So maybe, for the moment, don't say anything. Give us a chance to talk to her. Give us a chance to see what she'll do with it and to see what the colonel will do," he added, with a wince. "Then we'll go from there. What I do need you to do is keep an open mind."

At that, she whispered, barely able to get the words out, "Rick really committed suicide?"

Egan slowly nodded. "Yes, I'm sorry."

And, with that realization, Berry's tears broke through and came down in a flood. "He was such a great guy. But … he made a mistake. He made a mistake with my sister, and I couldn't forgive him for it," she stuttered, forcing the words through her sobs. "What does that say about me?"

"You were a wounded young lady betrayed by your sister and a boyfriend you were serious about," he snapped, his tone immediately harsh. "Don't even start blaming yourself for that."

She shook her head. "I don't even know what to say."

"Remember. Don't say anything right now. Just relax and try to let some of that information funnel through your head and see what comes up."

"Okay. I'll try."

"Did you move all your stuff out of your room?"

"Yes, I did," she said, then winced again. "But nobody'll believe that, will they?"

"They will if we can prove it," he stated in a soothing tone.

"Go search my new room then," she stated immediately. When he hesitated, she added, "No way will that fly, Egan. You need to because I didn't have anything to do with it, and I don't want anything you're doing to be tainted by a relationship between us. That will just make it look as if I am hiding something," she explained.

When he turned to leave, she called out to him, "You better not do the search yourself. Get somebody else to do it."

He nodded. "That would probably be best, but I was really hoping to not have to go there."

"That is no longer an option, is it?" she asked, staring at him, trying to figure out how to even begin to handle this. She hadn't done anything wrong, yet it still felt wrong.

"If I could have woken you up and done something about this," Egan shared, "it would have been fine. If we had searched Cherry's room and not found anything, it would have been fine."

"But you did find something," she said.

He nodded.

"Therefore, it's not fine."

He winced and nodded. "That would be everybody's take on this, yes."

"Dear God," she whispered. "I don't want to think that my sister could possibly be involved in this."

"None of us want to consider it. I just don't know that we have any choice at the moment. Especially since she's not cooperating."

Berry took a deep breath. "Can I talk to her?" When he stared at her, she shrugged. "That might be the easiest answer."

Just then, there was a knock on the door, and Magnus poked his head in. "We really need to be doing something here, Egan. You need to get started."

Berry faced Magnus. "Before that, could you go search my room?" Magnus frowned at her intently. "I have nothing to do with this, but, if my room isn't searched, you know people will say otherwise."

Magnus considered that for a moment and then nodded. "Good point."

Sydney stepped back into the room and looked at her in a commiserating way. "I'm sorry, Berry."

"Me too. I don't even know what I'm sorry for though. This whole mess is just too unbelievable. We don't know that she used the date-rape drug on anyone, right?"

"No, we don't," Egan replied. "What we also don't know is whether it has anything to do with why Yegorahn was killed."

Berry nodded slowly. "It seems as if there's absolutely nothing I can say to make it any better, but I just can't understand how or why Cherry would have had anything to do with this."

"I'm not sure she did," Egan told her. "Remember. There's still a chance that it was planted there."

"Maybe, and yet ..." Berry stopped.

"Yet what?"

She looked at him, wordless. "If it wasn't for Cherry's involvement years ago with Rick Mendas, I would agree with you 100 percent that it had been planted. However, due to the fact that it's the same drug, could that be a coincidence?" she asked, looking hopefully from Egan to Sydney and back again, but their expressions weren't very encouraging.

"Anything is possible," Sydney murmured. "The real question is a difficult one, both to ask and to answer. How much did your sister hate you?"

Tears came to her eyes, as Berry whispered, "I would hope the answer to that question would be not at all, but apparently I've been closing my eyes to some pretty rough realities—but I don't get to do that anymore."

At that, Sydney sat down beside her, wrapped Berry up in her arms and whispered, "I'm so sorry."

Berry held on for a long moment, then slowly loosened her grasp, looked up at the doc, and smiled. "What I don't know yet is whether there's really anything here for me to be blamed for. Is there something that I should have done, not done? I don't know. It's just … right now I feel—"

"You feel completely confused, and that's normal," Sydney told her.

Berry looked back at Egan. "I guess there was no other way to do this, was there?"

"If Cherry talked to us, it would sure help," he said.

At that, Berry stiffened. "Let me talk to her. Even if you guys are there, let me talk to her because, if nothing else, I'm the one who will push her buttons. Even though she may not want to say what she ends up saying, chances are she'll blurt out something, … good or bad."

At that, Sydney looked over at her and nodded. "I think, in this case, you're probably right."

Just then Magnus walked back into the room. He looked over at Berry and smiled. "Nothing's in your room."

Her shoulders sagged with relief. "Thank you for that much, at least."

"That still doesn't mean that some people won't talk about your involvement. They won't know that we've cleared you in some way. However, you moving out of your shared bedroom does mean you had a falling out with your sister, which might work in your favor to offset any gossip otherwise."

"I get all that," she replied. "And thank you for searching my room. I'm grateful to know nothing in my room shouldn't be there."

He just nodded, then turned to Egan. "The colonel is ready." Egan nodded, and the two of them headed out. She watched as they left, then turned to look back at Sydney. "This is big, isn't it?"

"Yeah, it's big." Sydney snorted. "Not only is it a drug, it's an illegal drug, and frankly one of the worst things anybody would want to see on a base like this. What I don't understand is why your sister would have it."

"I don't either, and I guess I won't be allowed to talk to her."

"No, not until they come back anyway. Then maybe they'll take you to talk to her, with them along of course. Do you think she would talk to you then?"

"I don't know," Berry muttered. "I guess it depends on whether she's innocent or not."

At that, Sydney hesitated, then sat down beside her. "Do you want to tell me what happened way back when?"

"Not really. It's not something I've ever really talked about. I explained it to Egan last night, but I didn't go into great detail." Berry sighed. "It's painful." Then she quickly explained about her sister having had an affair with Berry's college boyfriend, her long-term boyfriend.

"We had plans," she added, with a soft smile. "Serious plans. We would travel, get married, the whole enchilada. … Then I found out that he slept with my sister, and my world came crashing down."

"Of course it did," Sydney whispered, shaking her head.

"Then throughout that whole nightmare—and I don't even know how it came about—but somehow he was searched and found to have a date-rape drug on him." She was silent for a moment.

"Was the search done at college?" Sydney asked. "As in one of the classes, not his dorm room?"

She nodded. "Yes. During class. So humiliating."

"So why would he have it while he was at class? During the daytime?"

"I don't know, and of course that started a whole big nasty mess. Rick was suddenly not exactly Rick because of it all, and he kept saying that it wasn't his, that he had nothing to do with it, but nobody believed him."

"And why did nobody believe him?"

She stared at Sydney, and tears came to her eyes. "I suspect nobody believed him because of my sister. Cherry was quite vocal with her complaints against him. Because he'd been found with it, I guess that's all they needed back then. I don't know," she muttered, tears in her eyes. "Egan just told me that Rick, my college boyfriend, ended up committing suicide, probably because of that whole thing."

"Do you ever recall seeing him with drugs?"

"No, not at all," she replied, "and I did tell the police that, even though at the same time I was hurting because he'd turned around and had slept with my sister."

"Do you think there's any chance that it wasn't consensual?"

"No, she told me that she'd had a bad moment and went to bed with him."

"A bad moment?" Sydney asked delicately.

"Yeah, I know my sister," she said, sniffling. "It was presented as no big deal, a one-time thing, a momentary lapse in judgment. I guess, at the time, I wondered if it involved the date-rape drug because that would allow me to not blame my sister, but I'm not sure that's the case."

"No, it sounds as if it may not have been. I guess the hard question that needs to be asked of you is if there is any chance your sister may have set him up?"

"Set him up?" Berry asked, looking at the doc in shock. "What do you mean?" The words came out broken, and she was too numb to hear them.

Sydney winced. "Set up as in, what if he didn't have the date-rape drug himself? What if maybe somebody put it in his possession without his knowledge?"

"Are you suggesting that my sister may have done that?" she asked.

"That will be one of the questions, yes."

"Jesus," Berry wailed, "how did this get so messed up?"

"When people start lying and cheating, things tend to get messed up."

"Right. And that would be my sister, Cherry. In light of the recent events and all, as much as I hate to say it, I can see her doing that. Would she have done it? It's possible. But did she? Who knows. I walked away from all that at the time. I was broken-hearted and couldn't handle any of it, but my sister said that he …" She didn't know how to get the words out. "She left just enough doubt in my head that I wondered if the drug had been used on her, and that's why the sex happened between them. I was looking for an easy answer anyway. I didn't want to believe that the two of them did that to me. She told me just yesterday in her latest little truth session that she had seduced him. I look back at poor Rick now and realize that in no way was he prepared for somebody like my sister."

"It doesn't seem anybody could be," Sydney noted. "It sounds to me that she only cares about one person."

"Yeah, herself, and believe me, I've thought about that a lot, especially after she told me all that. But how much of that confessional talking was the drugs?" she asked, turning to look at Sydney. "Will she turn around and deny it all now?"

"I don't know," Sydney acknowledged, "but I suspect that you know that better than I do. Drug withdrawal does do some messed-up things, but I wouldn't expect random confessions to be one of them."

"Right, I guess I'm looking for excuses again."

"Of course you'll look for a way to excuse Cherry's behavior, but that doesn't mean you'll find one."

"*Great*," Berry muttered. "That's not exactly the answer I was hoping for."

Sydney chuckled. "No, and we're at a time and a place where this won't be easy. You need to keep that in mind."

"Absolutely nothing about this has been easy," she stated painfully. "I can't say I appreciate having my past heartache dredged up."

"Worse now with the knowledge that the young man took his life," Sydney pointed out.

"And I feel terrible for even considering anything other than that back then, and now with all the trouble up here?" she added. "And the stupid thing is, I'm only up here because my sister really wanted to come. I only agreed because she begged me to come along. She wanted to come up here, but she didn't want to do it alone."

"Is that normal for you?"

"No, not at all. The two of us haven't gotten along for a very long time, but she told me that it would give us a chance to bond, with the two of us out in the middle of nowhere. So, we would have no choice but to sort out our differences," she shared, with a half smile. "For some stupid reason I believed her. … What really concerns me in all this," she stated, as she looked up at Sydney, "is how would she have gotten access to that drug?"

Sydney winced. "Unfortunately in this day and age, it's pretty easy to get anything off the internet, and it'll be untraceable too. Particularly if she didn't identify the parcel and had it mailed to your parents' place for instance," Sydney explained. "It's not really that hard."

"*Great.*" Berry reached up a weary hand and brushed her hair off her forehead. "That really sucks."

"Yes, it absolutely does, and I'm sorry that you're caught up in the middle of it all. Again."

"Yeah, me too," Berry whispered. "I still struggle with the thought that Cherry would have had anything to do with that, after what we went through in college."

"Which is why I guess I wonder if she could have set up Yegorahn too."

Berry frowned at the doc for a long moment. "You're starting to make my sister sound like a monster."

"No, not at all, but we need some understanding, medically and legally, where your sister is at mentally in all this."

"Why?" Berry asked bitterly. "It seems as if none of us even know what she's capable of. Imagine how naïve I was back then. I can't even believe this."

"And yet you came up here with her."

"Sure, I was interested in the training too. I always enjoy trying anything like this. She knew that. I think I took it to mean that she also wanted to potentially have a chance to bond again. We're twins, after all, and everybody always says we're supposed to be super close." Berry shrugged, shaking her head. "Obviously I'm reassessing everything now."

"Of course," Sydney agreed, "and with good reason. I don't want you to think all of this is coming down against you either because that's not the intent here."

"No, but how do I not feel that way? Knowing that so much evil could be going on in my sister's head, to the point that this is even a possibility?"

"That's really what we have to ask because is it, or is your sister being set up as well?"

EGAN STEPPED OUT of the colonel's office and looked over at Magnus, waiting for him in the hallway. "What do you think about having Berry talk to Cherry?"

"I think it's the next step," Magnus replied, "and will likely be rough on both of them. Her sister was pretty angry at the accusations, so I'm not sure she'll take Berry's involvement in this investigation any easier."

"And yet do we have any reason to believe that Cherry might have been set up in this?"

"That's the question we have to really look at, isn't it? Because, if she was set up, she had nothing to do with it. And vice versa. If she had nothing to do with it, then her being set up is a possibility."

"*Maybe*," Egan hedged, with a wry look over at Magnus.

"Do you like her? Cherry?"

"No, I don't like her at all, but now I know from an insider perspective a little more about what she's been involved in, specifically as Cherry inserted herself into her sister's life, and that has made me judgmental," he admitted, with a wince.

"So, yeah, I get what you're saying. The problem is, I'm not sure anybody else will be less judgmental," Magnus stated. "A lot of upset is happening right now, and an awful lot of people are looking for answers. I'm not sure that some of them are even particularly worried about getting the right answers."

"*Right*." Egan grimaced. 'Still, if Cherry had anything to do with these deaths …"

"Absolutely," Magnus agreed, "there's no forgiveness."

"You and I both agree on that, but it's not even that there's no forgiveness," Egan clarified. "It's that there has to be something else to this, in order for this whole thing to not be a complete crock of shit."

Magnus chuckled. "It sounds like a complete crock of shit no matter what, unless you have another way to define it."

"No, I don't." Egan groaned. "I don't seem to have any way to define any of it. I've never seen anything like this before in my life," he muttered. "I guess the worst thing that I'm worried about is that in some way she'll be implicated."

"You mean Berry?"

"Yes, though I absolutely love the fact that she immediately asked you to go search her room."

"Sure, but you also know that just makes her look a little more suspicious."

Egan stopped, turned, and looked at him. "Seriously?"

"Yeah, seriously," Magnus stated, with a nod, "because that's how suspicions work, right? Say, for instance, what if Berry's the one who planted it in her sister's luggage, over all the bad feelings that the two of them have had between them all these years?"

"Jesus," Egan muttered, "is that even possible?"

"I don't know." Magnus laughed. "You tell me."

"No, it isn't. I don't understand this thought process at all," he stated. "And I can't imagine that anybody would think Berry was a part of this."

"I would agree with you, but you also know how people think. If they can blame one twin, they'll blame the other."

He nodded at that. "*Great*, so we need to get to the truth and not only that, … we need to clear Berry."

"I'd love to," Magnus confirmed, "but have you got any idea how to do that?"

"I think one of the first things is to get Cherry to open up—and that might very well take Berry's help—because if there's one thing that the two of them do, it's sparking fires against each other."

"If you want to show me a way to make that happen, I'm all for it," Magnus told Egan. "Otherwise, we're limited to simple questions."

"And yet Berry has asked to talk to her sister, so I think we should let her," Egan noted, turning to Magnus. "Agreed?"

"Agreed. Let's go do that now then, and we'll see where it goes from there."

And, with that, they headed back to the medical clinic. As they walked in, Berry hopped to her feet and looked at Egan hopefully. "Can I talk to her?"

He nodded. "Yeah, I think so."

The relief that washed over her face made him feel guilty for not being able to clear her name right away. "You also need to be prepared and understand that she might throw you under the bus."

Berry stopped, turned, and stared at him. "What?"

He laughed. "I know you don't think along those lines, but it's quite possible that she's already found a solution to her nightmare, and that solution will be to throw you under the bus."

"I guess she could try," Berry replied, puzzled, "but I don't know how."

"It's easy enough for Cherry to lie, to say that you're the one who put the drugs in her room, particularly after you found out about her sleeping with your past boyfriends."

She stared at him, then shook her head. "God, I don't even know if she would do that. You're not making me feel very good. Even contemplating such a thing just makes me sick, but thank you for the warning," she murmured. "Now, I really need to talk to her."

"Egan and I will both be present," Magnus declared.

She winced and nodded. "Fine, then let's go see what my sister has to say."

DAY 8, LATE MORNING

BERRY WALKED INTO the back room, the guard having been excused, since both Magnus and Egan were present.

Cherry looked up at her and glared. "Come to gloat, have you?"

"Why would you think that?"

"Why wouldn't I? This is your doing obviously. So now you've come to see the results of your labor."

Berry stopped and stared at her in shock. "You know, Cherry, they told me that, once you'd had a few minutes to get your head straightened away, you would turn around like a cornered animal and pin this on me, but I couldn't believe it."

"It wasn't me," Cherry declared flatly. "I don't have any connection to that drug."

"Say whatever you will, but you do have a connection to that drug," Berry argued, "If nothing else, just because of Rick alone. Remember Rick Mendas?"

"I do, but why is that my problem?" she asked, with a laugh. "That's your problem. After all, he was your boy-friend."

"Who you were sleeping with."

"Who you were angry with that I slept with."

"And yet, at the time, you also told me that you were

wondering if maybe he had given you something, and that's why you did what you did."

"Obviously that's how the drug works. I just woke up the next morning and found myself in bed with him," she said, with a wave of her hand. "I didn't know how or why."

"So you immediately put the blame on him and the drug, rather than on your own behavior and poor judgment."

Her sister looked at her, injured. "Jesus, Berry, you can't really think that I not only set him up but that now I've set you up too?"

"I don't know whether you were trying to set me up or not," Berry admitted, "because the bottom line is that the drugs were found in your room."

"Right, so you're the one who set me up," Cherry stated, with a nod. "That makes sense."

"How is that something that makes sense?" Berry asked, again staring at her sister in shock.

"You've always been jealous of me." Cherry sneered. "This is really just more of the same."

"Good God, Cherry, I've never been jealous of you. Not for a moment."

"Sure, you are. I'm the pretty one."

"You already told me how you felt about that."

"I take it back," she said immediately. "It was the drugs making me talk."

"I see." Berry frowned. "So it was the drugs that made you apologize for all that shitty behavior?"

"Yeah, consider the apology revoked." Cherry stared at Berry in anger.

But was that a touch of fear in her expression? Berry slowly nodded. "I'll take that into consideration. Now that

Yegorahn is dead, his friends did confirm that some criminal activity was going on here, but they didn't know what. Only that Yegorahn was part of it."

"He told me that he would go talk to somebody. I told you that already," Cherry said in exasperation.

"Yeah, and I don't know how much of that was the truth and how much of it was you just BS*ing* your way through this."

"BS*ing* my way through? That's rich. Look at you standing there, all high and mighty, pure as the driven snow."

"Oh, I'm definitely not that, but at least I can say I've never utilized that drug."

"No, of course not," she snapped, with a sneer. "Doesn't mean other people haven't used it on you though."

At that, she stiffened, and, then seeing the immediate joy in her sister's face, she nodded. "That's what this is all about, isn't it? You bought that date-rape drug for somebody to give to me." Berry sagged into the chair, staring at her sister in horror.

Cherry stared right back at her and then shrugged. "Maybe it was in the back of my mind," Both men behind her stiffened but refrained from interfering. "But I never used it," she rushed to say. "But, yeah, maybe it was something I considered, you know, like when you pissed me off."

"So, your plan was to arrange for somebody to use that drug and rape me?" Berry asked, frowning at her sister, wondering how two genetic twins could be so different.

She shrugged. "Yeah, for all you know, that's what Rick did."

"No, Rick did not. We were already lovers long before that. He didn't need to use the drug."

"Maybe not"—she smirked, then turned and glared at

her—"but you'll never know that, will you?"

"Has it been used while you've been here? Did you use it as a trial on anybody else?" Berry asked Cherry.

Her sister shrugged and then caved. "Look. I'm not that much of a bitch."

"Oh, I don't know about that, since what you're saying right now is that you obtained the drug and that you've hung on to it all this time, looking for an opportunity to use it against me." Then she frowned. "Is that what Yegorahn was planning?" she asked, with a note of revulsion.

Cherry didn't say anything but grinned. "You really hated him, didn't you?"

"I was fine as long as he was your partner," Berry replied, "but I didn't want anything to do with him."

"And he knew that, which was one of the reasons why he was looking into it, why he was considering it. He knew that I wanted it, that I was looking forward to seeing it happen," Cherry said delightedly.

"*Seeing it happen?*" Behind her, Egan took a step forward, his face revealing the fury he felt.

Berry reached out and grabbed his hand to push him back and then whispered to her sister, "Do you hate me that much, Cherry?"

She shrugged. "It's not that I hated you that much. I just wanted to drop you down below me," she muttered painfully.

"What does that even mean? Good God, Cherry, is that how low your own self-esteem is? Do you hate yourself that much?" Her sister glared at her, and Berry nodded. "That's what this is all about, isn't it?"

"Rick was yours, and you knew how much I loved him."

She stared at her. "No, Cherry, I didn't. He was my boyfriend, and I had no idea you cared in any way."

"It's not as if I would sit there and go on and on about it, but, yeah, I did care. I really did. I cared about him."

"And yet you set him up?"

"I didn't set him up, at least not at first," she muttered. "But then, when he wouldn't see any sense, I seduced him, and he still wouldn't see any sense."

"He didn't see any sense?" Berry repeated, staring directly at her sister and hearing another horrible, painful truth. "Because you used the drug on him, didn't you?"

Her sister nodded slowly. "Yes," she muttered. "And I've felt like shit over it all these years. And all that it's really done is made me angrier and angrier at you."

"Angrier at me?" Berry repeated, shaking her head at her sister in horror. "How the hell am I even responsible for this madness in any possible way?"

"Because everybody prefers you," she snapped. "Everybody, absolutely everybody prefers you."

"No, that's not true," she disagreed. "No way that's true."

"It is true," Cherry declared, as she glared at her sister, "and I, for one, am really fucking tired of it."

"But we're twins."

Cherry gave her a hard grin. "I'm really glad you mentioned that," Cherry stated, with a mocking look. "Because you're right, we are the same."

"No, we're not. We may look alike, but we are not the same, not in that way."

"You just said we're the same. You just don't want to acknowledge it."

"How can I acknowledge that? It's not possible."

"It is possible, and it's real." Cherry gave a hard look to

her sister. "But what's all this? Why are you making it into a big deal, when it's really just a sister issue?" Cherry turned to glare at the men in the room. "What it isn't is anything about a murder," Cherry noted. "I did not murder Yego-rahn." At that, her eyes teared up, and she added, "In many ways, he's the only one who ever understood me."

EGAN DIDN'T KNOW what to even make of this right now. It was just too hard to even contemplate how so very different the two twin sisters could be. He just kept shaking his head; then suddenly it hit him, and he turned to Magnus. "In spite of all this, there is one other truth that needs to be sorted."

"Only one?" Magnus asked, staring at him. "Right about now, this whole thing is a bloody mess."

"And it's getting bigger every turn we take," Egan added. "But I guess what I'm trying to say is that there is still another problem."

"Such as?"

He thought hard first to compose his words and then spoke carefully, "Those missing men, who went out on an Arctic walk, and we never found them. They just disap-peared, except for Terrance so far. What if"—he turned and stared at Cherry—"What if they were drugged, and they were just taken out into the winter elements and dumped?"

Cherry stared at him and shrugged. "I don't know. If anybody did that, they did it without my knowing."

"Are you sure about that?" Egan gave her a cold stare. "I'm not so sure you're innocent in all this."

She stared at him in frustration. "I am." She glared at

him. "I didn't have anything to do with that shit."

At that, Berry cried out, "How the fuck can we know that for sure now? How can we trust you after all the shit you've lied about?" She almost bellowed again. "How can we trust *anything* you say?"

Her sister turned and glared. "Because you know me."

"I don't know you at all," Berry whispered into the quiet room. "I don't know anything about you right now," she murmured. And, with that, she looked over at the others and pleaded, "If you'll excuse me, I need a few minutes." Then she turned and ran out of the room.

Sydney walked into the room, then looked over at the two men, frowning.

Magnus raised an eyebrow. "Problems?"

She shrugged. "That bottle of the date-rape drug," she began, "it's half empty."

He looked at Sydney, then at Cherry.

She immediately said, "No, no, no, no, no, it was not half empty. It was full," she stated, staring from one to another, "and I never used it."

"You may say that," Egan noted, "but how are any of us supposed to believe you now?"

"I didn't do anything," she snapped. "I didn't use it on anybody."

Sydney just nodded. "But that doesn't mean somebody else didn't use it."

"I know that Yegorahn didn't," she snapped. "He was pretty upset at the concept. I was talking him around though."

"But was he really?" Egan asked, with a snarl. "So far we haven't heard anything come out of your mouth that was the truth."

"You did mention he wanted to use it on Berry, and you wanted to see that happen." Magnus chipped in from the side, and she glared at him.

"On the other hand," Sydney added from behind him, "if somebody else was using it, that would have made it particularly easy to take out Yegorahn. He was a big man, after all, and I always wondered how somebody got the jump on him."

Cherry looked at her wide-eyed and shook her head. "No, I had nothing to do with his death. He was my ticket out of here."

At that, Magnus asked waspishly, "How the hell did you expect that to work?"

"He wanted out too. He didn't have any confidence in this whole mess, and he wanted out. He told me that he had a way and that the drug I had would make it happen." She was breaking up now, staring at each of them.

"Good God." Magnus shook his head. "So your date-rape drug had nothing to do with some criminal activity going on here?"

She nodded. "Yes, it did, but Yegorahn had a way to make that work in our favor."

"So, he would blackmail him? This other person, whoever he was?"

She winced and nodded. "I think so."

"And yet you have no idea who might have taken Yegorahn out."

"No, I wish I did."

"Really? Why is that?"

"Because I'm still here, goddammit," she snarled, "and this is the last fucking place I want to be." At that, she slumped onto the bed and leaned against the headboard.

"Just leave me alone, will you?"

"Why?" Egan asked, trying to understand her urgency. "Do you really think we don't need to know what happened to your boyfriend?

"Sure, you need to know," she snapped. "I always suspected his team, but I don't know that."

"Why would you suspect his own team?" he asked.

She looked at him and sighed. "Because he wouldn't take them along when we escaped, and one guy in particular wanted to go, but Yegorahn wasn't open to the idea."

"Why was that?" Magnus asked.

"Because Yegorahn hated him," she muttered, fatigue in her voice.

"Do you think Yegorahn may have had something to do with the other Russian deaths?"

"I don't know, but now that you've mentioned that the bottle is half empty, and, since I didn't touch it, it's obvious that somebody's been using it," she said, with a shrug. "Unfortunately the minute anybody knew it was here, they could have taken it anytime. Whenever I was having a meal or on a training session outside, it's just been sitting there."

"How many people would have known?"

She shook her head. "I have no idea but too damn many."

DAY 8, AFTERNOON

BERRY SAT ON her bed, curled up in a ball, her arms wrapped around her knees, just rocking back and forth. So much horrific information so fast, and all of it so confusing that she didn't even know which way to go or where to look anymore. She wanted to find the goodness in it all, but she didn't see any. She wanted to find the joy she had felt last night with Egan, but she didn't know how it was possible now.

She wanted to find something, something she could hang on to in some way to move forward and to make peace with her sister, but Berry didn't see how.

When a knock came on her door, she called out, "Come in," certain it would be Egan. However, when one of the Russians stepped in, with an apologetic look on his face, she was a bit taken aback.

"Hey, sorry," he murmured. "I didn't want to disturb you, but I understand they're doing another investigation."

She nodded and wrinkled up her face. "Yes, but, if you're asking me for any answers, I don't have a clue what's happening here."

He nodded. "I don't think anybody has any answers right now, and it's pretty-darn frustrating for all of us."

"I know."

He held out a cup of coffee for her. "I saw you come in,

and they had just made fresh coffee," he murmured, "so I brought you one."

Surprised at his kindness and at the fact that he had always been easy to get along with, she thanked him and clutched it in her cold hands. "I'm sorry about your teammates," she murmured. "This assignment is hard enough as it is, but I can't imagine losing the lives of your teammates on top of it."

"I know, but Yegorahn was not a good man."

She looked at him. "Why do you say that?" she asked, curious.

"He had drugs. Drugs he would use on you."

She winced. "Yeah, my sister just told me." She rubbed her free hand on her face. "I can't believe everybody knew."

"Yegorahn told me, and I got angry at him, told him it wasn't right, how it wasn't fair. It just wasn't the way that things should be done. He told me to knock it off and that he hadn't decided if he would do it or not. It was just something he was contemplating."

"*Great*. So nice to know people were planning all this crap behind my back."

He smiled and nodded. "Yes, yes, I know, and I'm sorry about it," he said.

As he stepped back, she asked ruefully, "Did Yegorahn tell anybody else about it? Do you know?" she asked, looking up at him, worried.

He shrugged. "I think just me, but I don't know for sure. It's just very sad."

She nodded. "That I would agree with. Thanks for the coffee."

He nodded and stepped out and closed the door . She just sat here, hugging her coffee. When another knock came on her door, she groaned. "Come in." Although why she wanted anybody in her room, she didn't know. As it was, Egan stepped in and smiled at her.

"Hey, feeling any better?"

She stared up at him. "To even think that my sister would have brought that drug, knowing what it did, and what it could do to somebody like me makes me sick. Then knowing in the back of her mind how she had planned to get somebody to use it on me? What the fuck?"

He winced and nodded. "Believe me. We're all of the same opinion."

"And yet she'll walk away, free as a bird."

"No, she won't." Egan shook his head. "She might think she will, but, no, she isn't."

"You sure about that?" she asked, staring at him. "Not that I'm trying to get her in any more trouble because God only knows she's in enough trouble as it is, but, man, I don't even know how to deal with her latest admissions."

"No, and you shouldn't have to think about it," Egan noted. "That's the thing. Nobody should have to consider such a thing happening in your life."

"Yet how do you not, when it was a very real possibility?" she whispered.

He walked over, sat down on the bed beside her, and held her close.

"Hey, at least you got coffee. I came to suggest we go get some together."

Berry smiled. "Yegorahn's teammate Raffi just brought me this cup."

He frowned at her and asked, "Really?"

She nodded.

Egan asked, "Why?"

"He offered condolences over my sister and told me that he'd heard about *the plan*."

Egan stared at her for a long moment, then told her to hang on a second and snatched the coffee and quickly disappeared.

She stared after him, crying out, "I could have used that, you know?"

"I'll get you another one," he called back. And, just like that, he was gone.

She sat here, still curled up, wondering what the hell that was all about, yet not really caring. Life was a lot of things right now, but none of it made sense.

When Egan returned a few minutes later, he asked her, "Which guy was it?"

"Raffi. I told you that already," she said, frowning at Egan. "You know. The one with the brush cut. Well, everybody has short hair up here, but he's the one with the broken nose."

He nodded and quickly stepped out again.

She cried after him, "Why? What happened? What the hell is going on?" When she got no answer, she decided to follow Egan.

Egan headed down the hallway to Raffi's room and found Magnus getting there first. They knocked on the door, but, when nobody answered, they opened it up and stepped inside.

Berry peered around them, but the room was empty. She looked at the men. "Okay, do you want to explain this?"

"We'll explain it after we find him."

"He gave me coffee, so maybe he went and grabbed himself one."

And, with that, they headed down to the kitchen area,

and, sure enough, he was standing there with a coffee, speaking with somebody else.

He turned and saw them and immediately shook his head. "No, no, no."

She looked at him and asked, "What's the matter?" Then he objected even louder. She turned and stared at Egan. "Somebody needs to explain to me what's going on," she declared in a loud voice.

With the two men now flanking Raffi, Egan turned to look at her. "That coffee you were given was laced with a heavy dose of GHB."

She frowned, then spun to look at Raffi. "You did that to me?"

He stared at her, then seemed to crumble in front of them. "I didn't mean to," he cried out. "I didn't want to do it."

"You didn't mean to what? You didn't mean to lace it with enough drugs to knock me out?" she cried out.

He sighed. "I was hoping it would take the suspicion off your sister."

Dumbfounded, she stared at him. "What, and put it on you? How was that a good thing?"

"Because I love her," he said sadly, "but she won't have anything to do with me."

"Good God." Berry studied him. "You're the one who killed Yegorahn." He looked at her in shock, but she nodded. "It was always about jealousy, wasn't it?"

He nodded again. "If he had loved her, I would have left him alone," he cried out. "But, when he started talking about maybe using the drug, and I could see that it both fascinated and repulsed him at the same time, I knew he was getting closer to wanting to use it," Raffi said, trembling with emotions. "And, if that was the case, then he didn't care about Cherry and shouldn't be with her," he stated immediately.

Berry let out a hard exhale. In shock, she asked, "Jesus, Raffi, were you trying to kill me?"

"No, no, no," he argued, "I just thought that maybe it would look as if you had done it deliberately."

"So I commit suicide because of what? Because I'd been the one out there killing people?" She stared at him, stunned.

He winced. "I didn't have much time to think it through."

"You didn't think anything through," she cried out. "All you thought through was saving my sister."

"At least I did that. You were ready to throw her to the wolves."

"Do you realize she brought that drug here to be used on me?" she bellowed, causing a ripple all around her. Hearing a collective gasp, she realized they'd amassed quite the crowd.

"She's the one who brought that date-rape drug here and was toying with the idea of having Yegorahn use it on me," she declared bitterly. "My own sister, my twin, who absolutely does not in any way, shape, or form give a crap about me, tried to get someone I couldn't stand to drug me and to rape me." Berry was on the verge of tears again. "Good God, what is wrong with people?" And with that, she looked over at Magnus. "There's your answer to that question, at least."

"Yeah, to that question, but I don't know about anything else."

Raffi immediately shook his head. "No, no, not me. I didn't do anything else. It was only Yegorahn."

"Yeah, so you say," Magnus muttered, as he hauled him up and headed down to the back locker room with him. "I'm not sure anybody believes you anymore."

Berry turned and ran to her room, then threw herself onto the bed, sobbing her heart out. To even think that this had just happened was beyond anything she had ever imagined.

When the door opened, and she was pulled into Egan's arms, she shifted to bawling into his heavy shirt.

When she finally had no more tears and lay quietly against his chest, he whispered, "It'll take time, a lot of time to get past this."

She looked up at him, her face covered in still-drying tears, and whispered, "Why does she hate me so much?"

"I don't know that she does," he suggested. "I just don't think she has anything left to give to anybody, outside of herself."

"But to bring a date-rape drug to be used on me?" she cried out in horror. "I still can't believe it."

"I know," Egan agreed, "and the trouble is, there's a lot of this still to go over yet."

"And it'll be ugly, won't it?"

"It could be, yes, and we need to get several people air-lifted out of here, just to keep the peace."

"And you also need to interview Raffi to see if he had anything to do with the rest of it."

"I know," he replied, "but tonight I'm not doing any-thing but holding you close. We'll figure the rest of it out as we go." Then he added, "Given what you've been through, you've got a good reason to leave, if you want to."

She looked up at him and slowly shook her head. "I probably should get out and run away as far and as fast as I can," she muttered. "Yet it feels like bailing out in the middle of this training session, and I don't want to do that. Will the brass keep my sister here?"

"No," Egan stated. "Your sister will be one of those removed and shipped out—in handcuffs or restraints. Sorry, Berry, but she will face a court-martial for her drug use, insubordination, bringing an illegal drug to this base, all for starters. No telling what all she's done here—or before in her life. She most likely will be ordered to be held in a psychiatric hospital, pending her dishonorable discharge, losing all her military benefits."

"Oh my God. She doesn't get away with anything this time, does she?" Berry asked.

"Nope. About time, is all I can say. She's a danger to herself and others, Berry. And has been for many years, as you have now found out. I hope you can see how a stay in a psych hospital is the best thing for Cherry."

"I'm sorry this all lands on her all at once. She'll have a hard time adjusting. … And I can't help her with any of this. Not effectively. … However, yes. The psychiatric ward is probably where she needs to stay. Is it wrong of me to say, thank God she's getting help?" she asked, trembling.

"Not at all," Egan said. "Believe me. Everybody here would understand."

She looked up and smiled. "Are you staying for the full term of this training session? You were brought in to deal with this mess, and you've managed to sort out at least some of it."

"I'm staying here for sure."

She smiled at him. "Then I'm staying too." He frowned, looking worried. She placed a finger against his lips. "No, you're not responsible for me, but it will be good for me to stay here and to see this to the end," she whispered. "There's just enough going on that I don't want to leave it as is."

He pondered that and nodded. "I can put in a recommendation, but there's no guarantee that you'll be allowed to stay."

She nodded. "If that's the case, then I'll see you when you get back stateside. Otherwise I highly suggest we work on our relationship here."

"That sounds good to me." Egan smiled. "God only knows what the next stage of this investigation will bring."

"That's okay." She curled up against him, wrapping her arms around him, cuddling closer. "Whatever it is, we'll get through it just fine—together."

EPILOGUE

AT DINNERTIME BARRET Dillinger walked into the dining area of the Arctic military base and stopped, surveying his surroundings. He understood from Mason some of what had just gone down. Sure enough, off in a corner, he saw four heads, two males and two females, huddled together at a table. Smiling, Barret walked over and sat down beside them, without any warning. Immediately the nearest woman stiffened, but he gave her a reassuring smile. "The name is Barret," he greeted her gently, then turned and looked at the men.

Magnus smiled at him. "You're here to help, aren't you?"

"If that's what you call it," he replied, with a casual glance around. "Not that anybody is supposed to know that," he added, with a warning.

Magnus nodded. "However, you'll find out very quickly that nothing stays quiet in this scenario."

"Of course not." Barret looked back at the women. "Which one of you is Berry?" Immediately the smaller of the two held up her hand.

"I'm Berry. This is Sydney. She's the doctor here."

"Honored," he said, "to meet you both." He looked around and added, "Sounds as if you guys have been having fun. You should share all those good times."

"Now you can take over. I've had all the fun I want,"

Berry declared, with a shudder. "Personally I'm okay to just have some peace and quiet for a while."

"And yet you're staying." Barret frowned, his gaze intent as he studied her.

She took a deep breath. "Yes, I am."

He nodded, not arguing with her at all. People had all kinds of reasons for staying after trying times such as this, and maybe she was in the right of it after all.

As another woman walked in and headed to the table, the woman grew nervous, her steps choppy. She looked over at Magnus. "May I speak to you for a minute?"

Magnus immediately stood. "Of course."

She pointed him toward the hallway.

At that, Barret joined him. "I'll come too, if that's okay."

She hesitated and frowned. "Sorry, but you're new."

"I am, indeed. Therefore, I'm not connected to anything already going on." He watched as that worked its way through her thoughts, then she ignored him.

"Fine, as long as he says it's okay." She pointed to Magnus, who nodded.

"It's fine," Magnus murmured. "What's going on?"

She shook her head. "I haven't been able to find Scott anywhere."

Magnus stared at her. "Scott, as in kitchen assistant Scott?"

She nodded. "We're both new here, having come in a few weeks ago as replacements. Scott was here to help Chef, and I'm mostly doing reports and supplies for the compound. The base isn't very welcoming, so Scott and I just stuck together. Scott wasn't expecting this weather or the isolation. It's really bothering him, so I check on him throughout the day," she shared, with a side glance at Barret.

"I step into the kitchen sometimes to give him a hand, but, when I went there a couple times already today, I saw no sign of him. Now I just talked to Chef, and he hasn't seen Scott all day."

"All day?" Magnus repeated.

She nodded. "Chef told me that Scott wasn't feeling well and went to lie down. I talked to him this morning, and he said he just needed some fresh air. This place, the isolation, being stuck inside, … he found it very claustrophobic."

"Ah, shit," Magnus said, as he turned toward Barret. "Nothing like jumping into the deep end."

"I'm all for it," Barret replied, still studying the woman. "What's your name?"

"Avalon Pritchard," she said, with a smile. "Please help Scott. He's a nice guy, and honestly he's not like a lot of the men here."

"When you say that, what do you mean?" Magnus asked.

She shrugged. "He's definitely not the alpha type. He's quiet, studious, shy, and a really nice guy. I'd hate for something bad to happen to him. Since arriving, we'd heard all kinds of horror stories. With all the shit that's been going on around this place," she explained, "when somebody goes missing …"

"*If* anybody goes missing," Barret corrected her immediately, then turned to look at Magnus. "I suggest we do a full-scale internal search and then head outside."

"Yeah, already on it," Magnus noted, with his phone up. "We'll set up the sirens and send out a full search party," Magnus added for Avalon's benefit, with a smile.

Barret turned to face Avalon. "Thanks for letting us know."

"Just find him please. I'd really hate to think of something else happening here." And, with that, her arms wrapped around her chest, she walked slowly back to the kitchen.

Barret turned to Magnus. "I guess you weren't expecting that, *huh?*"

"No, but we also don't know that it isn't a false alarm. Scott could just be out with the dogs or something."

"Ah, maybe I'll start there," Barret offered.

"Sure, you do that, but we can't waste time. If he's there, that's great. If he's not there, we'll be hitting the road real fast, before we lose out on any sunlight hours. In these temperatures, without proper outerwear and supplies, in twenty minutes you're done."

"Got it," Barret stated. "Considering that Scott might have been missing since sunup today, he's already well past that point."

"I know," Magnus acknowledged, his voice dark. "Yet we can't assume anything, not yet."

This concludes Book 3 of Shadow Recon: Egan.

Read about Barret: Shadow Recon, Book 4

Shadow Recon: Barret (Book #4)

Deep in the permafrost of the Arctic, a joint task force, comprised of over one dozen countries, comes together to level up their winter skills. A mix of personalities, nationalities, and egos bring out the best—and the worst—as these globally elite men and women work and play together. They rub elbows with hardy locals and a group of scientists gathered close by …

One fatality is almost expected with this training. A second is tough but not a surprise. However, when a third goes missing? It's hard to not be suspicious. When the missing man is connected to one of the elite Maverick team members and is a special friend of Lieutenant Commander Mason Callister? All hell breaks loose …

A teammate goes missing right as Barret arrives at the camp of horrors. Immediately he heads out to help in the search for the missing man – to no avail. And once again the numbers go down by one. No explanation, no body…

nothing. Are drugs involved? Blackmail? Or stupid bets? There's too many options and none of them make any sense.

At least Avalon is there, a woman who caught his interest on the first day. Although she's just as confused and worried about what's going on in the arctic camp, she's level headed and with a great sense of humor.

Subbed in for someone who couldn't make it, Avalon ends up helping out in the kitchen. At least there she's warm and can keep busy. Until someone falls ill from suspected food poisoning and all eyes turn on her. She knows she hasn't done anything wrong, but tempers are short and she's an easy scape goat.

It's going to take both of them to keep her safe and get her out from under the cloud of suspicion. Thankfully Barret has no problem helping a damsel in distress…

Find Book 4 here!
To find out more visit Dale Mayer's website.
https://geni.us/DMSSRBarret

Author's Note

Thank you for reading Egan: Shadow Recon, Book 3! If you enjoyed the book, please take a moment and leave a short review.

Dear reader,

I love to hear from readers, and you can contact me at my website: www.dalemayer.com or at my Facebook author page. To be informed of new releases and special offers, sign up for my newsletter or follow me on BookBub. And if you are interested in joining Dale Mayer's Reader Group, here is the Facebook sign up page.
http://geni.us/DaleMayerFBGroup

Cheers,
Dale Mayer

About the Author

Dale Mayer is a *USA Today* best-selling author, best known for her SEALs military romances, her Psychic Visions series, and her Lovely Lethal Garden cozy series. Her contemporary romances are raw and full of passion and emotion (Broken But … Mending, Hathaway House series). Her thrillers will keep you guessing (Kate Morgan, By Death series), and her romantic comedies will keep you giggling (*It's a Dog's Life*, a stand-alone novella; and the Broken Protocols series, starring Charming Marvin, the cat).

Dale honors the stories that come to her—and some of them are crazy, break all the rules and cross multiple genres!

To go with her fiction, she also writes nonfiction in many different fields, with books available on résumé writing, companion gardening, and the US mortgage system. All her books are available in print and ebook format.

Connect with Dale Mayer Online

Dale's Website – www.dalemayer.com

Twitter – @DaleMayer

Facebook Page – geni.us/DaleMayerFBFanPage

Facebook Group – geni.us/DaleMayerFBGroup

BookBub – geni.us/DaleMayerBookbub

Instagram – geni.us/DaleMayerInstagram

Goodreads – geni.us/DaleMayerGoodreads

Newsletter – geni.us/DaleNews

Also by Dale Mayer

Published Adult Books:

Shadow Recon
Magnus, Book 1
Rogan, Book 2
Egan, Book 3
Barret, Book 4

Bullard's Battle
Ryland's Reach, Book 1
Cain's Cross, Book 2
Eton's Escape, Book 3
Garret's Gambit, Book 4
Kano's Keep, Book 5
Fallon's Flaw, Book 6
Quinn's Quest, Book 7
Bullard's Beauty, Book 8
Bullard's Best, Book 9
Bullard's Battle, Books 1–2
Bullard's Battle, Books 3–4
Bullard's Battle, Books 5–6
Bullard's Battle, Books 7–8

Terkel's Team
Damon's Deal, Book 1
Wade's War, Book 2

Gage's Goal, Book 3
Calum's Contact, Book 4
Rick's Road, Book 5
Scott's Summit, Book 6
Brody's Beast, Book 7
Terkel's Twist, Book 8
Terkel's Triumph, Book 9

Terkel's Guardian
Radar, Book 1

Kate Morgan
Simon Says… Hide, Book 1
Simon Says… Jump, Book 2
Simon Says… Ride, Book 3
Simon Says… Scream, Book 4
Simon Says… Run, Book 5
Simon Says… Walk, Book 6
Simon Says… Forgive, Book 7

Hathaway House
Aaron, Book 1
Brock, Book 2
Cole, Book 3
Denton, Book 4
Elliot, Book 5
Finn, Book 6
Gregory, Book 7
Heath, Book 8
Iain, Book 9
Jaden, Book 10
Keith, Book 11

Lance, Book 12

Melissa, Book 13

Nash, Book 14

Owen, Book 15

Percy, Book 16

Quinton, Book 17

Ryatt, Book 18

Spencer, Book 19

Timothy, Book 20

Hathaway House, Books 1–3

Hathaway House, Books 4–6

Hathaway House, Books 7–9

The K9 Files

Ethan, Book 1

Pierce, Book 2

Zane, Book 3

Blaze, Book 4

Lucas, Book 5

Parker, Book 6

Carter, Book 7

Weston, Book 8

Greyson, Book 9

Rowan, Book 10

Caleb, Book 11

Kurt, Book 12

Tucker, Book 13

Harley, Book 14

Kyron, Book 15

Jenner, Book 16

Rhys, Book 17

Landon, Book 18

Harper, Book 19

Kascius, Book 20

The K9 Files, Books 1–2

The K9 Files, Books 3–4

The K9 Files, Books 5–6

The K9 Files, Books 7–8

The K9 Files, Books 9–10

The K9 Files, Books 11–12

Lovely Lethal Gardens

Arsenic in the Azaleas, Book 1

Bones in the Begonias, Book 2

Corpse in the Carnations, Book 3

Daggers in the Dahlias, Book 4

Evidence in the Echinacea, Book 5

Footprints in the Ferns, Book 6

Gun in the Gardenias, Book 7

Handcuffs in the Heather, Book 8

Ice Pick in the Ivy, Book 9

Jewels in the Juniper, Book 10

Killer in the Kiwis, Book 11

Lifeless in the Lilies, Book 12

Murder in the Marigolds, Book 13

Nabbed in the Nasturtiums, Book 14

Offed in the Orchids, Book 15

Poison in the Pansies, Book 16

Quarry in the Quince, Book 17

Revenge in the Roses, Book 18

Silenced in the Sunflowers, Book 19

Toes up in the Tulips, Book 20

Uzi in the Urn, Book 21

Victim in the Violets, Book 22

Lovely Lethal Gardens, Books 1–2
Lovely Lethal Gardens, Books 3–4
Lovely Lethal Gardens, Books 5–6
Lovely Lethal Gardens, Books 7–8
Lovely Lethal Gardens, Books 9–10

Psychic Visions Series

Tuesday's Child
Hide 'n Go Seek
Maddy's Floor
Garden of Sorrow
Knock Knock…
Rare Find
Eyes to the Soul
Now You See Her
Shattered
Into the Abyss
Seeds of Malice
Eye of the Falcon
Itsy-Bitsy Spider
Unmasked
Deep Beneath
From the Ashes
Stroke of Death
Ice Maiden
Snap, Crackle…
What If…
Talking Bones
String of Tears
Inked Forever
Psychic Visions Books 1–3
Psychic Visions Books 4–6

Psychic Visions Books 7–9

By Death Series
Touched by Death
Haunted by Death
Chilled by Death
By Death Books 1–3

Broken Protocols – Romantic Comedy Series
Cat's Meow
Cat's Pajamas
Cat's Cradle
Cat's Claus
Broken Protocols 1-4

Broken and... Mending
Skin
Scars
Scales (of Justice)
Broken but... Mending 1-3

Glory
Genesis
Tori
Celeste
Glory Trilogy

Biker Blues
Morgan: Biker Blues, Volume 1
Cash: Biker Blues, Volume 2

SEALs of Honor
Mason: SEALs of Honor, Book 1

SEALs of Honor, Books 7–10

SEALs of Honor, Books 11–13

SEALs of Honor, Books 14–16

SEALs of Honor, Books 17–19

SEALs of Honor, Books 20–22

SEALs of Honor, Books 23–25

Heroes for Hire

Levi's Legend: Heroes for Hire, Book 1

Stone's Surrender: Heroes for Hire, Book 2

Merk's Mistake: Heroes for Hire, Book 3

Rhodes's Reward: Heroes for Hire, Book 4

Flynn's Firecracker: Heroes for Hire, Book 5

Logan's Light: Heroes for Hire, Book 6

Harrison's Heart: Heroes for Hire, Book 7

Saul's Sweetheart: Heroes for Hire, Book 8

Dakota's Delight: Heroes for Hire, Book 9

Tyson's Treasure: Heroes for Hire, Book 10

Jace's Jewel: Heroes for Hire, Book 11

Rory's Rose: Heroes for Hire, Book 12

Brandon's Bliss: Heroes for Hire, Book 13

Liam's Lily: Heroes for Hire, Book 14

North's Nikki: Heroes for Hire, Book 15

Anders's Angel: Heroes for Hire, Book 16

Reyes's Raina: Heroes for Hire, Book 17

Dezi's Diamond: Heroes for Hire, Book 18

Vince's Vixen: Heroes for Hire, Book 19

Ice's Icing: Heroes for Hire, Book 20

Johan's Joy: Heroes for Hire, Book 21

Galen's Gemma: Heroes for Hire, Book 22

Zack's Zest: Heroes for Hire, Book 23

Bonaparte's Belle: Heroes for Hire, Book 24

Noah's Nemesis: Heroes for Hire, Book 25
Tomas's Trials: Heroes for Hire, Book 26
Carson's Choice: Heroes for Hire, Book 27
Dante's Decision: Heroes for Hire, Book 28
Steve's Solace: Heroes for Hire, Book 29
Heroes for Hire, Books 1–3
Heroes for Hire, Books 4–6
Heroes for Hire, Books 7–9
Heroes for Hire, Books 10–12
Heroes for Hire, Books 13–15
Heroes for Hire, Books 16–18
Heroes for Hire, Books 19–21
Heroes for Hire, Books 22–24

SEALs of Steel

Badger: SEALs of Steel, Book 1
Erick: SEALs of Steel, Book 2
Cade: SEALs of Steel, Book 3
Talon: SEALs of Steel, Book 4
Laszlo: SEALs of Steel, Book 5
Geir: SEALs of Steel, Book 6
Jager: SEALs of Steel, Book 7
The Final Reveal: SEALs of Steel, Book 8
SEALs of Steel, Books 1–4
SEALs of Steel, Books 5–8
SEALs of Steel, Books 1–8

The Mavericks

Kerrick, Book 1
Griffin, Book 2
Jax, Book 3
Beau, Book 4

Asher, Book 5
Ryker, Book 6
Miles, Book 7
Nico, Book 8
Keane, Book 9
Lennox, Book 10
Gavin, Book 11
Shane, Book 12
Diesel, Book 13
Jerricho, Book 14
Killian, Book 15
Hatch, Book 16
Corbin, Book 17
Aiden, Book 18
The Mavericks, Books 1–2
The Mavericks, Books 3–4
The Mavericks, Books 5–6
The Mavericks, Books 7–8
The Mavericks, Books 9–10
The Mavericks, Books 11–12

Standalone Novellas
It's a Dog's Life
Riana's Revenge
Second Chances

Published Young Adult Books:

Family Blood Ties Series
Vampire in Denial
Vampire in Distress
Vampire in Design

Vampire in Deceit

Vampire in Defiance

Vampire in Conflict

Vampire in Chaos

Vampire in Crisis

Vampire in Control

Vampire in Charge

Family Blood Ties Set 1–3

Family Blood Ties Set 1–5

Family Blood Ties Set 4–6

Family Blood Ties Set 7–9

Sian's Solution, A Family Blood Ties Series Prequel
    Novelette

Design series

Dangerous Designs

Deadly Designs

Darkest Designs

Design Series Trilogy

Standalone

In Cassie's Corner

Gem Stone (a Gemma Stone Mystery)

Time Thieves

Published Non-Fiction Books:

Career Essentials

Career Essentials: The Résumé

Career Essentials: The Cover Letter

Career Essentials: The Interview

Career Essentials: 3 in 1